UNTEACHABLE

LEAH RAEDER

ATRIA PAPERBACK

NEW YORK   LONDON   TORONTO   SYDNEY   NEW DELHI

ATRIA PAPERBACK

A Division of Simon & Schuster, Inc.
1230 Avenue of the Americas
New York, NY 10020

First Atria Paperback edition October 2014

ATRIA PAPERBACK and colophon are trademarks of Simon & Schuster, Inc.

For information about special discounts for bulk purchases, please contact Simon & Schuster Special Sales at 1-866-506-1949 or business@simonandschuster.com.

The Simon & Schuster Speakers Bureau can bring authors to your live event. For more information or to book an event, contact the Simon & Schuster Speakers Bureau at 1-866-248-3049 or visit our website at www.simonspeakers.com.

Interior design by Kyoko Watanabe
Cover design by Lucy Kim
Cover art by Getty Images; Shutterstock

Manufactured in the United States of America

10 9 8 7 6 5 4 3 2 1

Library of Congress Cataloging-in-Publication Data

Raeder, Leah.
    Unteachable / Leah Raeder. — First Atria Books trade paperback edition.
        pages cm
    1. Teenage girls—Fiction. 2. College teachers—Fiction. 3. Secrets—Fiction. 4. Teacher-student relationships—Fiction. 5. Illinois—Fiction. I. Title.
    PS3618.A35955U58 2014
    813'.6—dc23
                                                            2014009068

ISBN 978-1-4767-8640-7
ISBN 978-1-4767-8641-4 (ebook)

Praise for
UNTEACHABLE

"With an electrifying fusion of forbidden love and vivid writing, the characters glow in Technicolor. Brace yourselves to be catapulted to dizzying levels with evocative language, panty-blazing sex scenes, and emotions so intense they will linger long after the last page steals your heart."

—Pam Godwin,
New York Times bestselling author of *Beneath the Burn*

"*Unteachable* is a lyrical masterpiece with a vivid story line that grabbed me from the very first page. The flawless writing and raw characters are pure perfection, putting it in a class all by itself."

—Brooke Cumberland,
USA Today bestselling author of *Spark*

"Leah Raeder's writing is skillful and stunning. *Unteachable* is one of the most beautifully powerful stories of forbidden love that I have ever read."

—Mia Sheridan,
New York Times bestselling author of *Archer's Voice*

"Edgy and passionate, *Unteachable* shimmers with raw desire. Raeder is a captivating new voice."

—Melody Grace,
New York Times bestselling author of the Beachwood Bay series

"A simply stunning portrayal of lies, courage, and unrequited love. Raeder has a gift for taking taboo subjects and seducing us with them in the rawest, most beautiful way."

—S.L. Jennings,
New York Times bestselling author of *Taint*

For Lindsay and Ellen,
who are bad influences

UNTEACHABLE

WHEN you're eighteen, there's fuck-all to do in a southern Illinois summer but eat fried pickles, drink PBR tallboys you stole from your mom, and ride the Tilt-a-Whirl till you hurl. Which is exactly what I was doing the night I met Him.

It was the kind of greenhouse August heat that feels positively Jurassic. Everything was melting a little: the liquid black sky, the silver-gel-penned stars, the neon lights bleeding color everywhere. All summer there's a carnival a mile from my house, in a no-man's-land rife with weeds and saw grass, a sea of flat earth. It felt like the edge of forever out there. I cracked a tallboy and it echoed like a rifle shot. I took a swig of that pissy weak stuff, savoring the coolness. I was sitting on a picnic bench, watching the roller coaster go up and down and up again, the joyous screams phasing in and out like a distant radio station. Roller coasters scare me, and it has everything to do with me losing my stuffed bunny George when I was five.

George fell from a hundred feet in the sky when I threw my hands up in cruel, careless glee. Mom sewed new eyes on, but I cried and cried and said he was dead until she let me bury him in the backyard. We made a coffin out of a Froot Loops box. Mom, so drunk she was crying, too, gave the eulogy.

So maybe part of why I was out here tonight was because I was tired of being a kid, stuck with kid fears and kid memories. Senior year would start in two weeks. I wanted to go in already an adult.

I pounded the last of the beer and crushed the can on the bench.

My name's Maise, by the way. Maise O'Malley. Yeah, I'm Irish as hell. But you probably knew that from the drinking, right?

I went into the carnival. Apparently, a breaking news bulletin had just gone out about my legs: three pairs of wolf eyes looked over instantly, then moved down, up, down, the old broken elevator gaze. It's always the older guys, too. But I'm kind of screwed up from growing up without a father, and I like when they try to daddy me.

Try being the operative word, as Mr. Wilke says.

But we'll get to him.

I smiled at no one, sauntering past stalls stuffed with popcorn and pretzels and corn dogs, snow cones and cotton candy. The air was drugged with sugar and salt. It made my head spin. A bell rang nearby and someone whooped triumphantly. I passed the rigged games—milk bottles, darts—where people stubbornly threw money at the carny, desperate to win some giant lice-ridden teddy fresh out of a Taiwanese sweatshop.

Mr. Wilke says I'm both cynical and worldly for my age. I choose to take them both as compliments.

I wasn't ready to face the roller coaster yet, so I rode the merry-go-round for a while, going for the full Lolita effect as I lifted a leg high and slowly, slowly draped it over a painted horse, reveling in how uncomfortable I made all the parents. One man kept glancing in my direction until his kid pulled his sleeve and snapped, "Dad!" I raised an eyebrow coolly. Too bad I didn't have any bubble gum.

Finally the beer had charged up my blood. I marched over to the YOU MUST BE THIS TALL sign. The line was short. It was getting late, for a weeknight.

Then I saw the name of the roller coaster.

Deathsnake.

I almost turned around right there. Stupid, yeah, but PTSADS doesn't care how stupid a trigger is.

If you need me to spell that out, it's Post-Traumatic Stuffed Animal Death Syndrome. I thought it was pretty funny. Mom and the psychologist did not. The psychologist said I had substituted George for Dad and I actually had post-dad syndrome. I told her George was a fucking bunny.

Anyway, Deathsnake.

"You getting on?" the carny said. He had so much acne he looked like a halftone comic, like when you peer really close at a newspaper and everything that looked solid is just little dots.

I gave him my ticket.

The assholes on this ride had decided to take every single car except the front. Again, I almost turned around. I did turn, actually, and saw a guy behind me, so I turned back and got into the empty car because I was not going to chicken out in front of the entire universe. Best-case scenario: I close my eyes for four minutes and get a free blow-dry. Worst-case scenario: I fall from a hundred feet in the air, and there's no sewing my eyes back on.

The door to my car opened.

It was the guy. He raised his eyebrows questioningly, and I shrugged. He got in.

At least I might die next to a hot guy.

Revised worst-case scenario: I throw up on him, we both die.

"You're pretty brave," he said, lowering the bar over us. "Must be a veteran, sitting up front."

"It's my first time," I said. Well, first time on my own terms.

He smiled. It lit his face like a camera flash. "Mine too."

Then Deathsnake lurched forward, toward doom.

It's a trick, the way it starts. There's a loud, creepy ratcheting, like some massive clockwork grinding beneath you, but the car just farts along inconspicuously. People behind us were talking about stupid shit. Some girl told someone to put away his phone and I prayed that he wouldn't and that it was expensive. The guy next to me looked out over the fairgrounds as we ascended, and I peered past him, but my attention was split. Beyond him, a confetti of lights and fey music, all the ugly carny weirdness rendered magical thanks to distance. But my eyes kept catching on his face. From below it was traced with red neon, from above with metallic moonlight, sketching out a bold, almost sulky chin, lips that looked too soft and sensitive for a man. His eyelashes were a fringe of furry gold. I couldn't see his eyes from this angle.

He looked over suddenly and I whipped my head away. "What a view," he said.

"Tell me about it," I mumbled.

I could feel him smiling.

"Oh, shit," someone said behind us.

And we dropped.

I'm not going to do the whole roller-coaster/falling-in-love metaphor. I didn't fall in love with him up there. Maybe I fell in love with the idea of love, but I'm a teenage girl. This morning I fell in love with raspberry jam and a puppy in a tiny raincoat. I'm not exactly Earth's top authority on the subject.

But when we crested the first peak and the world sprawled beneath us like a tangled-up string of Christmas lights and then we plunged toward it at light speed, the guy and I reached for each other's hands spontaneously and simultaneously.

And I felt something I've never felt before.

You can call it love, or you can call it free fall. They're pretty much the same thing.

When Deathsnake glided to a stop, we both looked like we'd stuck our fingers in electric sockets. Einstein hair, Steve Buscemi eyes. The guy had screamed more than I did. I mostly laughed, at his screaming, at my fear, and finally at how good it felt to be alive right then and there. Not once had I thought of George or my mother or my sad life.

The guy—who I mentally upgraded to The Guy, capital letters—offered me a hand out of the car. We still had shit-eating grins plastered on our faces.

"Thanks," he said.

"For what?"

"Helping me lose my roller-coaster virginity."

I don't think he meant to flirt, but he blushed anyway. He looked at me a little closer.

This is the part where they realize you're jailbait.

"How old are you?" he said, right on cue.

"Old enough."

I love what that does to their faces. Old enough to . . . fill in the blank.

But The Guy only smiled. "I don't want your parents to think I'm some creep."

He could have said, *I'm a teacher,* and everything would have been different.

"I'm here by myself," I said. "All that matters is whether I think you're some creep."

"Do you?"

"Let's test that hypothesis." And I headed for the exit.

I knew exactly what he was seeing from the rear view. The cutoff jean shorts, the creamy legs sleek and slender as a filly's, the tight tee, the cascade of burnished chestnut hair. I was, perhaps, very slightly, flouncing. Normally I'm cool and collected. But I was giddy from the heights and this beautiful man paying attention to me. I still hadn't really seen him head-on, so in my mind he became a pastiche of male models and movie stars.

"How do you feel about centrifugal force?" I said over my shoulder.

"Totally against it."

"Great. Next up is the Gravitron."

The line here was longer, and when he caught up we turned to each other, and I did a double take.

There was the sensitive mouth I'd seen earlier, the lips that looked made for poetry and murmuring sweet French nothings in cologne commercials. *Je te veux, mon chéri.* But now there was a whole face to go with them, and that face—oh my god. You know when a swimmer gets out of a pool, and they're radiant and flushed, mouth open a little, eyelashes dewy and sparkling, squinting like they've just come back from another world? He had that look, permanently. Like he wasn't really from here. He was some beautiful thing coming up from a beautiful place, squinting amiably at our brightness and filth. I could give you the technical specs—cheekbones high and chiseled, straight patrician nose, tall forehead, boyishly handsome—but it was the expression that made him beautiful.

He'd said something to me and I was just gaping like an idiot. "What?"

That smile again. Like a flashbulb going off, freezing you in the moment.

"Did you know you can walk on the wall while it's spinning?"

"Really?"

"It's nuts. You'll feel like a superhero. They won't let you do it now, but if you hang around till closing and slip them some cash, they'll look the other way."

My eyes must have lit up at this. The Guy leaned in suddenly, tilting his face.

Heart attack.

But he just stared at my eyes, as if searching for a stray eyelash. A free wish.

"What are you doing?" I whispered, hoping I didn't have beer breath.

"Green," he said, and leaned back. "I wanted to know the color."

"Why? So the police can identify my body later?"

Thankfully, he laughed. We handed over our tickets.

"Five bucks says you scream," I said.

"Deal."

They lined us up against the wall. Lights went off. Marquees blinked on. The giant steel saucer began to spin. They were really going for the UFO effect here.

"Someday they'll make spaceships like this," I said. "So the astronauts can walk around."

"Like in *2001: A Space Odyssey*."

"What?"

"The movie. You've never seen it? It's a classic."

That was the first time I felt the difference in our ages.

"How old are you?" I said.

"Old enough," he said, and we both laughed.

My bones stuck to the wall like magnets. I tried to raise my arm, but it weighed a hundred pounds. The boards we stood against rose off the floor, our feet levitating. A girl near me giggled uncontrollably. The saucer was still accelerating, flattening my insides, making me feel both weightless and infinitely heavy. I tensed my legs and raised them straight out, sitting in midair. The Guy grinned at me. His gaze lingered on my legs, and the edges of his grin softened, and even though my stomach was a pancake, something in it fluttered. Little two-dimensional paper butterflies.

The UFO reached maximum velocity. I let my legs slam back down. I wanted to feel like this all the time, like I was rushing through the universe, everything intense and pressed right up against my skin. The Guy gave a wild, jubilant yell. The giggling girl sounded like she was drowning. At that moment I knew every single person on the ride wanted it to go faster, faster, blood pooling at the backs of our skulls, until we were tingling and dizzy and flew apart into a million particles of happiness.

I had trouble getting my balance when we came down. The Guy rooted in his pocket for something. He took my hand.

"What—"

He pressed a five-dollar bill into my palm. "You win."

I felt weirdly sheepish. I didn't want to take his money. "I was just kidding."

"I'm a man of my word."

Yes. You're a man, a very pretty one who's being very nice to me, and I don't know what the hell I'm doing.

"Fine. Let's support the economy," I said, waving the bill at the game stalls.

We decided the least-rigged game was the water gun race, because it had a winner every round. I paid up and sat next to a little boy whose mom stood behind him, maneuvering his arms like a puppet. On my other side was a fat drunk guy who smelled like sausage. He leered at me.

This would be cake.

I grabbed my WWII-era machine water gun and took aim at the bull's-eye dead ahead. The carny counted down. Three. Two.

I brushed Fatso's bare leg with my calf.

One.

Fssssshhhhhh.

The little boy lost before it even began. He started crying, and his mom snapped at him and seized the gun. She only managed to squirt out a tragic, flaccid little stream before her kid burst into wails and she pulled him off the seat.

"And Seven drops out," The Guy announced, as the carny stared at us with sullen boredom. "A sad day for Team Seven. Six has the lead now, but Five is gaining fast."

I hit my bull's-eye flawlessly. My marker rose smooth and steady.

Fatso had pretty good aim, too. We were neck and neck.

I rubbed my calf along his hairy shin.

"But wait! Five is falling behind! He seems to be losing focus. Can he pull it together?"

I hooked my foot around the back of Fatso's leg. Dragged my toes up his meaty ham hock.

Ding ding ding!

"Winner! Number Six by a landslide."

I turned a huge smile on Fatso. "Sorry, mister."

He wasn't mad at all. His piggish eyes gleamed. "I got another game you can beat me at."

"Dad," I said brightly, "this man wants to play a different game with me."

Fatso heaved himself off the stool, his hands up in the surrender/I-didn't-touch-her position, and backed into the crowd.

"You're a dangerous girl," The Guy said softly.

I made a gun with my fingers and blew imaginary smoke away.

My choice of prize was a weepy-eyed velvet pony. It was the look on its face—soulful, hopeful, earnest—that appealed to me. I crushed it to my chest, getting my smell all over it as we strolled aimlessly through the crowd. Mostly older, drunker people now. Two veiny guys yelling, inching into each other's faces. A man chasing a woman who kept saying it was too late, he blew it.

"I'm thirsty," The Guy said. "You want something?"

I shrugged, which apparently meant yes. He bought two plastic cups of beer.

"How old are you?" he said again as he watched me drink.

"Twenty-one."

"When's your birthday?" he said fast.

My reply was just as quick. "August seventeenth, nineteen

ninety-two." I've memorized dates for getting into clubs since the dawn of time. Last year I was born in 1991.

He relaxed, smiling, sipping. "Congratulations. You can do everything now but be the president."

I thought about why he was so fixated on my age. What he was thinking of doing.

"Are you in college?" he said.

"Dropped out."

"Why?"

"To strip."

His eyebrows rose. I laughed.

"Kidding. I never went."

We still hadn't told each other our names. It was beginning to feel deliberate.

"You're not from around here," I said.

He gave me a funny look, half flattered, half perplexed. "Why do you say that?"

"For starters, stripping is a respectable profession in these parts. It's gainful employment. Plus you don't have an accent."

"Neither do you."

"Well, golly, Mr. Man," I drawled, "you sure are right about that."

He laughed. "So you hide it. You've reinvented yourself. A self-made woman."

I think he'd been drinking earlier that night, like me. His eyes were glassy and a bit feverish.

"Maybe," I said mysteriously, trying on the idea in my head. A self-made woman. I threw back the rest of my beer. The Guy stared at my throat, and I swanned for him as I swallowed. When my head came down my eyes were lazily half-closed, my mouth pouty. That fuck-me look I've used to great effect on other men.

The Guy averted his eyes. Took a drink. Scanned the crowd. I felt stupid. I hugged the stuffed pony under my arm.

"Why are you here alone?" I said.

"What?"

"I said—"

He touched my elbow and bent close. "You want to go somewhere quieter where we can actually talk?"

"Yes."

He didn't let go of my elbow, and I thanked a whole pantheon of gods for that. It felt different now. His skin on my skin caused a chemical reaction. My cells were rioting.

We walked out of the carnival into the night sea of grass and stars.

I did a suave little twist of my arm until our hands joined. I pulled him through the darkness toward the picnic table, then let go and hopped up, hugging the pony between my knees. He stopped a foot away.

"You look incredible," he breathed.

A rush of sweet blood to my head.

"So do you," I said, my voice also gauzy.

He moved toward me. Cool platinum starlight played off his hair, the gold sheen on his arms. He wasn't super tall, maybe five foot ten, but his frame was elegantly made, lithe muscle knitting around finely sculpted bones. That muscle rippled beneath his T-shirt and the jeans that molded to him. I pressed my palms to the splintered wood but I could still imagine them running down a hard thigh. I'm going to fuck you, I thought. Somewhere not far from here. Maybe the back of your car. The only question is how we'll get there.

"Did you bring me out here to talk," I said, "or for something else?"

He looked chagrined. He sat beside me on the table. The

rides were shutting down, great mechanical dragons folding their wings, coiling up their segmented tails. I propped the stuffed pony behind my head and lay back, looking up at a perfect planetarium sky.

"You asked why I'm here alone."

I glanced over at him. He stared straight ahead.

"I see the lights every night. It seems like the whole world has figured out how to be happy, but no one's letting me in on the secret."

There are moments, when you're getting to know someone, when you realize something deep and buried in you is deep and buried in them, too. It feels like meeting a stranger you've known your whole life.

"Why'd you get on the roller coaster?" I said.

A little comma formed in the corner of his mouth, a half smile. "I'm starting a new job soon, and . . . I'm terrified, honestly. I thought that if I faced another lifelong fear, it'd give me confidence."

"You didn't seem scared."

"You don't remember me screaming."

I grinned. "Au contraire. August twenty-first, twenty-thirteen. Never forget. But you seemed happy."

It should have tipped him off that I didn't talk about his job, I talked about feelings. I was too young to care about boring adult jobs. I was still testing out how my heart worked.

He was smiling at me now. I imagined him putting a knee between my legs, holding me down. The sky felt like a huge hot aquarium, swimming with tadpole stars.

"How about you?" he said. "Why tonight?"

"I'm starting a new job, too, actually."

"What kind of job?"

High school senior.

"It's sort of an unpaid internship. Anyway, I guess I wanted to do something the old me wouldn't have done."

"Would the old you have done this?"

I sat up slowly. My body was languid and light. We were very close, mostly by accident. His stubble glittered like gold dust. The ledge of his lips cast a shadow I couldn't look away from. "What am I doing, exactly?"

I felt the heat of his hand before it touched me, and shivered. He laid it on my bare knee. Didn't stroke, didn't squeeze, just placed it there like a card he'd dealt, waiting for my move.

"This?" I said. My voice had lost all body again, becoming air contained in a thin envelope of words. I mirrored his movement, rested my hand on his jeans. The denim was smooth-worn and warm.

His other hand cupped my face. Somehow he'd gotten closer without quite kissing me yet. There was a carnival smell still on us, beer and popcorn and motor grease, but all of that faded into a kind of white noise, and now I smelled him. Something between suede and smoke. The clean tang of sweat mixed into his cologne, turning into a musky alcohol. Pure delirium. I couldn't breathe any more of this. I couldn't get enough of it.

My body was on autopilot. Mouth opening, face tilting, everything yielding. "What am I doing?" I whispered again, and knew he felt my breath in his own mouth.

"Seducing me," he said.

My eyes opened all the way. My bones regained solidity. Blood pumped furiously into my throat, my temple, fleeing my hands and every part of me that had wanted to be touched by him. I pulled away.

His brow creased. If we'd known each other's names, he would have said my name then with a question mark.

Was that what I was doing? Seducing him? Another throwaway fuck?

Was that all this was?

"Did I say something wrong?"

I shook my head. But I stood up anyway, grabbed the stuffed animal, mangled it in my hands.

Again, that pained pause on his face where he wanted to say the name of this girl who was clearly upset. Funny, how our own names soothe us. It's okay, Maise. You are yourself. Whoever that is.

"I'm sorry," he said.

"Don't be sorry. I'm sorry."

"Why?"

"I wasn't trying to seduce you."

The tension went out of him. It wasn't his fault. It was just the crazy girl and her crazy girl-feelings.

Was that unfair? Maybe I wanted to be unfair.

"Hey," he said. He came close, his hand hovering over my shoulder blade, waiting for clearance to land. "I didn't mean it in a bad way. If you weren't trying, it would've happened anyway. You are so beautiful." The hand retreated. "I've upset you."

"No, you haven't."

He rocked on his toes a few times, back and forth. I'd learn later that it was his nervous habit. It endeared me to him, a little—instead of retreating from anxiety, he psyched himself up to face it. "I don't want the night to end like this. Can I take you home?"

I nodded.

He walked at my side, never ahead or behind. Our bodies aligned naturally. I never had to guess where he was going.

He drove a Chevy Monte Carlo built before I was born.

It looked like something out of a Tarantino film. I don't read too much into people's vehicle choices. Mom drives a minivan, and she's never taken me to soccer practice or gymnastics. Her van is her office. Only clients get to see the inside.

The front seat of his car was a solid piece of old leather. It smelled dizzyingly masculine. When he got in the seat dipped toward him, peeling away from my skin.

"Where do you live?"

I turned to him. I was breathing hard. He noticed and his hands came off the wheel, his body angling toward me.

We met halfway.

Before this goes any farther, I should tell you I've slept with older men before. Some much older than me. Like, times two and up on the multiplication table. One was almost times three.

Thanks, Dad, for leaving a huge void in my life that Freud says has to be filled with dick.

I don't blame it entirely on him, though. I am the master of my fate, I am the captain of my soul, and all that jazz. Obviously I'm compensating for something, but I think even if I'd had a normal childhood, I'd have grown bored of boys my age. They're like oversensitive car alarms. A brisk breeze is enough to set them off. I should know, since I lost my virginity to one in freshman year. I didn't even realize it when he came—I thought he was still trying to get in.

Okay, I thought. Bad first pick. The next will be better.

The next one lasted twenty-four seconds. I counted. He said if I really wanted to feel something, we should try anal.

At some point you realize they're still children, and it starts to feel weird and pervy.

So when a guy in his late twenties flirted with me at a gas station, I got into his car, and he fucked me on a bare mattress in a stuffy one-room apartment that smelled like ashes and beer. He made sure I came first, and he didn't whine about wearing a condom. He called me gorgeous and bought me a burger before he dropped me home.

I could get used to this, I thought.

So I did.

———

It seemed like the kiss would be frantic, urgent, but when our lips actually met it was soft. Restrained softness. All the urgency went into our hands, perched on each other's shoulder and neck like talons. My heart was ecstatic. He wanted this as much as I did and also wanted to not fuck it up, to not let it become a gross sloppy drunk screw. I kissed him slowly, indulgently, feeling the pillowed satin of his lips, the gritty scatter of stubble all around them. It took serious willpower to go slow. Beery bitterness in our mouths, but it just made everything sweeter—this was something we wanted no matter what imperfections tried to deter us.

His hand circled my skull, pulled me into him. I tilted my face further, my mouth at a right angle to his, opening for his tongue. God, when had I last been kissed like this? Had I ever? It felt like being fucked, but sweetly, more personally, somehow. Inside my veins my blood glowed the same neon red as those carnival lights. He pulled back, pulled gently at my lower lip. Opened his eyes and looked at me.

"I'm not trying to seduce you," I said in an absurd gasp.

He smiled. Not the ultrabright public smile from earlier, but one just for me, small and sly, one corner of his mouth higher than the other.

It was pretty obvious who was seducing whom here.

Some part of my old self wrested control. She curled her hands in his shirt and yanked him toward her. She lowered her body to the long seat and hooked her legs around his, let his weight settle atop her. They kissed again, her and him, and this time it was urgent and frantic and all the things they'd been holding back. Teeth now, and nails. She felt him get hard, the thick ridge of it pressing through his jeans against her inner thigh. She felt our body, mine and hers, getting wet, the sweat between her breasts, on the back of my neck, between our legs. We grasped the zipper of his fly.

The Guy pushed himself up on his elbows, panting. "Wait."

Then I was me again, hair sticking to my face, flushed. "What?"

He closed his eyes. I could tell breathing was a conscious effort on his part. He lowered his face, grazed my cheek with his sandpapered one. "I want you," he whispered into my hair, and a million filaments of electricity raced across my scalp. "But I want to know you. I don't just want a hookup."

When he raised his head again, I felt that same weightless drop I'd felt when our hands first touched a hundred feet above the Earth.

He combed a hand through my hair, untangling it. "Is that too old-fashioned for you?" A self-deprecating smile. His forehead furrowed when he smiled like that.

"No," I said.

"You are so beautiful. God, I just want to touch you." He sighed, his chest moving against mine. Sodium light slanted through the windshield, painting the side of his face with warm lemon. "You know why I was happy up there? Because I completely forgot where I was. All I could think about was you."

I couldn't wait anymore.

I took his face in my hands and brought it back to me. We kissed with closed mouths, then tongues again, and he pressed me down, his knee between my legs, like I'd imagined him doing. I felt his kiss all the way through me. I felt it in every hollow place, filling me with summer heat, starlight, sweat, and abandon. When he broke away I said, low and steady, "We can do both. It doesn't have to just be a hookup."

His expression was pained, but he didn't argue this time.

I raked my fingers through his sweat-damp hair. Wrapped my legs around his. His weight made my breath shallow. I felt the rotation of the Earth, our bodies pulled together by gravity. "I want to fuck you," I said.

The pained look melted away.

I'd burned off my alcohol. The drunk feeling that surged in me now was self-generated. I didn't even think of where we were parked, if anyone might walk by. I didn't care. He kissed my throat, my collarbone, pulled the tight sticky tee off with more grace than I would have. His stubble tingled against my breasts. He opened my bra, pressed his hot mouth to my skin. Every string in me tightened and hummed. There was some jerky shifting as I tugged off his T-shirt and he took off my shorts, then our bodies rejoined, skin on skin. Every time an article of my clothing came off, he would spend a moment exploring the revealed area with hands and mouth, then he would kiss me again. Something was spiraling wildly inside of me, more and more out of control. My usual clinical approach to sex wouldn't work here. He kept confusing it with these tender, adoring gestures. Just fuck me, I wanted to say. But I didn't want him to just fuck me. I wanted this to keep going on forever, never running out of clothes or new places to be touched.

Finally his fingers slipped into the waistband of my underwear. I popped the button of his jeans, and he didn't stop me this time. He didn't stop me as I unzipped his fly, either. Or as I slid my hand around his dick. It's almost surreal, the first time you feel it and realize this man is going to fuck you with it. It was thick and hard, entire degrees hotter than the rest of him. As I touched him his eyes closed, his eyebrows slanting upward, toward bliss. I love that. I love how absolutely helpless they get when you touch them. I pulled him out of his jeans, pressed my thighs around him. My underwear was still on.

He reached out for something. Flipped the glove box open, extracted a foil wrapper. Pressed it into my hand.

I love when they let me do this, too.

I tore it open, rolled it over him. There's something so final about it that makes my insides turn to water. No going back. No more excuses. It's going to happen.

He ran a hand through my hair again, his eyes almost sad. Tucked both thumbs into my underwear and pulled it down. I didn't let him take it all the way off. Too cramped inside the car anyway. I wanted it to feel desperate, difficult, necessary.

"Fuck me," I said. My voice shook.

He pressed himself against me, but not inside. We both grimaced. Then again, letting me feel the length of him. The condom was instantly slippery. I breathed through my teeth.

He clamped one hand to the side of my face and said, "Tell me your name."

Oh, fuck. He was going to do this, make it real.

I bit my lip and rolled my hips against him.

His breath flooded over me. I felt each muscle in him flexing, his abs crunching against my belly, his thighs stretching inside of mine. He slipped his arms beneath my back, pulling me closer to him. That hard dick right up against me was making my brain explode.

"Fuck me," I said again. No shake. A growl.

"Tell me your name."

It wasn't easy for him. I probably could've waited him out. He probably would've given in. But I said, impatiently, "Why?"

"I don't want this to just be sex. I want to know who you are."

Men have a thing I call sex logic. When they're horny, which is most of the time, the rules of logic change. Instead of being an organized system of reasoning, logic becomes the shortest path to getting what they want. In my present situation, I also succumbed to sex logic. It's not like he could find me with a first name, anyway. Even in a town this small. Even with a name this uncommon.

And maybe a part of me wanted to let him in. Really let him in.

"Maise," I said, shaky again.

Something shifted in his face, a puzzle piece sliding into place.

"Hello, Maise," he said.

"Hi. What's yours?"

"Evan."

"Evan," I said, "please stop talking and fuck me."

He kissed me first, and held my lip between his teeth, sharply, when he did it. I cried out, not from pain but relief. I'd been aching for this, and it wasn't until he was inside me that I realized it. He fucked me slowly, his eyes open, on my face. My fingers and toes curled and then sprang loose. The funny thing was that his kiss had felt like fucking me, and his fucking me felt like being kissed, everywhere, every bit of my body unbearably warm and buzzing. I had to turn away, close my eyes. Shut down some of my senses. I heard my own voice, the breaths I vocalized without meaning to, and I sounded so girlish and young that it excited me. I was getting off on myself. Crazy. Evan—oh god, he had a name now—lowered his mouth to my breasts, kissed them, sucked at a nipple as he thrust into me, and I felt like I was being turned inside out. Everything became a confusion of overlapping sensations. I hadn't even realized I'd slipped my hands into the back pockets of his jeans, pulling him deeper into me. Fleetingly I was aware of my bare foot splayed against the cool window. The smack of my skin against leather. Eventually the outer world fell away and all that remained were pressure points. His hands cupping my ass, holding me still, making me feel all of him inside of me, filling me with hardness and heat. You start feeling crazy things when you're close. All the inhibitions dissolve. I wanted him in every part of me, my mouth, my ass, between my breasts, every place that could be fucked. He went still inside of me and I could have screamed. When he started fucking me again he was so slow, so fucking slow I felt every inch of him, sinking in all the way to the hilt, pressing my clit, and my eyelids fluttered and I said, "I'm gonna come, I'm gonna come," and he kept fucking me steadily and I let go, every coiled bit of tension shooting out of my nerves in an electric storm. He came with me, his whole body seizing up, monstrously strong for a heartbeat, his fingers digging into my ass and his dick a startling hardness inside me when I was already softening, melting. He pumped into me, softer and softer, his head falling, body going slack, until his weight hung there, poised on the fulcrums of his elbows.

Planets moved in their orbits. Dawn broke in the United Kingdom. A car door slammed like a typewriter key.

I looked up at his face. He was already looking at mine.

When was the last time the man who'd just fucked me wanted to see my face after he came?

Neither of us blinked or seemed to breathe. He was still inside me, soft now. I didn't know what to do. They usually pulled out immediately, or I disengaged and started looking for my clothes. I couldn't move, trapped under him.

He brushed my cheek with the back of his hand.

Oh god. Please don't say something cheesy. Please don't talk.

He leaned in and kissed me.

I could deal with this. I closed my eyes, kissed him back. An aimless, unhurried kiss, not wanting anything from him now. As he kissed me he pulled out, gentle. I made a little sighing sound. He tucked his dick into his fly, leaving the condom on. His eyes moved over my body but now, unlike earlier, they lingered on my face.

Panic.

He was looking at me like he knew me. Not in the biblical sense—obviously we were past that—but in a you-are-more-than-a-quick-fuck sense.

I sat up, forcing myself to reach casually for my clothes. Underwear up. Bra on. I couldn't get into my shorts without almost kicking him in the face, which made him laugh and grab my leg and rub his cheek against my calf. I tried not to let the prickle of his stubble send fireworks through my nervous system, but you try arguing with endorphins.

The car smelled like bleach and sweat, that magical sex musk that isn't so magical after it's all over.

How the hell was I going to get out?

The pony stared at us lugubriously from the dashboard. Jesus. Little fucker had watched the whole thing.

"Maise."

My spine crackled when he said it. I pretended to find something interesting in the side mirror. "Yeah?"

"Just trying it out."

Would it be too rude to open the door right now?

Fingertips grazed my forearm, the fine peach fuzz there. "Are you okay?"

"Yeah."

"Maise."

I turned to him. I guess that's all he wanted—to say my name and get a response. He tilted his head, that otherworldliness shimmering in him. God, he was a beautiful man. And he was so nice to me. And I had to get out of his car before I choked.

"Hey," I said with forced cheer, "I've got an idea."

His eyebrows rose hopefully.

"I'm going to see if there's anyone left to bribe at the Gravitron." I made myself smirk. "You should get cleaned up. Meet me there?"

I'm a pretty good liar. Key skills: eye contact, confidence, not caring about the outcome.

But here was the problem. Somehow, in the two or three hours since I'd met him, Evan had gotten to know me well enough to see through the bullshit. Maybe he heard some undetectable crack in my voice, saw a furtive glint of desperation in my eyes. Because instead of joking or blushing or anything normal, he looked at me like I'd just said I never wanted to see him again.

Never mind that that was exactly what I was saying.

"Okay," he said quietly.

Key skill: follow-through.

"Great," I said, and leaned in to peck his cheek.

He grabbed my jaw, holding my face still. My heart thumped like a vampire kicking his way out of his coffin.

Evan just looked at me. He ran his thumb over my mouth, my cheek, as if he was memorizing them, knowing it was the last time he'd see them.

I didn't have the heart to give him a fake kiss. I lowered my head and got out of the car.

———

My bike was chained to the cyclone fence behind the Tilt-a-Whirl. It was quiet inside save for a few drunk carnies messing around with the strongman hammer. I swung onto my seat, wincing at the sweet burn between my legs. God fucking dammit. I had to stand to pedal out of the tall grass and dirt, and of course every push reminded me of what I'd just done and how good it had felt and how bad I felt now.

Yeah, I hook up with older guys. And then I leave them, before they can leave me.

Thanks for the abandonment issues, Dad. Fuck you very much.

When I reached the blacktop my eyes were blurry. It was just the wind. Really, it was.

2

MISSION: Remake Myself.

The movie cliché is to cut off my hair. Well, fuck that. Not too many Irish girls can boast about dark, silky tresses.

I'm also not going to buy a whole new wardrobe (broke), get a pet (can't support a dependent), a boyfriend (see previous), or a makeover (Mom's whorepaint inspires me to stay au naturel).

What I *am* going to do:

Delete all the numbers in my phone. No more skeezy geezers, no more high school skanks who think talking to me means we're friends, or that we are even in the same genus.

Apply for college. This has nothing to do with Evan asking me about it.

Face my fears, at least one per month. I've already done my duty for August. In September, I'll tell Mom she has a drug problem. If I make it to October, clowns.

Get a job. Don't expect Mom to give a flying fuck that I want to go to college, or to have any idea what I'll need.

Stop using men. Stop. Stop. Stop.

Maybe see that psychologist again. Or one who doesn't have such a bunny fetish.

Live, instead of numbing myself to life, like Mom.

Stop thinking about Evan.

———

They made me register for classes late because O'Malley technically starts with an O, not an M. Which meant everything I wanted to take was gone by the time I sat down with the registrar.

"I'm sorry, Maisie," the woman droned. She looked half asleep in the swampy AC. "It's full."

"Maise," I corrected. "Short for Maisie, which is a name for a little girl. And you don't understand, I reserved Film Studies last year."

I caught a reflection of her laptop screen in her bifocals. She was playing Angry Birds.

"I'm going to film school," I explained. "I need this class."

"You're going to be an actress?" she said, tepidly interested.

"No, I'm going to *make* movies."

"You're pretty. You could be an actress."

I started to say, *It takes more than that,* but depressingly, she was right. "Can't you just look up the reservations?"

"Class is full."

A red bird went rocketing across her glasses.

"How about Drama 102?"

"I don't want to fucking act," I muttered.

"Excuse me?"

"Look, one of those seats was reserved for me. Maybe

someone bribed you. I'm not judging. I'm sure they don't pay you enough to put up with this shit." I leaned across her desk. "But this is all I'm passionate about. If I don't get this class, the only way I'll get into film school is by sleeping with the dean of admissions. He'll probably make me blow him in his Porsche. Him and all his douchey adjunct friends. That's the future you're deciding right now. Think about it."

Mrs. Bird stared with her round, rheumy eyes.

I raised an eyebrow.

Click, click. The laser printer whirred. "Seems I was mistaken. A seat just opened up."

Mrs. Bird handed the paper over, peering at me above her glasses.

"You should seriously consider acting."

"Thank you, ma'am. I will."

I beamed as I walked out to my bike, imprinting the schedule like a proverb on my heart.

FILM STUDIES. M-TH-F 10:15–11:45. E WILKE. RM 209.

I was so absorbed in it I didn't notice the maroon Monte Carlo with the sad-eyed pony sitting on the dashboard, its coat shining sleekly in the sun.

———

If you're a film buff, right now you're probably thinking, *She wants to go to film school and doesn't even know Kubrick?*

First: that's why I wanted to get into Film Studies, duh. I admit, my tastes skew modern. I'm more into Lars von Trier, Terrence Malick, and the anime films of Miyazaki than the stuff you're supposed to say you like—Kubrick, Hitchcock, the good ol' boys. I'm no hipster, though. I love Peter Jackson and J. J. Abrams just as much as the arthouse darlings.

So yeah, epic fail on my part when I didn't recognize one of Kubrick's most iconic works, *2001: A Space Odyssey.*

You think my Film Studies teacher would let me forget it, either?

I see the lights every night, he'd said.

I couldn't get those words out of my head. He lived or worked somewhere near. In this flyover, flyaway town that barely topped five figures, one of them was a man with an angel's face, a man who'd asked me my name before he fucked me in his car on a fearless August night.

I couldn't get him out of my head.

I biked up to the water tower on the hill overlooking the prairie. Climbed the rust-eaten struts up to a crow's nest some stoners had hammered together out of Mississippi driftwood. It wasn't as hot tonight, and a restless wind raked through the grass, smelling of loam and barley. From here the carnival lights looked like fireflies swirling madly in place, trapped under an invisible jar. Just like me.

So, I thought. Am I feeling good after sleeping with a nice guy and leaving? Is that hitting the spot? Or am I feeling more alone than ever?

Rhetorical questions.

Maybe it was time to admit that being wanted intensely for a few hours wasn't enough. It got me through a few days, a few weeks here and there, but when the emptiness returned it felt bigger, hungrier. I kept thinking it was the guy—once I found a nice guy, it would be different. Fulfilling. But I left the nice guy like I'd left all the others, and I was still empty. And I covered it up with cockiness and bravado and kept telling myself that this was life, this was how things really were. Nobody was happy. Nobody was fulfilled.

Evan thought there was some secret to happiness, but he was wrong. The secret was to harden yourself. Not let the emptiness get inside you.

But I was failing pretty spectacularly at that.

Rustling in the grass below. A sharp crack.

I jumped up, wishing for a knife. Some tweaked-out psycho rapist?

"Who's there?" a boy called.

Shit. He was standing right next to my bike.

"Go away," I said menacingly.

Silence, then a low laugh. "It's okay. I won't hurt you."

"Don't touch my bike," I said. "And go away."

A cigarette cherry glowed in the darkness, an angry orange eye. "Rude."

The longer I stayed up there, the more scared he'd think me. I climbed down smoothly, jumping near the bottom and landing on nimble feet. The boy was a good head and shoulders taller than me, but scarecrow skinny. I couldn't see much of him except a huge Adam's apple when the cigarette flared.

I knew most kids my age, and I'd seen this boy around school. A loner type, sorta weird.

"Hi," he said.

I picked up my bike.

"You're just going to leave without saying hi?"

"Hi," I said. "Bye."

He laughed again.

I swung my leg over and bit into the dirt with my tire.

"I'm Wesley," he said.

"I'm not looking for new friends."

"That's a weird name."

I laughed, despite myself. Dammit. The ground was all rutted and lumpy. Would've been faster to walk my bike out.

"I've seen you here before," Wesley said, following me with a cloud of herbal smoke. Clove cigarettes.

"Great," I said, "so you're a stalker."

"It's not stalking if I was here first."

I stopped, my shoes slapping into the dirt. "Look. Whoever you are, it's nice to meet you, but this isn't going to work out. I don't want a friend, boyfriend, groupie, or big brother. Whatever you're thinking, it's not going to happen."

The cherry arced off into the darkness. "You're M. O'Malley, aren't you?"

Ice in my heart. "What?"

Crinkling. He opened something white and fluttery in front of my face. Moonlight turned it bluish. I could just make out laser print.

"They dropped me from film class. Someone took my seat. The lady in the office said it was a girl who looked like Snow White. She went on and on about how 'talented' you are."

"Shit," I breathed.

"I'm not mad," Wesley said. "But the least you could do is tell me why you need that class so bad."

I didn't even know about E. Wilke yet. How it would feel to need someone. Right then, I just wanted something of my own. Something I'd made. Something no one could take away from me.

I stuck out my hand.

Wesley frowned at it, then shook. His skin was dry and rough, like a corn husk.

"Maise," I said.

"Huh?"

"That's my name."

I gave it easily, freely, no strings.

You remember these things later, when they matter.

"And the reason I need that class," I said, "is so I can get the fuck out of this town."

He smiled, a big, crooked grin. "Good. That's a worthy reason to fuck me over."

Wesley walked me home. Not intentionally, but the conversation just kept going. Turned out he's into movies, too, but more the technical side: cameras, cinematography, video editing. I respect people who get nerdy as fuck about something they love. He spent most of the walk explaining the difference between twenty-four, thirty, and forty-eight frames per second, and how human eyes work. How our brains fill in the gaps between frames. How when we're watching a movie, half of what we "see" isn't even real—we're making it up in our heads.

I thought about seeing Mom at one frame per day. The way I blurred her life into something to fill the gaps.

I wondered if Evan was doing the same to me in his head.

When we got to my house, Wesley pulled out his phone. "Want to trade numbers?"

I didn't want to say yes too easily. High school boys are so presumptuous. "Are you going to guilt-trip me about that class?"

He shrugged. "If I miss anything life-changing, you can tell me."

We traded numbers.

"You lied," Wesley said, grinning.

"About what?"

"Not wanting new friends."

"We're not friends," I said coolly, walking toward the porch.

Mistake. I thought I was being flippant, not coy. This isn't fourth grade. We're not going to instantly become BFFs because we have the same cartoon character on our backpacks.

But what Wesley heard was, *I have not ruled out the possibility of fucking you.*

You're never saying what you think you're saying.

———

First day of school.

It felt like life was beginning all over again. That September sun, still a smoldering summer ember but starting to fail, to slant a little more heavily. The shadows of leaves flickered like pixels on the sidewalks. All the voices were relaxed, happy to shake off the terrible freedom of summer and slip back into comfortable straitjackets, schedules and routines. Everything had a golden powder coat, the autumn decay setting in slowly, breaking the world into molecules of sun and dust.

7:55, First bell, bright and comforting. My insides arranged themselves obediently, preparing for the role we were going to play for the next ten months. I waded through suntanned bodies, the ocean mist of gel and perfume. Everyone's face was jammed against a phone, getting in their last few precious minutes of airtime before they severed all contact with the outside world. I tossed mine casually into my locker. Wesley had texted me: *Lunch 4th period?* And I said, *See you there.*

So began the first day of my "new job," as I'd told Evan. I wondered where he was, if he'd started his yet.

In retrospect you want to scream at yourself: Don't you

feel it? Don't you feel that strange edginess in your blood, the way it vibrates, as if some nearby force is disturbing it? Don't you notice the disturbance, Luke?

I slammed my locker closed.

A Mean Girl stalked past, lip curled. Her eyes slid down my body like a viper's tongue.

Okay, I hadn't *totally* remade myself. I wasn't Mother freaking Teresa. I wore shorts a hair's width within dress code regs, and a button-up boy's shirt that I hadn't buttoned very diligently. The funny thing was, even in my hillbilly attire and zero makeup, I looked ten times better than this girl, who'd spent all morning tweezing and abrading just to end up resembling a chihuahua. I smiled at her sweetly, and her sneer deepened. You could almost see the circuits sparking behind her eyeballs as she scanned me: *Target acquired. Terminate.*

8:00–9:05, Calculus. Save the worst for first, as Mom says. I was alert, assiduous. I took old-school paper-and-pencil notes. Some kids tapped at laptops and tablets. This is a dual lesson in class stratification, I thought.

9:10–10:10, World History. This involved numbers, too, but not enough. My mind wandered. Here's a history of the world: Girl meets boy. Girl fucks boy. Girl gets scared and skips out on boy. Boy builds civilization to lure girl back.

After class I made a beeline for my locker to text Wesley, but froze up. What's the polite way to say, *I need comfort but am unwilling to share any titillating details?* Whatever. We didn't even know each other. Who was getting presumptuous now?

Chin up, sport, I told myself. Next class was Film Studies. My first taste of the future. And then I'd have an excuse to text Wesley and gloat about what he'd missed.

As I swam upstairs through the crush of bodies, I thought

about what Evan had said. *It's a classic.* Well, mister, if it's such a classic I'm sure we'll study it.

Like watching a lamb prance cluelessly toward the knife.

Room 209 was at the end of a hall, a huge window beside it like a portal straight to the sun. I spent a second soaking in the light, photons beaming through my eyelids. When I walked into the room my vision danced with microscopic explosions of blood vessels, a hazy red sparkle.

I saw him first.

I didn't blink. Everything inside me came to a full stop. He wore pressed slacks and a collared shirt, clean-shaven, hair combed neatly, a silver watch gleaming on his wrist, but it was undeniably him. I knew those hands. I knew that mouth. I'd pictured that face, grizzled with stubble, his eyes half shut, nuzzling at my neck as I lay in bed and got myself off.

I knew instantly, unequivocally. Evan Wilke. Starting his new job as a teacher at Riverland High.

My teacher.

10:15–11:45, Intro to the End of the World.

He raised his head and swept a generic, acknowledging smile over the room, starting with the far side. It took all of two seconds to reach me but I felt it coming like thunder, sensing my imminent doom and yet paralyzed, unable to run.

He reached me and paused. His face fell. Not into dismay— all expression went out of it. Shock.

A kid nudged me aside and walked in. I stood stupidly in the doorway. It felt like a series of small eternities, but it was only seconds.

Evan stared at me dazedly. I think he was confused. I don't think he realized I was a student yet. I made myself step in and took the seat nearest the door.

His mouth opened slightly.

What did we do wrong, Your Honor?

I was eighteen. He wasn't my teacher yet.

I drank. Everyone drinks.

He purchased alcohol for me. I lied about my age. Not his fault.

I rest my case.

My eyes were open, but I wasn't conscious of having seen anything for a minute. A gray-out, Mom called it. You didn't pass out but you just . . . weren't there for a while.

The room was starting to fill up.

Evan shuffled papers around his desk. Then he stood there, staring at the surface, only his eyes moving, a rapid back-and-forth like REM.

Was this a dream? It felt distinctly nightmarish.

He straightened and walked toward the door, pausing beside me.

"Can I see you outside?"

Soft, discreet. No hint of emotion.

I stood without looking at him, feeling exposed. I hadn't brought anything to this class. I thought I had everything I needed in my head.

He waited in the sun. Kids streamed past in and out of a bathroom. All their noise seemed fuzzy and far away, behind glass.

I'd imagined what I'd do if I ever saw him again. Rush into his arms. Apologize for skipping out. Touch his face. Kiss him, kiss him.

Instead we stood with two feet of solid sunlight between us.

"Maise," he said.

My head rose as if his voice had lifted it.

"Is that your real name?"

"Yes."

"I am so sorry."

I wasn't prepared for this. I'd expected anger. *You lied to me. You ran off.* "Why?" I said.

He only shook his head.

"I'm eighteen," I said quickly. Darted a glance at the kids around us. No one seemed to see anything out of the ordinary—just a teacher talking to a student. "I was eighteen then, too. So—don't, you know. Be sorry."

"Are you okay?"

I think I'm starting to be. "Yeah."

He rocked on his toes. It made him seem young. God, how old was he, anyway? I figured past his twenties, but I had no real fucking idea. Two feet of sunlight wasn't enough to block out that suede smell, tame and subtle now, but unmistakable.

"I don't know what to do," he said. "You tell me what you want. You can transfer to another class. Or I can—I can submit my resignation, right now. I'll do it. Just give the word."

He was talking crazy, and it made my heart expand like a balloon. You're guilty, I thought. Flustered. You know this will be a disaster if we pretend like nothing happened. Because you still feel something.

The warning bell rang. One minute.

Evan didn't move. His gaze focused unerringly on me.

"You didn't do anything wrong," I whispered, conscious of the emptying hall. "And I don't want to transfer to another class."

"Maise," he said. Just my name.

"And I'm the one who's sorry. I shouldn't have left like that."

Thirty seconds. Lockers slammed. Footsteps hurried.

"I don't know if I can do this," he said.

"It'll be fine." I swallowed every bit of spit in my mouth to add, "Mr. Wilke."

We were staring at each other when the final bell rang. Together, we walked back into class.

It was both the longest and shortest hour and a half of my life, and at the end of it all I remembered was him saying, "See you Thursday," and eyeing me a heartbeat longer than anyone else.

———

Wesley gaped at me. "Holy shit."

I guess he was staring at my boobs. I'd totally forgotten them. I'd forgotten my entire body. It was just this cloud of blood floating beneath me, an occasional warmth.

"I see what that lady meant now," Wesley said. "You're *very* talented."

"Shut the fuck up," I said lazily. I could not stop grinning.

"What are you so happy about?"

I pushed my gigantic smile at him, knowing how my face looked: rapturous, flushed, the sort of pupil-dilating ecstasy that makes guys lose it. I didn't care if it was teasing. I gave zero fucks. "Life," I said. "Being alive."

"Creepy."

I laughed, and spun my lunch tray on the slide counter. A Tater Tot went sailing into oblivion.

Mr. fucking Wilke.

At the beginning, you're grateful to simply be near them. To look. To bask. It's a gift fallen from heaven, accidentally nudged off a golden table, still glimmering with stardust.

I didn't have insane ideas about janitor closets and locked doors yet.

I was just happy.

Wesley took out his phone while we ate and started filming. It was expensive, recorded in HD. I was so high on myself I let him. I leaned against the cafeteria window, squinting, looking for Mr. Wilke's car. It gave me an obscene thrill. My sweat was in that car. I'd come in that car. It was out there somewhere, in the middle of all this wholesome kiddie shit.

My skin seemed to inflate with blood. I felt everything pressing against me: air, voices, eyes. Like being on X. I wanted to touch everything, be touched everywhere. I wanted everyone to know how alive I was.

Wesley watched me through his phone camera.

"What are you looking at?" I said.

"Escaped mental patient."

I loomed close to the lens. He tried to edge away. "Joke's on you," I said. "I never escaped. This *is* the asylum."

"You're fucking crazy," he said admiringly.

"Just you wait."

On my way home I saw Mr. Wilke's car in the lot, from a distance. I stood in the gravel, eyes out of focus, remembering how the leather stuck to my bare skin, until someone honked. I don't remember biking home. I don't remember anything. Was it even a day, or merely an interval of sunlight and bells and doors until I was alone, Mom out on a sale, the house blissfully quiet and dark? I took a bath for the first time in forever. Pinned my hair up, found an old bottle of orange oil. We always have candles. Count on a drug house for candles. I lit a few and slipped into water so hot it could strip me to the bone. Dragged a loofah along my shins, my upper arms, slow as sin. My skin needed stimulation.

My everything needed stimulation.

When I get myself off, it's usually a utilitarian thing. Sex logic. The shortest path to what I want.

Not tonight.

I parted my knees, let a hand trail along my thigh and settle where gravity decided. My eyes closed. The memories came flooding back. The gritty, scratchy feel of his face against my breasts. That soft hot mouth pulling at my nipples. I sank lower in the tub, letting the weight of the water cover me, crush me, like his body had. Ran a finger over my lips beneath the water. It wasn't the same. I craved the hardness of him, that smoky leathery smell, that overwhelming sense of masculinity all around me, forcing its way inside of me. Candlelight flickered at my eyelids. I touched myself the same way, lightly, flickeringly, warm water swirling around my fingertip. It could almost have been a tongue. I remembered him teasing me with the head of his dick, making me tell him my name first. I breathed faster. Bit my lip. Slipped my finger inside. Water lapped at the porcelain, a wet smack like skin. God, if only he was the one fucking me right now. This was his finger, I thought. Not mine. This was him, shoving me against the classroom wall, his hand inside my underwear, his finger snaking inside me, fucking me as I grew tighter around him. His thumb circling my clit without touching the tip. His finger sliding in to the knuckle, stiff and quick, that I took as deeply as I could, that made me ache in a place tucked so far inside it didn't seem real, the root of me. His finger fucking me and filling my belly with heat that built higher and higher until I couldn't contain it anymore and it spilled over in a white-hot rush. His hand making me come, making my thighs tighten and my voice cry out and my honey spread all over him, giving myself up to the water, to this man in my head.

Tuesday.

Carrot sticks and cream cheese.

Me spending way too much fucking time checking my hair between periods in case of an Evan sighting.

My PE teacher: "Yes, I'm a lesbian. No, that is not a job requirement."

Wesley filming a fight in the hall. Blood gushing from a guy's nose, a long red creature that keeps crawling and crawling out, endless.

A sudden, cold rain drenching me on the way home. My invincible skin not even feeling it.

Wednesday.

The familiar smell of clove cigarettes.

A girl in history asking if I want to work on a report together.

Lingering storm clouds, turning the world below into zinc and aluminum.

Wesley showing me a video of a homeless guy downtown who keeps crossing the same intersection, back and forth, back and forth.

Thursday.

He looked up when I walked in. I waited and let a few other kids go in first, so I could walk in alone. So he could look up nervously and see me and break into a smile, that smile I remembered from the car, the small, private one. He looked down quickly at his desk, but his lips were still curved.

"Maise."

What the fuck was Wesley doing in my class?

"What the hell?" I said.

He pouted. "Nice to see you too."

I sat down next to him and shot anxious looks between him and Mr. Wilke. Could he know? Was this some kind of intervention?

"What are you doing here?"

"I was on the waiting list. Someone dropped."

"Oh."

The disappointment in my voice didn't go unnoticed. Wesley kicked the desk in front of him. I tested the edge of a fingernail with my teeth, a bad habit.

Worlds colliding. This never ended well on sitcoms.

"I just wasn't expecting to see you here," I said.

"Clearly."

He didn't look at me. I looked at my desk. Someone had carved RIHANNA = SLUT. I thought about adding CHRIS BROWN = DOMESTIC ABUSER, but Mr. Wilke probably would've caught me before I finished.

I was not going to entertain the insane detention fantasy that instantly popped into my mind.

All my stoked-up happiness had evaporated. I wasn't the self-made teacher-seducing minx who'd walked in. I was a banal teenage girl with depressingly typical problems.

I glanced up at Mr. Wilke. It was like he had Maise radar: his eyes rose to mine immediately. Or maybe he'd been looking at me more often than I realized. I remembered the bathtub and blushed, but didn't look away. I can do this, I thought. I can't touch you but I can eye-fuck you. He wore his collar open today, his hair a little mussed, and I wondered if it was for me. I let my eyes move over him, shoulders to waist, then a slow return. His stayed steady on mine.

Movement in my peripheral vision. Wesley, training a video camera on me.

"Jesus," I snapped, whirling away. "Will you fucking ask me first?"

"I was capturing a moment."

My heart throbbed in my throat. "What moment?"

"Homicidal rage."

Despite myself, I laughed, relieved. Wesley was not a bad guy. Socially awkward, probably a virgin, possibly latching on to me in an unhealthy way. But right then, that sort of teenage boy angst was comforting. Familiar. A simple toy I could pick up and understand, instantly. Ballast against Mr. Wilke and whatever was happening between us.

The final bell rang.

My teacher stood up, smiling. An open, ordinary smile. He spoke to us, asked questions, spent more time listening to our answers than he lectured. Showed us film clips on YouTube, tropes that popped up time and time again. Grinned and nodded enthusiastically when we began to recognize them for ourselves. Asked about our favorite directors, actors, composers. I managed to answer like a normal human being. I got into a debate with a guy about whether *Alien* was a feminist movie. Wesley pointed out that Ripley was originally written as a man, and someone called him Wesleypedia (brilliant), and Mr. Wilke let me go on a five-minute rant about Hollywood infantilizing women and not giving us a female-helmed *Die Hard*. He listened to us earnestly, his face filled with curiosity, amusement, respect. He was smarter than us but not smug. He shared his intelligence like a secret, making us conspirators in it. I could feel the whole class falling in love with him.

And every time his eyes touched me, the air jolted.

Heat lightning.

I'd started to follow Wesley out of class when Mr. Wilke called my name.

Wesley raised his eyebrows. I shrugged, pretending to have no idea what it was about. "I'll catch up. Buy me a taco."

"You've got five minutes until I eat it."

"Pig."

I was dragging it out. I was nervous. This could be something amazing, or this could be the turning-in-my-resignation/ you'll-be-better-off speech.

And this would absolutely be the first time I'd been alone with him since the night we met.

I turned around. He stood behind his desk, a solid obstacle preventing untoward contact between teacher and student.

"Close the door."

My heart did a kickflip.

I closed it, lingered over the lock, left it open. Walked slowly toward his desk, wondering where I should stop. My knees hit cool steel.

"Hi," he said.

We hadn't talked until now. All that stuff in class had been between other selves.

"Hi."

He seemed about to say something rehearsed, eyebrows up, mouth ajar, but he just looked at me and it melted away. And he kept looking.

"Is this weird for you?" he said finally.

"Yes. Is it weird for you?"

"Yes."

"Good."

The corner of his mouth lifted. My stomach mimicked it. My center of gravity grew wings and took off.

"I keep hoping this is some elaborate practical joke," he said.

I swallowed. "Life is an elaborate practical joke."

"How do we make this work?"

My eyes widened.

"Shit," he said, laughing. "I didn't—I mean, how do we have a class together without it being weird?"

"I don't think that's possible."

"If it ever gets too weird for you, tell me. Anything you need, I'll do it. No questions asked."

I hated that he was treating me like a victim. Someone he needed to make reparations to.

"What about you?" I said, propping my hip against the desk, folding my arms. "What happens if it gets too weird for you? You just get to pack up and leave?"

"It's not like that."

"What is it like?"

"And it's already too weird for me," he said, ignoring my question. "I have no memory of this week. There was the moment you walked into my class, and there's now. Nothing else."

My mouth opened, an involuntary breath coming free.

"But I don't want to impose that shit on you. It's not your problem."

"Impose," I said.

He winced. Put a hand on his desk, leaned into it. The space between us was finding ways to close, even with solid objects intervening.

"I don't want to screw your life up, Maise."

"Do you have a class fourth period?"

"No."

I unfolded my arms and before he could do anything, I took that open collar in my hands, lifted on my toes, and kissed him across the aircraft carrier he called a desk. He didn't fight. He kissed me back, oh so lightly, lips barely parting. Careful. He tasted like mint creme, kind of like Bailey's. His face felt somehow rougher without stubble.

"This is dangerous," he said against my mouth.

"I know," I said.

He pulled me onto his desk and I swung my legs across to his side. We never stopped kissing. One hand at the back of my neck, the other gliding between my thighs. My legs tightened but my mouth opened in response, as if my wires had crossed. I thrust my hands into that hair I'd wanted to mess up so badly. I was short of breath but kept kissing him anyway, not getting enough of that creamy mint, those lips that were somehow firm and yielding at the same time, opening me, parting me. Giddily I thought, Have you been eating mints on the off chance this would happen? Have you been obsessing about this as much as I have?

A knock at the door.

Hands instantly demagnetized. I hopped off his desk, smoothed my shorts. He dropped into his chair and crossed his legs. "Yes?" he called, deep and steady.

I stepped back to an appropriate distance, but our eyes never left each other.

Thank fucking god, it was just some random kid. "You got the projector in here?"

"No," Mr. Wilke said. "It's in 208."

"Sorry." The door closed.

We both breathed audibly.

"We can't do this here," he said.

"Where can we do it?"

He laughed. "Nowhere," he said, but his words were at odds with his eyes.

"Don't give me the fake Boy Scout routine," I said. "You're sitting there with a hard-on."

My bravado was slightly spoiled by my breathless delivery. The way he looked at me from under his eyebrows, slightly sheepish, slightly intense, turned every girl part in me to jelly. I clenched my hands to keep them from idle evil.

"What happens now?" I said.

"I don't know, Maise."

Say my name. God, keep saying it.

"You won't break me," I said, my voice low. "I'm not a doll. I'm not fragile. And you can't possibly screw my life up any more than it is."

That furrowed look, the mournful angel observing human tragedy. "It's not just about damage control. It should be more than that."

"Then give me more," I said.

The fourth-period bell rang.

I walked out, but my heart stayed right there where I'd planted it, a tender little seed waiting for sun.

———

Friday looked like rain. That sneaky summer rain that waits for a still moment and sucks the air out of the world *Backdraft*-style and explodes the sky into water. For the first time in eons, Mom drove me to school. We sat in the van like strangers on a plane, making awkward small talk.

"You still talk to Melissa?"

"Who?"

"That Melissa girl you went around with. The blonde."

"I haven't talked to her since freshman year."

"Oh."

Traffic light. Yellow. Red.

"Got lunch money?"

"Yeah."

"Where you get it?"

"Turned a trick."

"Watch your fuckin' mouth."

Green.

"Can you get out here? I got a pickup."

I opened the door wordlessly.

"Babe."

I looked at my mother. She had my face, under crayon makeup. She had the hick accent I'd ironed out of my voice. She had the dead-end future I would never, ever have.

"Let's go out this weekend. You and me."

Drop dead.

"I'm going to be late," I said.

"Love you."

I slammed the door. Pictured it closing on her face. The clown stamp she'd leave on the glass.

You wondered why I lied to you, Mr. Wilke? Because I'm never going to be her.

"We're going to do things differently in this class," he said.

I sat next to Wesley, my attention drifting outside. A big old granddaddy black oak shivered in a sudden breeze, a thousand leaves clicking dryly, like castanets. The smell of gunsmoke drifted through the open windows. The world was tense and desaturated, waiting for the catharsis of rain. I knew exactly how it felt.

Wesley filmed Mr. Wilke. Mr. Wilke said it was okay, as long as he had the subject's permission. Permission was very important.

Remember that.

"I'm not a believer in tests or quizzes or any of that bullshit," our teacher said. *Bullshit* got my attention. I turned to him. Casual today, jeans and a plaid shirt. He wore glasses sometimes, simple plastic frames, the narrow lenses emphasizing that crinkling thing his eyes did.

I was not the only girl in class who noticed this. Hiyam, a girl with skin the color of butterscotch toffee and hair like liquid midnight, kept crossing her legs this way, then that.

Wesley held the camera on Mr. Wilke, but he was looking at Hiyam now.

I rolled my eyes.

"I'm only giving you one assignment this semester," Mr. Wilke continued. "You're going to make a short film. Any genre, any style, any subject. It can be a documentary about your three-legged cat. It can be a classic sci-fi genre film." His eyes touched me, and I blushed. "Whatever. It's up to you. Minimum three minutes long, max ten. You can group up or tackle it solo. I strongly encourage you to group—that's how most films get made."

He leaned against his desk. I thought about that body atop mine on the long front seat of his car. Hiyam yawned, stretching her arms above her head. Cleavage shot.

Wesley dropped his camera.

"I'm so not working with you," I murmured.

"However," Mr. Wilke said, looking straight at me, raising all the blood to my skin, "if you're some kind of mad genius auteur, you can go it alone. It's all up to you."

Hiyam narrowed her eyes at me, like a cat.

"This project is due by winter break. We'll watch and grade them together. You may not ask me any questions about it. I've told you all you need to know. If you weren't paying attention, I'll post a copy to our class folder online."

"Hear that, butterfingers?" I told Wesley.

He grinned. "Wanna be partners?"

"No."

"I've already got an idea for ours. It'll be sick."

This boy, I swear.

I dallied when the bell rang, hoping Wesley would leave without me, but he waited, faithful, puppyish. On the way out the door I glanced back. Mr. Wilke watched me, his face angled partially away, shadowed. Our gazes struck like flint and steel. And I realized that gunsmoke smell wasn't ozone. It was us. We burned.

———

Wesley ate my chicken nuggets as I stared into the parking lot, moon-eyed. Here and there a dash of rain shot down, a meteor streak of water. The sky clenched, desperately holding itself in. There's something so terrible about wanting something you've already had. You know exactly what you're missing. Your body knows precisely how to shape itself around the ache, the hollowness that wants to be filled.

Jesus Christ, this was only the end of the first week of school. No fucking way would I make it to winter break, let alone June.

"Hey, Maise."

I glanced at Wesley miserably.

You know, he wasn't terrible-looking. He had character. Deep-set eyes, bruise blue, intense. Shaggy dark hair that always looked windblown. Big Adam's apple, big mouth that flexed easily into a lupine grin. If he ever gained any weight or body hair, I might've—no, I still wouldn't. But other girls would.

"What?" I said.

"You've got a crush on our teacher."

My belly tightened. *Crush* was understatement of the year. But it might be good to know how it looked to an outsider. "Why do you think that?"

"Cuz you've been walking around with that I-want-to-be-fucked face all day."

I laughed and sat across from him, plucking a nugget from his tray. It looked vaguely like a deformed rooster. "Hiyam likes him, too."

Wesley made a disgusted sound.

I dipped into the honey mustard. "You don't think he's hot?"

"He's a million years old."

"You are so childish."

"Would you seriously fuck a guy that old?"

Decision time. Do I let Wesley know the real me, or do I make up a persona for him, a suit of armor I can take on and off? As if there was a choice. As if I wasn't burning up inside with this. Every time I opened my mouth, flame licked up my throat. I could have razed villages, kidnapped princesses.

"Yeah," I said. "I would."

His eyebrows rose. He leaned forward. "Have you? With a guy that old."

I smiled enigmatically and ate my nugget.

"Holy shit."

"You don't even know what old is," I said. "Mr. Wilke is probably like, thirty. That's nothing."

"He was in high school before we were born."

My heart paused. Little factoids like that cut right to the bone of reality. "So?"

"So, he was probably fucking high school girls when we were little kids."

"Why do you have to be gross?" I said, and shoved his tray at him. "You are such a boy."

Wesley blinked at me. I think he understood what I actually meant. Not, *You are so male*. Rather, *You are so young*. He was still seventeen, a December birthday, but the gulf between us was more than four months. It was generations.

"What makes you such an authority?" he said.

I shook my head and stood up, the armor going on. But I didn't want it to end like this. "I'll be your partner," I said. "If you still want me to."

Wesley shrugged, eyes on the tray. "Yeah."

"Good."

We needed something, I thought. A *thing* we could do to show we hadn't meant to hurt each other. On impulse, I flicked his earlobe. He jumped so hard the table rattled, and I laughed.

"By the way," I said, "we're officially friends now."

I was waiting at his car when he came out. Some teachers stay late on Friday, catching up on papers, making plans to hit the bars together. Mr. Wilke headed for his car exactly fifteen minutes after the last bell.

I could tell when he saw me, the hitch in his step, the quick, guilty scan for witnesses. In the student lot kids yelled and honked as they took off for the weekend, but the faculty lot was quiet. I sat on the hood of his car, one foot propped on the fender beside it. A tiny, distorted version of myself swirled in the hubcap chrome: a Southern Snow White, all skim-milk legs below my cutoffs, red toenails and sandals. The silver sky wrinkled with storm clouds.

He stopped in front of the hood. His hand tightened on the strap of his messenger bag, his knuckles white spurs.

"Do you need to talk?" he said in a muted voice.

I shook my head, slowly.

His chest rose and fell with a deep breath. He went to the driver side, unlocked it. Stood there unmoving.

"We can't do this," he said, but it sounded like he was talking to himself.

I hopped off the hood and he got in the car. But he just sat there, keys glinting in a limp hand. Then he turned and looked at me through the passenger window.

My eyes skipped to the dashboard. Somehow, in my daze, I hadn't noticed it. The stupid velvet pony with its too-human eyes. I looked back at Mr. Wilke.

There was something very boyish about him at that moment, despite the five o'clock shadow, the blue rivers of veins mapping the back of his hand, the entire adult world he was part of. He looked lost. Maybe it was hypocritical, but the boyishness I barely tolerated in guys my age was exactly what drew me to him. He was like me: not fully part of the adult or child world. An exile, watching wistfully from the outside.

Something sharp and cold struck my shoulder.

A car drove past, a face turning to us.

We were utterly still.

Another icy dagger, this time hitting the crown of my head.

Then it all came at once, the sky exploding into water.

Thank you, Jesus.

Mr. Wilke sat there watching me. He didn't take his eyes

off mine for a second, even when my hair plastered itself to my face and my shirt turned to cling film, and I stood motionless, expressionless, knowing I was going to win.

He leaned over and opened the door.

I got in.

Rain drummed on metal, a hundred wild heartbeats surrounding us. Mist came off my skin as if I was some ethereal creature. Our bodies faced forward, our faces angled toward each other.

"You kept it," I said.

A long pause before he said, "It smelled like you."

Everything solid in me evaporated, leaving only breath. I weighed nothing.

He started the car. I felt the engine rumble in my belly. I was a very thin, transparent piece of skin, everything going right through me. A sheet of nerve endings. I pressed my palms to the seat and drank in the smell: the old leather of the seats, the new leather of his skin, and, startlingly, me. My presence suffused his car. Rain and orange oil, the creamy body lotion that was coming off on the seat. I wiped wet hair out of my face and Mr. Wilke caught my hand.

I waited, wide-eyed, ready for anything.

His fingers curled around mine, painfully. His whole arm was rigid. Tension corded up into his neck, his jaw.

No words. Just that crushing grip.

He let go.

"Where do you live?"

It rained ruthlessly. I had no sense of time passing, of moving through space, only the zircon curtain clattering against the windows and the heat of his body so close to mine. I knew he was barely paying attention either because he almost ran a red. He slammed the brakes so hard the tires screeched and I caught myself on the dashboard, his arm tangling with mine.

"Killing us both is one way to solve it," I said.

He drove more carefully, his hands strangling the wheel.

The closer we got to my street, the faster something accelerated inside of me, a terrifying urgency. How could I stall? How could I wring more out of this moment before it was over?

He parked several houses down from mine. I didn't tell him to, and there was room in front of my house. My heart stuttered.

Car interior. Afternoon, heavy rain. Two people turn to each other. Raindrops crawl over the windows and paint shadows across their faces.

Action.

"Evan," I said.

It was the first time I'd said his name since that night. It hit him like an electric shock, opening his eyes wider, stiffening his muscles. There was power in it and I wanted to play with that power. But not yet.

"I'm sorry I left that night," I said.

He and the pony looked at me sadly. I felt a childish urge to hug it.

"Why did you go?" he said.

There was no choice here of putting on the armor. This man had already seen the real me.

"Because I was scared," I said. "Because you made me feel like being myself wasn't such a bad thing. Like it might even be special. I didn't know how to deal with it, and I panicked."

I grimaced, hearing my words.

"This sounds stupid."

My left hand lay on the seat. He covered it with his.

"No, it doesn't. You're being honest, so I'll be honest, too." His fingers contracted. "This feels wrong, Maise. I'm your teacher. It's not just about getting caught. It's how our lives will get screwed up even if no one finds out. Sneaking around, secrecy, paranoia—"

"You're seriously underestimating how much I like espionage. And it's just until school ends."

"Is that how you want to spend your senior year?"

"I don't want to spend it wondering what could have been."

His expression turned morose, inward-looking.

"Evan," I said again, and he focused on me. "If I hadn't left that night, if this kept going . . . would you still think we should stop now?"

"I don't know."

"Do you really want to stop?"

"No," he said softly.

There was no desperate collision of bodies this time. We moved in small increments, my fingers lacing through his, my neck craning toward him. My gaze fixed itself on his jaw, the place just under his lower lip where sandy stubble graded into smooth skin. His free hand came up and touched my mouth, traced it, fingertips pushing in, against my teeth. Again I grimaced. I saw him through my wet eyelashes, blurrily. Unbearable. All this restraint, everything furled and reined in, while the rain came down with pure wrath.

A car roared past, throwing a tsunami against his door.

We both started. It must have broken the trance, because then his arms were around me and I was on my knees, kissing him, pressing his back to the window. I tasted glassy rain and my own wet hair tangling across my face. He didn't stop me to fix the shot. He wanted me as I was, raw, unedited. His hand ran up the back of my bare leg, his fingers stroking the inside of my thigh. I gasped against his mouth. Lost a sandal. Rubbed my face against his jaw, hard, feeling the grit. Mark me, I thought. Give me something to take away with me. Something I can touch when I'm alone, remembering this.

When we stopped to breathe he took my face between his hands. "You don't know what you do to me. I can't look at you in that classroom."

"You look at me all the time."

"And do horrible things to you in my head."

My blood was wildfire. I felt my swollen mouth, my sharp teeth digging into my lip, my dreamy half-shut eyes, and knew what I looked like to him. "Do them to me," I said. "Take me somewhere."

He gave a long, long sigh. His lips were bright red from my attentions. "I want to. You have no idea how much I want to." Two fingers on my chin, pinching gently. "This is moving very fast. We should think it through. Think about how to be less conspicuous."

My face lit up with dark glee. "I can be discreet. I can be Harriet the fucking Spy."

His hands moved to my ribs. Palms cupping my breasts, rubbing my wet shirt into my skin. It chafed, but I didn't want him to stop. I wanted this. Imprint yourself on me, I thought. It felt like he held all of me, gathered there next to my heart, small enough to fit in his hands.

"I wish I could take you away," he said in a rough, eerie whisper.

I shivered. "How am I supposed to make it through the weekend?"

"I was wondering the same thing."

We kissed for a while, soft, sweet good-bye kisses. We

traded numbers. We touched each other's faces, hands. The glass had gone opaque, glowing with fuzzy spots of color, the way a camera blurs background lights. We kissed again. I tried to think of another excuse to stay in his car, and he smiled, reading my thoughts.

"I don't know what I'm doing with you," he said.

"That's okay," I said. "Just don't stop."

I stood in the rain, watching his car go. A string tied to it looped around my heart and pulled tighter and tighter until it sheared clean through.

3

AT seven Saturday morning I woke to Mom's voice, a raven screech ravaged from cheap alcohol and ciga-rettes.

"Babe! I made breakfast. Let's go shopping."

I pulled my pillow over my face, wondering if I had the discipline to suffocate myself.

"Get up, lazybones."

Curtain swish. Holocaust sunlight ignited my bed, seep-ing through the pillow.

"Go away," I groaned. I'd been having a weird dream about being chased through a cornfield by a wild dog. I couldn't see it when I looked back, just the ripple through the stalks. But when it growled I felt its breath on my neck, hot and toxic.

By "made breakfast," she meant bought McDonald's. At least it wasn't her usual liquid meal. I scarfed an egg sandwich and observed the woman who gave birth to me. Sunlight was not kind to her face. Her eye shadow looked greasy, not covering the dark circles so much as completing them. Her lipstick was thick and tacky. No one still wore magenta except ironically.

Once upon a time, this witchy skeletal creature was a teenage girl, like me. Her eyes were a clear peridot, her skin poreless alabaster. She was beautiful. Men and boys worshiped her.

I shuddered. I had the disturbing sense of looking into a mirror that showed the future.

"What do you need to shop for?" I said.

"For you, silly."

I eyed her suspiciously. "You never buy me things."

"It was a good week. We got some extra cash."

Translation: *I sold a lot of meth to kids your age.*

"And you're going to spend it on me." Not a question. A tentative statement.

"I can't stand looking at them ratty clothes. You need something nice."

Them ratty clothes were good enough for Mr. Wilke, I thought.

"You can just give me the money," I said. "I'll buy them myself."

Please, Jesus, don't go with me.

Mom smiled. Her porcelain caps shone brilliantly. The majority of her teeth were fake, the real ones rotted out by meth. "If I got to pay to spend time with you, I will."

Zip, thunk. Arrow right in the heart. It sank deep, quivering. I knew this woman cared about me in some delusional way. I just preferred when we both ignored that fact.

She chain-smoked in the van. I hung halfway out the window, texting Wesley. *Please kill me. Girls' day out with Mom.*

He texted back, *Who's the girl?*

Good old Wesley.

We drove through sleepy Carbondale, green lawns and campus commons, to the University Mall. Ice-cold AC, that soda pop smell in the slightly carbonated air. Mom took me straight to American Eagle. We passed a rack of pretorn, prefaded jean shorts, indistinguishable from what I was wearing except for the price tag. I raised an eyebrow. Translation: *Told you so.*

"Get what you like," Mom said. She held a mesh tank against her boobs, turning left and right.

"I'll meet you at the register," I said, slipping away.

Alone on the hardwood floors under champagne-colored lights, I'll admit it—I felt slightly glamorous. I couldn't stop looking at myself in the mirrors. I knew I was pretty. I'd never been one of those angsty girls who needed constant reassurance. When your mom's skeezy "business partners" hit on you when you're twelve, you learn fast. I'd been aware of male attention since before menarche. I knew I was desirable. I knew how to wield that as both a tool and a weapon.

I'd never really thought of myself as beautiful, though.

The girl in the mirror was beautiful.

Part of falling in love with someone is actually falling in love with yourself. Realizing that you're gorgeous, you're fearless and unpredictable, you're a firecracker spitting light, entrancing a hundred faces that stare up at you with starry eyes.

The girl in the mirror stared at me. She blinked slowly, knowingly. She seemed to be looking at something bright—chin raised, eyes distant, guarded. Button nose and full lips. Her mouth was open slightly, a sliver of white visible. She had the kind of effortlessly slender body older women hated her for. Despite what Wesley said, her breasts were average, even on the small side, but she carried them in a way that made you aware. She carried her whole body that way. Spine straight, each limb flowing loosely and easily. She had bones only when she needed them. Rich chestnut hair spilled over her bare shoulders, an elegant mess.

I looked at her and thought, I don't know who you are.

A group of girls drifted past, laughing in brazen tones. They smelled like a walking Bath & Body Works ad. They were moisturized and shining and tan, but beneath that was pudginess, acne, bulimia, self-hatred. They were processed. I was natural, uncultured and untamed.

My phone vibrated.

Britt, the girl from history class, asking about our project. After I'd responded and put it away, I still felt it. His number was right there, snug against my ass. Any moment, I could reach out to him, connect. For now it was comforting just knowing it was there. But I knew this kind of comfort wouldn't last. I'd need more.

Mom didn't bat an eyelash at the armful of clothes I dumped on the counter. I watched the register tick up, growing increasingly nervous as we hit $100, $150, $200. No way would she go for this. She'd stop the cashier. Oh god, she wasn't stopping the cashier. There was going to be A Scene.

Total: $242.18.

Mom pulled out a wad of twenties. I tried not to gawk.

One of the laughing bulimic girls watched us leave, her eyes glinting jealously.

I was too stunned to say thank you. I followed Mom to the food court, feeling like a delivery person, about to give this to some kid who really deserved it.

She bought us a huge plate of orange chicken and picked at it, eating like a bird.

My body tensed, expecting a blowup. It couldn't go this long without turning ugly.

"Want to see a movie?" Mom said.

My mouth dropped. We hadn't done that since I was little. I cleared my throat, blinked. Something weird was happening in my chest. It was an actual feeling for this woman.

"I'm kind of tired," I said.

Her eyes widened. She looked like a sad raccoon. Her mascara made spider legs out of her eyelashes.

"Maybe a short one?" I conceded.

I couldn't believe myself. I knew she was manipulating me. I didn't know *why* yet, but I knew better than to buy her shit. Remember what she's done to you, I thought. Remember those nights she left you alone on the couch with a man who kept saying how pretty you were, who touched you, so she could squeeze more money out of him. Remember her going to jail for possession and sticking you in a group home for three months. Remember she's the reason you're so screwed up.

I didn't remember anything.

I sat with her in the refrigerated theater, smelling her cigarette breath and way-too-young perfume, watching a terrible movie, laughing.

———

That night I sprawled on my bed with my ancient laptop, ostensibly researching my history report but actually googling Mr. Wilke. Not much Internet presence. Some placeholder profiles on social networking sites. Some blurry JPEGs. Even those tiny, pixelated images made my heart spin like a top. I saved the best one to my desktop, glancing at him while reading about the Cold War.

Not good. I was becoming obsessed.

New search: Illinois age of consent laws.

We were legal.

That night at the carnival was legal, obviously, and even if it happened now, as teacher and student, when he was in a "position of trust or authority" over me, it would still be legal because the cutoff was seventeen. As an eighteen-year-old, I could legally fuck my teacher.

Of course, if anyone found out, they'd fire him in a heartbeat. He'd probably never teach again.

Something heavy thudded downstairs.

I put in my earbuds and lay back, eyes closed. The Constellations, "Right Where I Belong." Mellow and bluesy and bittersweet. Just how I felt.

A tepid breeze ghosted through the room, smelling of grass and dying summer. The cicadas were so loud I heard them through the music, the rattle of a million rainsticks. What are you doing right now? I wondered. What if I called?

Something heavy fell again. My bed vibrated.

I sat up, yanking out my earbuds.

Thump. Thump. Crash.

I stormed downstairs, calling for Mom.

A man stood in our living room. Rangy, gray beard, jeans so oily they looked like leather.

"Your mom had too much to drink," he said.

Mom was on the floor. He was trying to help her to the sofa.

"Jesus," I said, kneeling. Her skin was cool to the touch. "She wasn't drinking. She's cold. What did she take?"

The man gave me an unreadable look.

"Mom?" I shook her. She was breathing, but shallowly. "Mom, what did you take?"

I thumbed open an eye. Her pupil contracted in the light. She moaned, rolled away from me.

Thank fucking god.

I turned to the man. "Who are you?"

"Paul."

"Paul," I said curtly, "carry my mom to bed."

He carried her, and I held her head up. I pulled the cover over her. Turned on the lamp. Found her cell and pressed it into Paul's hand.

"You're going to stay with her until she comes down," I said. "Check her pulse every five minutes. If it slows, or she gets colder, or stops breathing, call a fucking ambulance. I can't do this again."

Paul had trouble paying attention to my mouth. He stared at my legs like they were talking.

"Hey." I snapped my fingers.

He looked up.

I took a picture of him with my phone. "Now I've got you on file. Don't fucking leave her until she comes down."

Paul's beard twitched.

I shut the bedroom door and leaned my head against the wall in the darkness. My throat twisted shut. Selfish bitch. She had never, ever let me be a kid.

A wedge of hot amber light fell across me. Paul stepped out of the bedroom. For a pathetic second I considered hugging this stranger. I needed to be hugged, by anyone.

Paul put a hand on my back. My shoulders knit. The hand slid down to the top of my ass.

I slammed my elbow into his gut. He gave a small, stifled gasp.

"Touch me again," I said, "and I'll fucking kill you."

I walked fast out of the hall, but once I turned the corner I ran for the front door. Slammed it behind me. Dropped onto the top step, breathing wildly.

God, my life was a fucking joke.

I pulled my phone out, intending to call Wesley, to beg him to meet me somewhere, but before I could a new text popped up.

From Mr. Wilke.

Just a photo, no words. A ribbon of fireflies zigzagging through the night. The fiery spokes of a Ferris wheel. The merry-go-round like a giant music box. Deathsnake, a sinuous line of lights rising into the sky, dropping off into oblivion. It looked like a small galaxy, a fog of colored light hanging around it like a nebula. He'd taken it from his house. The lights he saw every night.

My heart calmed. I stared at the screen, forgetting the life behind me. *Wish I was there,* I replied.

A moment later, his response: *Me too.*

Somewhere in the universe, two hearts reached out and connected.

Then a figure stepped into the light streaming from the house, a shadow falling over me.

I leapt up and ran for my bike in the garage. Pedaled furiously down the street to the highway. I headed for the water tower, racing as fast as I could, even when I was alone with the arctic starlight and the wind keening in my ears.

At the reservoir I jumped off my bike, letting it fall. Used my momentum to run up the hill. Breathless, sweaty. My blood sang in my veins at hypersonic speed. I climbed to the crow's nest, feeling savage. I could kill someone with my bare hands right now.

Wesley sat on the driftwood boards, a point of orange fire frozen beside his face.

"Maise?"

I collapsed beside him, rolling to my back and staring up at the fat-bellied tank. Drank air that tasted like clove smoke.

"What happened to you?"

I waited until I had my breath back. "My mom overdosed."

"Is she going to live?"

"Unfortunately, yes." I sat up. "Maybe. I really don't give a fuck."

I felt him looking at me. I slid to the edge of the platform, dangling my legs off. Thirty-foot drop to grass and dirt. Probably not fatal.

"What's your greatest fear?" I said, gripping an iron strut angling overhead.

Wesley exhaled. "Being alone for the rest of my life."

"That's a good one." My fingers flexed. "Mine is being my mom."

I kicked myself off the platform.

Wesley yelled something. My arms held; I swung out over space, light as air. It seemed I could let go and just float to the ground like ash.

Arms around my waist.

His attempt at "rescuing" me almost resulted in both of us falling. I kept telling him to let go, let go, but he wouldn't. We toppled backward, his arms still locked around me. I wrestled free.

"Jesus," I said. "You almost made that a murder-suicide."

"You're fucking crazy," he screamed.

I stared at him.

His cigarette lay smoldering on the boards.

"I'm not like you," he said. "I don't want to self-destruct."

"What?" I said in a soft voice.

"If you want to kill yourself, don't do it in front of me. Don't make me try to save you."

I watched, speechless, as he climbed down the ladder and stalked off through the tall grass.

Then I stood there alone. The cherry still burned. I stubbed it out with my toe and sat down. I felt empty, a sort of diffuse hunger, a gnawing sensation in my belly and lungs and throat.

The world shivered brightly.

Don't. Don't fucking cry.

I took my phone out. Lost myself in those lights, the stupid pixels that formed words that meant everything.

From up here I had a view of the carnival, too. I snapped a pic. Mine was farther out, a sprinkle of rainbow glitter. I sent it without a message. His reply, almost instantaneous, was what I'd expected, and I smiled.

Wish I was there, he said.

Me too, I answered.

I pressed the phone to my chest, a warm rectangle of light irradiating my bones. I wasn't sitting there alone. I wasn't alone anywhere anymore.

Something made me check the screen again. I'd read it fast, teary-eyed. It was different when I read it the second time.

What he'd actually written was, *Wish you were here.*

———

Wesley met me Monday morning outside calc with a carrot cupcake.

"Olive branch," he said.

I split it with him.

"Hey," he said, licking frosting from his lips, "if shit gets crazy at your house, you can come to mine. My mom won't try to give you advice. She'll just stuff your face."

On impulse, I hugged him. He was ungodly tall. "Thank you," I said somewhere in the vicinity of his xiphoid process.

When I let go he was blushing.

A pang of guilt. Had I been leading him on, by habit? Nip that in the bud. I flicked his ear. "Hiyam's having a homecoming afterparty. You want to go and drink her booze and stare at her tits?"

"Fuck yes."

I walked into Film Studies later that morning feeling more in balance with the universe than I had in a long time. Which meant, of course, that the universe had to swing a big rusty wrench straight into my face.

He wasn't there. A sub sat at his desk.

"Where's Mr. Wilke?" I said.

The sub shrugged. "His instructions say you can use this period to work on your semester project."

Wesley and I slipped out after she took attendance.

"This is fucking weird," I muttered.

"Why?"

Because he drove me home Friday. Because we made out in his car, in the rain. Because he said he thought of doing terrible things to me in his head.

"I don't know. He didn't seem sick last week."

"Mysterious illnesses often strike the elderly."

I kicked the back of Wesley's knee.

"Are you gonna spend the whole day pining for him?"

Yes. "Meet me in the lab in ten. We can start on our masterpiece."

Where are you? I texted Mr. Wilke when I was alone at my locker.

I waited for a reply. Five minutes. Ten. Then I sighed, and tossed it in, and buried myself in schoolwork.

He finally responded that afternoon. *Court date. Nothing major.*

I didn't reply.

A minute later, he added, *I miss you.*

I stood at my locker as kids milled around me and felt like I was on a movie set, surrounded by extras. Their lives were so small, so simple. So scripted. No one had a secret life like this. No one was texting the teacher they'd fucked, the teacher they were planning to fuck again.

I want to see you, I said.

I expected a brush-off. I did not expect him to say, *Can you meet me outside school?*

Yes. God, yes. *Where?*

He gave me an address not far away for a pickup.

And then where? I said.

Wherever you want.

———

I sat on an old cold case outside a derelict gas station half a mile from school. The sun banged off chrome pumps scabbed with rust, ricocheting into my eyes in bright bullets. Heat baked up from the cracked concrete. A tin sign pocked with BB holes creaked mysteriously, no breeze touching it. I reclined in a cool bath of shadow, my body relaxed, my mind going a million miles an hour.

He pulled up like a movie star, one arm propped on the headrest, mirrored aviators flashing.

I got in. The seat leather scorched my legs.

We didn't speak. He took his sunglasses off. His eyes were tender and soft beneath. He wore a pinstriped shirt and tie with jeans, sleeves rolled up, hair wind-tossed. Sun gilded the feathering of stubble on his cheek.

We didn't kiss.

Our hands met on the scalding seat between us.

I breathed fast. I hadn't been this scared since I got into that roller-coaster car by myself. This was the same thing, really—getting on a ride that might destroy us.

Worst-case scenario: He loses his job, I get kicked out of school.

Best-case scenario—

I don't know. What is the best-case scenario? Sneaking around, peering out of curtains? Lying to everyone we know?

I thought of that Robert Frost poem they love to ruin for you in high school. *Two roads diverged in a yellow wood.* This was where my life forked. I could only go one way; in the other, Gwyneth Paltrow plays my alternate self like in *Sliding Doors*, ending up miserable or happy. That was the question. Which one was she? Which was I?

I knew which one I was.

The fearless one.

I squeezed his hand.

The silence between us rang. It made everything so clear. I saw my thoughts reflected in his face, the trepidation fighting with a very simple, very biological need. He looked at all of me, my fresh teenage skin, my adult certainty, my old soul. No one had ever looked at me so completely. No one had ever seen me as such a whole, rounded person.

Yes, I thought. This is the road I want.

He squeezed my hand back, then took the wheel.

It's amazing how much you can communicate without words.

We drove onto the highway, through neat green rows of

soybeans raking to the blue horizon. My window was down, hair lashing my face. The air smelled chemical with a tang of sickly-sweet fermentation. A blade of sunlight lay across my legs, making my skin glow.

I glanced at Mr. Wilke. His look made something deep in me ache. I held on to the feeling, letting it open inside of me, blossoming, filling me from toes to fingertips with a tension somewhere between hunger and pain. By habit I put my thumbnail between my front teeth. I hadn't meant it seductively, but Mr. Wilke stared, a smile flitting around the edges of his mouth.

Great job, Lolita. Now you just need some heart-shaped sunglasses.

I felt his eyes on me, hot as the sunlight. I knew he was watching every move. I tilted my head back, eyes half-closing, the wind playing over my face. My heart beat a slow, bluesy rhythm. It felt like acting, like being onstage, every camera on me, bewitched.

The car slowed.

We both looked at the motel sign, then each other.

He turned.

Crunching gravel. Parking space. Engine off, ticking. Heat swarmed into the silence, becoming almost a sound, a high locust whine buzzing against my skin.

I heard him breathing. He wasn't quite looking at me, his gaze landing somewhere on the dashboard.

We knew what we were doing, Your Honor.

He put his sunglasses back on and popped the glove box, handing me a second pair. I laughed softly. Like this would hide anything.

Maybe it wasn't for other people. Maybe it was for us.

It was a lot easier to face him without seeing his eyes. My

reflection in his lenses: a girl without fear, her lips slightly upturned, knowing.

He got out and headed for the registration office.

Panic attack.

I flipped down the sun visor, clawed at my hopeless hair. What had I eaten since I brushed my teeth that morning? What planet had I been on? No memory of anything between waking and the moment I got into his car. I couldn't sit comfortably in my own skin. Every tendon was a violin string stretched taut, dying to sing out at the faintest touch. What if it was different? What if I'd ruined it by lying, leaving? God, what the hell could he possibly see in a screwed-up eighteen-year-old? How screwed up must he be to get tangled in my life?

Footsteps on gravel.

I slapped the visor up.

No more thinking.

I opened my door, slammed it shut loudly, defiantly. My senses focused on small things: the pumice scrape of his shoes, a splash of sun on a steel bumper. He opened 112 and went in first. I followed, closing the door behind me.

Dim inside, afternoon light straining through muslin curtains. There were heavy drapes to either side of the window that we didn't touch. I had impressions of square silhouettes in the murk but all I really saw was him. Taking his sunglasses off, setting them on the bureau. Moving toward me. Taking my glasses off, too. I blinked at the dust suspended in a cloud of sunlight.

I didn't realize I wasn't going to step further into the room for a while.

Mr. Wilke put his hand under my jaw, raising my face. My body pressed against the cool metal of the door. I ached like I'd been asleep or watching a long movie and needed to be pulled, stretched, used. It made my face sullen, made his eyes narrow. We looked at each other with that resentment you feel when you want something so much it's causing you pain, so much you start to hate it a little. There was a whiff of gasoline and the city on him and that smokiness I'd become addicted to. I put my hand on the knot of his tie. His mouth opened, as if I'd touched some live part of him.

Our lips met.

What happened felt more like chemistry than a kiss. Pure liquid heat on my lips, dissolving into me, trailing a hot line down my chest and pooling in my stomach. My heels rose off the floor. All of me rose, unanchored, held down only by his weight pressing me to the chilly slab of the door. We kissed as we could not have done until now—like lovers. He tilted my head, slid his tongue into my mouth, not urgent or hurried but in a way that made me feel the inevitability of this. The hand on my jaw moved over my chest, my belly, to the button of my shorts.

I'd had some practice unknotting ties.

When I tugged it free he pulled back, those full red lips slanting in a half smile. This made it easier to unbutton his shirt. He watched me, letting me have my way with him. Raised his arms obediently when I rolled up his undershirt. I wanted to press it to my face, smother myself with it like ether. But he took my wrists and pinned them above my head and something trembled in me, somewhere between blood cells and neurons, a liminal space where I wasn't quite mind or body. God, he was going to fuck me right here, against the door.

His hands let go and mine stayed raised, obedient. He unbuttoned my shorts, knelt to take them off. Warm breath sighed between my thighs, making me feel my own wetness. Large, careful fingers slid beneath my underwear, pulling, fingertips running down my legs. I bit my lip so hard I tasted sweet copper. He kissed my hip, moving along the soft crease of my thigh, moving lower as his hands spread my legs open. I couldn't. I couldn't anymore. I thrust my fingers into his hair and pulled his head back, making him look up at me. My face said it all.

He stood, unzipping himself, taking the condom from his back pocket as I pulled him out of his jeans. His dick felt huge and burning hot in my hand. I slid my palm around the base and he froze, the muscles of his chest chiseled against his skin, unmoving. My fingers stroked the fine silk over that hardness, pumping slightly in my hand. Just touching it made me curl up, everything in me going super tight. He put the condom on himself. Lifted me suddenly under the knees, making me grab him for balance. Then it was only my spine against the door and his dick thrusting inside of me, and I lost all breath, all function, all everything. For an endless moment all I felt was penetration. Slow and hard. Slow and deep. He made sure I felt every single thrust. I was hard inside, too, my body coiled and tense, and the first few moments were so poignant it was almost painful. Then the rhythm took over, and the world began to fade back in. My bare thighs rubbing against his jeans. The way his abs flexed, the muscle rolling, the little trail of bronze hair he pressed against my navel. The viperous motion of his body as he fucked me. He held me a few inches above him and raised his face, watching mine without kissing me. The way we looked at each other was more intimate than a kiss could have been. I saw his pupils dilating like pulsing black hearts. I saw every tremor of strain and pleasure that went through him. I watched what I did to him, how vulnerable he became as he gave himself to me, fucking me but also being fucked himself, that slightly lost, boyish look coming into his face as he got closer and closer. A fire built in me, leaping from cell to cell, setting my body slowly alight, but I made myself keep my eyes open and watch him. His eyes closed, his eyebrows rising helplessly. His fingers dug into the backs of my legs. His dick was so hard and thick inside me that all I felt was a sweet fullness in my core. Every time he sank in completely and compressed my clit, a bolt of pure electricity shot up through my belly. My eyes were open wide when the tension in me changed from resistance to surrender, and I started to gasp uncontrollably, and didn't tell him I was coming, but he knew. The fingers clenching my legs tightened like claws. I came so fast and hard it was like a flash of sheet lightning, a blinding white bliss, there one second and gone the next, and I gaped at the shadowy room, dazed. He kept going for a few more seconds, groaning, thrusting hard one last time and then rocking through the aftershock, settling against me, our weight easing limply against the door.

His head rested in the crook of my shoulder. I ran a hand over his back, light, unsure of myself yet, of this closeness. It was like an awful pounding clock had finally stopped ticking. The silence in the room was peaceful, melancholy. I breathed in the smell of him. Of us. My sweat on his body, my wetness on his jeans. I wanted to pause this moment and linger in it, looking around, memorizing.

He pulled out gingerly but didn't let me down. His arms tightened. He carried me to the bed.

My breath fluttered in my lungs.

He laid me down and lowered himself beside me, facing the ceiling. We reached for each other at the same moment, our hands linking in the small gulf between us.

Oh my god, I thought. Just that. A pleasant daze. My body was full of sunlight. No blood, just liquid blue sky.

I didn't know how much time had passed when his head turned to me. I looked over, feeling lazily magnanimous. Everything was golden and graceful.

I'd thought his eyes were blue, but in the September light they had a silvery, metallic look, like brushed aluminum.

"Hi," he said, soft and low.

Something lit up in me like a candle. I propped myself on an elbow, swung my leg across him, and crouched over his body. "Hi," I said.

It was the first time we'd spoken since Friday.

———

For a long time he held me atop him, looking at me. I kissed him but he broke it after a second. When I tried to get up, he pulled me back.

"Let me look at you," he said. "Before your guard comes up."

So I let him look. At first I was nervous, my eyes flickering away, suddenly aware that I wore nothing below the waist. I tucked my hair behind my ear and it immediately tumbled back into my face.

Then I eyed him askance. There was nothing in his expression but curiosity, so innocent it seemed almost childish. My anxiety melted. A slow, small smile took over me. Cocky, not shy. The way I'd smiled at the carnival. I owned every part of me, the nudity, the just-had-sex hair, every mistake I'd ever made, and wrapped myself in it.

Evan touched my cheek and pulled me closer against him. My hair fell around us, enclosing us in a dark veil. I ran my palm over his chest, the smooth-carved muscle, the patch of coarse gold hair across his pecs, the dense, solid bones. Let my hand move lower to the silky down on his belly. God, I thought. You are such a fucking *man*. His hands moved over me, outlining the slimness of my arms, my hips, stopping on my bare ass, his fingernails pressing into my skin. The innocent look was gone.

"Did you see her?" I said.

He raised his eyebrows.

"The real me."

"She's right here," he said, and kissed me.

The afternoon became a blur of this: of kissing him, and being held, and not leaving that bed. He stepped into the bathroom to clean himself up and brought me my underwear. I put it on but took my shirt off, and we spooned, his hands all over me. We talked as much as we kissed.

"Tell me everything about you," he said. "What's your favorite movie?"

"Oh my god. You can *not* ask me that."

"Why?"

I sat up, giving him a horrified look. "First of all, because I want to impress you. Second, because it changes on a daily basis."

"You have one, you just don't want to tell me. I'll tell you mine."

My lip curled with hostility.

He laughed. "Say it together, on three. Ready?"

"No," I shrieked.

"One. Two. Three. *Casablanca*."

"*Jurassic Park*."

He broke into a huge grin.

I flopped face-first onto the bed. "I'm going to die."

"A modern classic," he said, tickling my heel. "I remember

seeing it in the theater and thinking, 'Someday CG will be as real as real life.' My favorite scene was when the girl—"

"If you start quoting," I said into the mattress, "I will actually kill myself."

He laughed again. His laugh was nice. Not mocking like Wesley's but giddy, conspiratorial. I glanced at him over my shoulder.

"Tell me everything about you."

His laughter faded, but the smile stayed. He lay beside me, his fingertips tracing the curves of my back. "What do you want to know?"

"How old are you?"

"Thirty-two."

So I wasn't far off. He was fourteen when I was born. Maybe Wesley wasn't far off with his theory, either. And so what? I'd fucked guys older than thirty-two.

"Where did you go to college?"

"Northwestern."

I peered over my shoulder again. "You from upstate?"

"Just outside Chicago."

"Snob. Everyone says they're from 'just outside Chicago,' like towns don't have names up there."

"It's true. They don't. Very confusing for mail carriers."

He slid a finger under my bra strap and followed it up over my wing bone, cresting my shoulder.

"Why—" I started.

"My turn." His finger moved slowly toward my breast. "Why did you talk your way into my class?"

Fate, I wanted to say. Kismet. It was in the script.

"I reserved it last year, actually. They messed up the registration." I took a deep breath. "I'm going to film school."

His hand stopped. He sat up a little. "Really? Where?"

"I don't know yet. I mean, I have my top choices, obviously, but I'm trying to be realistic. Hopefully somewhere like USC, or UCLA. I'm kind of torn whether to focus on indie or commercial film. Commercial is safer, I think, because I'll get a broad view of how the whole process works. But focusing on commercial shit can turn you into a philistine who churns out garbage, so maybe I should focus on indie stuff. On storytelling, and art. But then maybe I'll be really naive when it comes to actually doing the work. I don't know."

I was rambling. I glanced back at him. He had a slightly dazed look on his face.

"You're serious about this," he said.

I gave a half shrug. "Well, yeah."

"What do you want to do? Jobwise."

"I'll take what I can get. I'd love to be a PA, get a general sense of how it all fits together. Because someday, I'm going to direct."

It was as if I'd said something enchanting, romantic. His eyes sparkled. "You're a creator."

I thought about that. It seemed too lofty for me. All I did was watch a lot of movies and daydream. But he'd given me an opportunity, one I hadn't even really acknowledged because I'd been so obsessed with him: our semester project. I could actually *make* something. If it turned out halfway decent, maybe I could include it on my college apps.

"I don't know what I am yet," I said.

An electric moment between us, balanced between honesty and fear. Because I was young. Maybe I had more drive than most kids my age, but I was still a "kid my age." And you know that, Mr. Wilke, I thought. That's part of what this is between us—the thrill of the taboo. Teacher and student.

"If you're going to film school," he said, "there's something I need to give you."

My heart skipped. "What?"

"An education."

The first thing he taught me was how to make love.

Before you laugh, know that I'd always hated that phrase. It sounded so corny, so *old*. Hippies made love. People my mom's age, though I preferred to believe I was an immaculate conception.

People my age hooked up, fucked, had sex. We didn't attach frilly ideas of oneness and eternity to a basic biological act. Most of us were from single-parent homes. Those who weren't wished they were when their parents screamed and beat the shit out of each other. We grew up sexualized, from toddler beauty pageants to the constant reminder that adults were waiting to lure us into vans with candy. The invention of MMS gave us a platform for the distribution of amateur porn.

That's a lot of conditioning to break through.

The afternoon light got that long slant to it, slowly folding into dusk. Half a day had passed since I'd eaten and I barely felt hungry. I didn't want to stop this thing, lying on a motel bed with this beautiful man, our hot skin always in contact, never breaking apart. He sat up and I sat in his lap, facing him, my legs wrapped around the long lean muscle of his back. I rubbed my palm against the bristle on his cheek. He wore a sleepy, smoldering look, his lower lip jutting out, and it completely worked on me. If he'd asked me to do anything right then, I would have. I kissed that sulky lip. I couldn't tell the taste of his mouth from mine anymore. Only warmth, softness, pressure.

"I want to see you," he said quietly. "All of you."

I breathed quicker. Disentangled myself from him, my eyes locked on his, and stood. I felt like I was in a trance. I'd undressed for other men, and I wasn't wearing much right now to begin with, but this felt different. He wasn't just going to see my body. He was going to see *me*. In the way I undressed, the way I stood there under his gaze, the way I wore my skin.

He moved to the edge of the bed.

I unhooked my bra, slipped it off one shoulder. Let it fall to the floor with cool disregard.

That was the easy part.

I was breathing hard now.

His eyes moved over me but hovered mostly on my face. That was almost worse. Who am I without this? I thought. Without the seduction I wear like armor, without my bravado and cocksure confidence? Am I really just a little girl under it all?

I tucked my thumbs into my underwear.

And I thought of myself getting into the front of that deathtrap roller coaster all alone. Of swinging out from the water tower. Of getting into my teacher's car.

I slipped my underwear down until it fell. Then I stepped out with one foot and kicked it away with the other. I never broke eye contact.

Evan's lips parted in awe.

I'd like to thank the Academy.

"Now you," I said.

He stood smoothly. His silhouette blocked the dregs of

sun filtering through the curtain. It limned the edges of him, a bronze arc of light on his shoulder, the tips of his hair turning white blond. His jeans clung tightly and he had to strip them off. He was hard again, totally hard, his briefs doing nothing to hide it. He slipped them off. My eyes didn't know where to stop. Apparently my hands didn't either because they were all over him, following the cascading slabs of his ribs, his abs, the smooth chevron of muscle that led to the hard dick I took and wrapped in my fingers. His hands came down on my shoulders, heavily. His breath was heavy, too. He leaned on me, eyes closed.

"I want you like this," I said.

He looked like he was drugged. I pushed him onto the bed. My knees fit to either side of his waist. We sat face-to-face again, but without any clothes between us. I was higher than him and he kissed my breasts, his dick stiff against my thigh. The heat of it drove me crazy, my blood percolating, a viciousness winding up in me like a cobra preparing to strike. If he didn't fuck me, I was going to force him.

He looked up at me. "Are you sure?"

"Yes," I said, my fingernails carving into his back.

I could have forced him. I had the leverage. But I wanted him to do it, and so I let him take his sweet, torturous time, teasing my nipples with his teeth, sliding the whole length of himself between my thighs, pushing lightly, agonizingly, right against the focal point of that horrible ache in me. At first it was an insane test of willpower. I hit my limit again and again, somehow always starting over, finding a new reserve of patience. Then I realized that he was going to test my patience until it stopped being patience. Until I stopped waiting to be fucked and just experienced this. I made myself let go, made my muscles unravel. Draped my arms languidly around his neck. Looked at his face without thinking anything but how light it made my heart feel, as if pumped full of helium. And when I started to zone out and he slipped inside of me, I made myself stay relaxed. I let him penetrate me so gradually there was never a moment when it felt like he was finally fucking me. It all sort of blended together, fluidly, dreamily. His arms circled my back, holding me against the soft rocking of his body. This was different. This wasn't being fucked. This was something happening to my entire self, not just the useful parts. There was so little tension in me I didn't think I could come, until a warmth spreading from my hips and belly became hotter and hotter, and I looked up at the ceiling, gasping like I was surfacing for air, saying, "Come inside me, please, come inside me." That was it. No holding back. The heat in me detonated in a gentle nuclear burst, annihilating all sensation with soft light. It came on slowly and faded slowly, leaving me tingling, buzzed. Evan kept going a little longer, and then he slowed, and stopped, and held me. He grimaced when he pulled out. He was still hard.

"You didn't," I said drowsily.

He kissed me.

I let it go on for a moment and then leaned back, clear-eyed. "Why?"

"I wanted it to be just for you."

It was as if he'd spoken in Greek. I stared at him.

And something very strange happened in my brain.

I rolled away and sat on the edge of the bed, curling my arms around myself. My hand clamped instinctively over my mouth. The room was dark now, its shadows tinted the color of rust and old blood by the parking lot lights.

"Maise?"

The shadows swam in my eyes. I squeezed them shut.

Evan laid a hand on my back. "Why are you crying?" he whispered.

"I'm not," I said, and sniffed. Perfect.

His hand stroked me tentatively. "Did I hurt you?"

"No." I laughed at myself, bitter. "I'm just a fucking head case."

"Why are you crying?" he said again.

"Because no one's ever done that before."

He swept my hair out of my face, tucking it behind my ear. "Done what?"

I don't think I was really crying about this. I think it was a cumulative effect, all the tension and anxiety of the past few weeks culminating in this perfect day, this perfect happiness. It was relief, not sadness. But he'd been the trigger, and I guess I owed him an answer.

"Done it for me," I said. "Just for me."

His arms were around me then, drawing me to his chest. He said something soothing, but it was merely sound. All I really heard was the deep submarine thump of his heart.

When I finally stepped outside it felt like walking into a different world. A million new roads stretched before me that I'd never seen before. We put our sunglasses back on in the car, grinning at each other. He took his off when he almost hit a streetlight. I laughed and said maybe he should let me drive, and surprisingly, he did. It felt both wrong and amazing to be driving my teacher's car. I stopped at a McDonald's and ordered fries and vanilla shakes, parking in an empty lot under the stars. Evan said he'd make a special syllabus to prep me for film school.

"Private tutoring?" I said, dipping a fry in my shake. "How scandalous."

He smiled, but after a moment his eyes went distant.

"How is it going to be on Thursday?" I said.

"I don't know. I was hoping I'd figure out some way to freeze time."

I gestured with my fry. "I'll be discreet. No one will know. I won't risk your job."

He looked at me. "It's not just about me. In fact, it's less about me than it is about you."

"What does that mean?"

"It means I won't risk your future, or your happiness, or your sanity."

"Good thing I only have one of those."

"I'm serious." He frowned. "Which one do you have?"

"Happiness," I said, and leaned over and kissed him. Vanilla and salt.

He looked at me a long time when I pulled away. It wasn't until later that I realized he'd hoped I'd say *future*. That's how you know someone loves you. When they want you to be happy even in the part of your life they'll never see. But right then I was too stuck in the moment, in the visceral pleasure of it all.

"Let's figure out our battle plan, comrade," I said.

I didn't get home till midnight, and getting out of that car was harder than it had ever been. He made me hug the stuffed pony until it smelled like me again. I sat there until I'd finished every last fry. I was ravenous, insatiable. I'd done nothing but fuck him all day and wanted to do nothing else for the rest of this week. Month. Life. When he drove away I took a picture of the receding taillights, and after his car was gone I stood there holding the photo up to the street, pretending. What is this feeling? I wondered. What is this hunger that grows worse the more I feed it?

They'd come up with a name for it a long time ago. But you already know what it's called, don't you?

4

WESLEY had texted me about eight zillion times.

"Where were you yesterday?" he said at lunch. "I texted you about eight zillion times."

I looked at him philosophically, brandishing a mozzarella stick. "Where is anyone, really? In a quantum sense, I was everywhere and nowhere."

"Are you high?"

I smiled.

"You're obligated to share with me, you know."

"I'm high on life. Take all you want. It's free."

His eyes narrowed. "You got laid."

I bit the tip of my cheese stick suggestively.

"Was it an old guy?"

"What is age, really?" I said, and Wesley groaned.

Before we went to our fifth-period classes, I grabbed his arm.

"I want to start working seriously on our movie."

"Okay."

"So I'm coming to your house after school."

"Okay."

"So hide your socks and titty posters."

"That's a sexist stereotype," he said.

I raised my eyebrows at him.

"Okay," he sighed.

I saw Mr. Wilke completely by accident. I didn't know he was here today—maybe they'd called him in as a sub—and I was walking between classes on the first floor when we spotted each other in the hall. We both stopped. It was as if the lights dimmed on the river of bodies streaming around us, and we were the only two people left in full color. Fiery, radiant color, singeing the screen. All noise and motion blurred away. It felt like a camera circled us, capturing this movie-perfect moment. I started forward again and so did he. We passed each other slowly. We didn't stop or speak. But our arms brushed, and for half a second our fingers curled together, then slipped free, like a secret handshake.

Leaves shook out of the trees and fluttered around me in gold and green flakes of summer. I rode slowly so Wesley could keep up, pushing my bike with my feet. The soft clack of the spokes, the groggy drone of bees and locusts, the honey-thick sunlight drizzling over us—I was in love with the world today. A big dumb smile climbed onto my face every time my mind drifted. The air tasted like sherry, sweet and light, a pleasant sting on my tongue.

Wesley gave me a weird look, but didn't deflate my good mood.

At his house, I leaned my bike in the rosebushes and leapt

up the stairs to the porch. There was a snap in my limbs like the lazy twang of a guitar, like when I'm drunk. Their place was huge and all painted wood, white and tomato red, with a wraparound veranda. As soon as I stepped foot inside I could tell what kind of mom he had: the kind who gave a shit. Braided rugs on polished oak floors. Couches more comfy-looking than chic. Family photos parading across the mantel, end tables, hallway shelves. I imagined opening a closet and getting swept away in an avalanche of cheesy frames: seashells for beach pics, little baby blocks spelling out WESLEY and NATALIE.

"Who's Natalie?" I said. Same dark, floppy hair as him, same deep-set eyes. She looked coolly knowing, sly.

"My sister. She's in college."

I had no idea he had a big sister.

"Stop looking at those."

"Hold on, I've almost seen every year of your life."

He dragged me into the kitchen. A pitcher of lemonade sat on the counter, sweating.

"What, no fresh-baked cookies?" I said.

A woman stood up in the garden and waved at us with a spade.

"That is not your mother," I said.

She brushed herself off and came inside. She was crazy tall, nearly six feet, and willowy, her skin pale as bone, her eyes a startling magnetic blue in a long, handsome face. Her nose was bold and hawkish, but it fit her. She smiled like she knew everything about me and was proud. She was beautiful.

"You must be Maise," she said in a low, mellifluous voice. "Thank you for not filing a restraining order against my son."

"Mom," Wesley said.

"Nice to meet you, Mrs. Brown," I said.

"Call me Siobhan."

I raised an eyebrow. "Are you Irish?"

She sighed, good-natured. "Before this one's father ruined me, I was Ms. Callahan."

"Seriously, Mom," Wesley said.

"My only consolation is embarrassing my children in front of their friends. That's why the oldest went to college on the other side of the country."

"Nat's at UC Berkeley," Wesley said, "learning how to make cyborgs."

"Biotechnology," Siobhan said.

"The Terminator," Wesley said.

"It probably involves a certain amount of naked men," Siobhan conceded.

I laughed and sat at the counter, watching them, fascinated. Wesley poured us all lemonade. "Mom, we're gonna work on that film project."

"What is your film about?"

"Yes," I said. "What *is* our film about, Monsieur Auteur?"

Wesley raised his hands defensively. "I've just been shooting B-roll. We haven't decided on a subject yet."

Siobhan leaned against the counter beside me. She smelled like warm soil and crushed flowers. "What sort of film is it?"

It was totally weird having a parent actually be interested in my schoolwork. Even someone else's parent.

"Docufiction," Wesley and I said together.

"It's like *cinéma vérité*," I said, "but with some narrative injected into it."

"Stories based on real events," he said.

"Inspired by," I corrected. "We're blurring the line between fact and fiction. It'll probably focus on the trials and tribulations of being a high school senior."

"Or a teacher."

Not something we had talked about. I glanced at him sharply.

"I see," Siobhan said. "But what is the story?"

"It's a slice of life," Wesley said.

"It's a lot of short, interconnected stories," I explained. "Vignettes. We're taking a scattershot approach. There's no grand design, just like there isn't in real life."

"But surely there's a theme," Siobhan said.

Wesley and I both opened our mouths, then looked at each other.

"Well, obviously," he said.

"We just haven't decided on it yet," I added.

"Maybe it will emerge while you work," his mom suggested.

A memory leapt to the front of my mind, unbidden. Evan and I in the motel, in each other's arms, moving together slowly, hypnotically. Jesus. So inappropriate in this chaste family kitchen. I blushed furiously, but I said, "When you don't force it, sometimes amazing things happen."

Siobhan peered at me. "Wise girl." She brushed my cheek with a cool, dry finger. "Lovely, too."

Please adopt me, I thought.

"Mom," Wesley said. Funny how that word was both censure and affection when he said it.

"I assume you two will be working upstairs? I'll trust you to keep it PG-13."

Wesley blushed. I laughed. Siobhan smiled.

"I love your mom," I said as I followed him upstairs.

"That's because you don't know her yet."

I plucked that word out of the air and clutched it to my chest. *Yet.*

His room was enormous, but the ceiling slanted, making him crouch half the time. Pretty much what I expected: huge TV, Xbox, movie posters. Instead of the usual boy funk there was a faint herbal scent, his cigarettes and some kind of incense, maybe patchouli. He had a custom-built computer with two monitors and studio-grade speakers. And about a dozen types of video cameras, in various states of disassembly.

"Are your parents rich?" I said, drifting to the windows. "Oh my fucking god."

"What?"

"You have a pool."

He shrugged uncomfortably.

"Wesley. Do you hate me?"

"No?"

"Please rephrase in the form of a statement. And if you don't hate me, why didn't you tell me you have a pool?"

Not once did it occur to me that it was because he couldn't handle seeing me in a bikini.

"It's too late to use it anyway."

"That's defeatist talk," I said, but I grabbed a chair and sat beside him at the PC. "Let's see the B-roll."

He had a metric shit ton. Half from summer: oceans of wheat rippling in the wind, trains silhouetted against bloody sunsets, even the carnival, eerily deserted in the rain. The rest was from the school year: a swarm of legs walking past, the fistfight we'd seen. And me. I was in most of those shots. Staring out windows longingly or giving him my lunatic grin. Sitting in class listening to Mr. Wilke. In every single one of them my yearning was crystal clear. It burned in me like fever, made my skin glow palely, my eyes blaze, a beautiful madness. I stared at myself, breathless. I wasn't hiding anything. It was all there in plain sight.

"Is this how you see me?" I said, almost whispering. "As an attention whore?"

"No. No way."

"Then why am I in all of these?"

"Because you're the only interesting person here."

I glanced at him. "You can't do much with this except make a film about me."

He eyed me sideways, too. "Is that a bad thing?"

"That's not me. I'm not some starlet. I want to make something, Wesley. I don't want to be objectified as some pretty face."

My words came out harsh and sibilant, like steam. I hadn't meant to sound so angry.

"Sorry," he muttered.

"It's okay. That's why we're here. To get some perspective."

He wouldn't look away from his keyboard, so I flicked his ear. He gave me a dirty look.

"Clean slate," I said. "High school in the American heartland. What darkness lurks inside this seemingly pastoral town?"

"Incest," he said.

"Cliché," I said. "But probably."

We brainstormed for a while, then decided to watch some stuff for inspiration. Unsurprisingly, Wesley was a huge David Lynch fan. We watched bits of *Mulholland Drive*, skipping around to our favorite parts. Mine: Betty arriving in LA, full of big dreams about to be mercilessly crushed. Wesley's: the lesbian sex scene. I laughed and asked if he needed me to leave the room for a few minutes. He threw a Blu-ray case at me. Siobhan made baked mostaccioli, and we all ate together, showing her some of his better footage on his phone. I'd plugged mine into his computer to charge.

"Someone's calling you," he said when we went back upstairs.

"Who?"

" 'E.' "

I grabbed my phone. "I need to take this. Outside."

"Who's E?"

"Hi, Dad," I said exaggeratedly when I answered. "Just a sec."

I could practically hear Evan's eyebrows go up with a little comic book noise. *Fwip.*

I raced downstairs, flung open the patio door. The pool lights were off, the water gleaming darkly in the oozing, sauvignon twilight.

"Hi," I said when I was alone. "Sorry about that."

" 'Dad'?"

"Thought you'd appreciate the Freudian irony."

He laughed softly. His voice, slightly metallic, ran down through my bones and settled warmly in my chest, like bourbon. "I can't stop thinking about you."

You read things in romance novels like *He made me melt*, knowing this is physically impossible. Girls are not pats of butter. Yet my body was doing a damned fine imitation of I Can't Believe It's Not Girl, dissolving against the side of the house.

"So you called to torture me?"

"I know it's late, but I want to see you."

My eyes widened. "Do we have time for that?"

He laughed again, a little guiltily. "I actually just want to see you. Even if it's only for a minute."

"Yes," I said.

"Yes what?"

"Yes, it's late. And yes I want to see you."

I pictured him smiling. "Can you meet me?"

Wesley was messing around online when I went back upstairs. "I've got to run. Family shit."

I had to convince him not to walk me home. I sang out a good-bye to Siobhan, and for a moment I was reluctant to leave that bright, happy house. But something even brighter was waiting for me.

———

I stopped at home to brush my teeth and change clothes, because I'm not above vanity. The lights were off, Mom's van gone. I wished she'd never come back. That Siobhan would pull into the driveway, saying, *Come with me to your new life, lovely girl.*

When I biked out to the water tower he was already waiting.

I hopped off and let my bike ride on without me and ran to him. He pulled me down on a blanket he'd spread on the grass. I ended up atop him, my hair in both our faces. He held me, his arms coiling and relaxing, again and again, one hand buried in my hair at the base of my skull. Crickets made a creaking heartbeat around us. Cool aloe musk rose from the grass.

"I've been thinking about this all day," he whispered.

I brushed my cheek against his. The earth sank beneath us, pressed by the weight of the whole universe above. How could it set us up like this, every planet precisely aligned, if it didn't mean for us to collide? His heart crashed against mine, fierce and steady.

I pushed myself up on my palms. "You've done something to me." My voice was quiet, too, a ribbon of breath threading into the breeze that stirred my hair. "I feel like I'm waking from a long dream, and everything is so much more beautiful than I remembered."

His eyes were pale and bright in the starlight. The hand in my hair pulled me to him.

I kissed my teacher in the shadow of the water tower, beneath the stars.

I've been pretty honest so far, haven't I? So I'll admit: it wasn't innocent, blind love. His age drew me to him in the first place; now it was his being my teacher that gave me a wild, terrified thrill every time we touched, infusing me with adrenaline, making my skin prickle. The danger was an electrode buried in my brain, lighting up my most primal fear and pleasure circuits. There was more to it, of course. Something was unfolding in me that had never opened before. But I wasn't kidding myself. The forbiddenness was part of it.

I rolled onto my back and stared up at the sky. We propped our knees side by side. A tiny cut of light opened in the star-freckled face of the night, a shooting star. I raised my hand and closed a fist over it. When I opened my fingers, it was gone. Part of me now. *You're a creator.* Wesley had seen the person he thought I was, some obsessive, narcissistic teenager. Evan saw both who I was and who I wanted to be.

"Why did you become a teacher?" I said.

He sat up, leaning on an elbow. "There are two types of teachers. The first kind always wanted to be teachers. They train for it. They're passionate, caring, good people." I could hear the smile in his voice, bittersweet. "The second kind wanted to be something else, but couldn't. Crowded field, not good enough, not driven enough. Whatever. But they have a lot of specialized knowledge, so instead of letting it rot, they become teachers."

"Which kind are you?"

"The third kind."

"As in *Close Encounters of*?"

He pinched my arm. "The kind who doesn't know how he got here or where he's going. I was on my way somewhere else, but a detour came up."

"Where were you going originally?"

"Promise not to laugh?"

I sat up, too, intrigued. "Maybe."

"You can't promise 'maybe.'"

"Cross my heart, hope to die."

"I was going to be an actor."

My jaw dropped. I could see it. That fucking gorgeous face. The way it filled with light, looking more alive, more feeling, more human than anyone else.

"Is that pleasant surprise, or 'don't quit your day job'?" he said.

I turned it into a grin.

Evan laughed, eyes downcast, actually shy. Or maybe acting shy. I looked at him as if seeing him for the first time. The lips that had been sculpted so delicately they stood out more than his other features, the eyelashes like gold dandelion seeds. I pulled out my phone.

"Tell me the story," I said.

"While you film me?"

"Can I? This can be your audition."

"For what?"

I couldn't resist. "The role of my corrupt teacher. Of the third kind."

He gave me an electric look. Even through the cheap phone camera it made my nerves tingle, lightning lacing up my arms. Our gazes met above the screen.

"I thought I already had the part."

"Not until I get you on the casting couch."

His eyes crinkled, his face folding into embarrassed laughter. "You're a predator. I'm pretty sure you're the one corrupting me."

I sat behind my phone, relishing this. My power over him. The strange dynamic of me as the observer, him the observed.

"Why don't you put that away?" he said.

"Why?"

"So you can corrupt me."

I put it away.

"You owe me that story," I said.

He tilted my face. Kissed me lightly on the mouth, then along my jaw, following it to my ear. My eyes half-shut, drifting to the carnival lights in the distance. The hot breath in my ear was unbearable, a chemical pulse straight to my spine.

Something rumbled out on the road.

We stiffened, listening. A car going past.

"Kids come out here," I whispered, thinking of Wesley.

Evan took my hands and pulled me to my feet. Scooped up the blanket. I walked my bike toward his car on the road shoulder.

"I can't last until Thursday," I said. "I need to see you."

He gave me that regretful wince, but it had become much less regretful lately, more longing.

"Rent another room," I said. "At a different motel. I'll pay for it."

"You don't have to do that."

"I want to. This is as much mine as it is yours."

We stared at each other over my bike. Far down the road, two red snake eyes winked in the darkness.

"Okay." His voice was a little strange. "When should I pick you up?"

"As soon as the last bell rings."

He reached over and lifted my face and kissed me, so intensely I let the bike fall against him. This was an old-time, black-and-white-movie kiss, with the orchestra swelling in my chest, hot tungsten lamps carving out our shadows. My bones turned to air, nothing holding me up but the fierceness of my desire. God, I just wanted to get into that car with him. Forget this whole fucked-up life and disappear somewhere together. I had to push him away, fight for my breath. Too much. I gave him an agonized look. When he spoke, his voice was guttural.

"I can't hold on to you. You're like that shooting star. Just a trail of fire in my hands."

And the Oscar goes to Evan Wilke, for putting the first fine, hairline crack in the ruby of my heart.

Before Nan died, she set aside a small nest egg for me. Six thousand dollars sitting in a trust fund, waiting for me to turn eighteen. *For your future,* she said, with a guilty tone that was clearly also an apology: *Sorry you were born to my daughter.* I'd made a promise to myself that I'd use it for college.

I ditched Wesley at lunch and got an off-campus pass and biked downtown to the bank. I wasn't going to pay the ATM fee at school, and I didn't want anyone—especially Wesley—seeing me take out money.

Key skill while having an affair with your teacher: discretion.

The bright-eyed, bushy-tailed teller made squirrel noises at me.

"I need to make a withdrawal."

Squeak, squeak.

I slid my bank card through the reader.

Squeak.

I pushed my ID under the window.

"Oh, you're Maise," the squirrel said.

"Right. Who else would I be?"

Puffy-cheeked smile. "Well, it's a joint account."

"With who?"

"Yvette."

Mom.

I waited as the squirrel counted ten twenties with her twitchy little paws, then I said, "Can you take Yvette off the account?"

"Unfortunately, no. It was opened for a minor. But you could start a new account."

I had all of ten minutes to get back to school. "Maybe some other time."

Squeak squeak.

As I walked out, tucking the wad of bills into my pocket, I suddenly felt my grandmother watching me withdraw my college money so I could shack up with my teacher. Jesus, when was the last time I'd actually felt ashamed of myself? I made two promises as I unlocked my bike.

One: I will replace this money before I go to college. Every cent.

Two: I will pay my own way with Evan, no matter what. I'm not a child. I'm an adult, in an unusual but no less adult relationship.

Key skill: denial.

———

Fast-forward.

Wesley flicking my ear in the hall and tossing me an apple.

Me and Britt getting kicked out of the library for laughing too loudly at a boy giving us googly eyes.

Evan in his aviators, picking me up at the ghost town gas station.

Me in the motel office in borrowed sunglasses, renting a room.

And then just us.

Press play.

Urgency and need, my skin hot as sun-baked glass, my fingernails clawing his back. Him taking out a condom and me saying I'm on the pill and him saying, "I don't want you to worry, ever," and I agree because I just want to be fucked. And I am. And then I can think again, a starving girl given her first meal in weeks.

Fast-forward.

Trading life stories in our underwear on a motel bed.

Burgers and fries spread across the blanket and his laptop playing *2001: A Space Odyssey*.

Evan doing the ending monologue from *American Beauty* and making me shiver.

Photos of us I take in the bathroom mirror: laughing at the camera, then his head turning to me, then mine to him.

Faster.

School days ending in motel rooms. Broken AC, humidity making the air cling like clear jelly. A thunderstorm releasing us from misery, and me running barefoot into the parking lot, screaming with crazed abandon. Evan taking my wet clothes off in the sudden chill of the room and getting into a warm shower with me. My hands unable to find purchase on his slick skin as he holds me against the wall and fucks me with his finger, the tiles printing a graph onto my back.

Wesley saying his mom invited me over to Sunday dinner, even though I know it's him.

Siobhan hugging me before I leave, and me stopping on a dark street to cry and smell her on my shirt.

Hiyam formally inviting us to her homecoming party.

Mr. Wilke and I talking to each other in class as if we're just teacher and student, though our jokes are a little too familiar, our glances a little too intense.

Making out with him in his dark classroom during fourth period while kids walk past the locked door.

Wesley asking why I smell like men's cologne.

Me listening to stupid sappy love songs nonstop, getting addicted to the Yeah Yeah Yeahs' "Wedding Song."

Another bank withdrawal, and me and Wesley applying for jobs together online.

Mom mercifully leaving me the fuck alone.

Finally, homecoming.

Siobhan said we'd regret missing the dance.

"It's just a bunch of idiots trying to conceive illegitimate children," I said.

"We're not missing anything," Wesley agreed. "Blood, fire, heads exploding. We can just watch *Carrie*."

Which we did.

Besides, I thought, who would we go with?

Insane fantasy of me and Evan showing up together, blowing everyone's minds.

At nine, Siobhan drove us to Hiyam's house. "Watch each other's drinks," she said. "Don't take any mysterious pills. Call me if you need anything." Her eyebrows rose with droll disdain. "And tell this child's parents they're trying too hard."

Hiyam's house could've been airlifted from Beverly Hills. There was nothing like it within a hundred miles. It sat on a dozen acres, surrounded by a wrought-iron fence. Inside was a brochure spread of flagstone paths, landscaped shrubs, illuminated accent pools. It took fifteen seconds of walking before we even saw the house, a pile of geometric debris.

"It looks like a parallelogram fucking an isosceles triangle," I said.

Wesley snorted.

Light bled from every window, clear chardonnay yellow. Silhouettes swam across it. The music was a murky underwater pulse that grew clearer as we approached. Kids sprawled in the garden, laughing drunkenly, lurking in shadows in various states of undress. Despite myself, I felt a flare of excitement. It seemed all two-hundred-odd members of our graduating class were here tonight.

I poked Wesley in the ribs. "Have your camera ready."

"Always do."

We walked through open French doors into the house.

Half the kids were still in formal wear, the rest in street clothes, like us—Wesley in a graphic tee and skater cargos, me in a tank and skinny jeans. The deejay had some Hot 100 shit on at skullfuck volume. I couldn't see much through all the skin and rayon and sweat, just flashes of onyx granite and oxblood leather, a cut-crystal punch bowl, platters of canapés. Every room flowed airily into another and people followed the circuit, moving, mingling. They were all sleepy smiles, shiny eyes, duckfaced girls making out with boys who had less hair on their face than I'd shaved off my legs, everyone drunk and dumb and happy.

We hit the drink table hard. A guy had smuggled in some

Grey Goose and I slipped him a twenty and Wesley and I matched each other shot for shot, one two three four until he stepped back, looking dizzy.

"Lightweight," I laughed.

"You're trying to take advantage of me," he said dubiously.

The room with the sound system was full of black lights. When I glanced at Wesley he grinned, showing me moon eyes and a mouth full of glowing teeth. I closed my eyes and grinned back.

"Creepy," he yelled in my ear.

The crowd split us for a moment, skeleton kids dancing with their arms in the air. The deejay spun some lame Kesha, but it was infectious. I slipped into the rhythm, let my body ride the music, vodka flooding my veins with sugar and fire. Wesley tried to sneak away and I caught him.

"I can't dance," he said.

"Neither can they." I took his hand. "Just let yourself go."

He was such a giant, it was hopeless. So I stayed close to him, and he faced me, and it worked. We were in our own little zone, surrounded by perfume and alcohol breath and damp young skin. A girl blew glitter in my face and instead of slugging her, I just laughed.

"This is so weird," Wesley said when the song faded to the next.

"I know," I said. "I feel like an actual kid."

I grabbed his hand again and pulled him to the next room.

Hiyam was there, surrounded by her royal court of Mean Girls. She smiled and beckoned us over. Her subjects scattered like roaches when we neared.

"Having fun?" she said to me.

"I don't know. Are we having fun, Wesley?"

Wesley stared at something across the room.

Hiyam's feline eyes flicked to him, then to our clasped hands. I let go of him, suddenly self-conscious.

"Oh," Hiyam said.

Jesus, awkward.

"I'll catch you later," Wesley muttered, slinking away.

I stood there feeling like an idiot. *There's nothing between us*, I imagined saying. *He's kind of got this big sister crush on me and I'm kind of sleeping with our teacher. Also, I'm kind of drunk.*

Hiyam was seventeen but looked midtwenties: lipstick, heels, cream-colored cocktail dress. She had a sphinx's face, stony and enigmatic. Her skin was amazing. Burnished bronze. I wasn't sure of her ethnicity—Turkish? Persian?—but I felt utterly childish in her presence.

"I wanted to talk to you anyway," she said. "Let's walk."

We drifted through the party, stopping occasionally for someone to talk to Hiyam. She listened with a half smile, her eyes half-lidded. Regal boredom. No one seemed to realize it but me.

"Ever feel like you don't belong with these people?" Hiyam said.

"Every day of my life."

She smiled knowingly.

We ended up outside, on a terrace overlooking a pool. This pool was usable, not decorative, and a guy and girl were currently using it to make out madly in the shallows. The house pumped music into the night.

Hiyam produced a pack of cigarettes from somewhere mysterious and offered me one. I shook my head. She leaned on the granite railing.

"Mr. Wilke," she said, exhaling a serpentine coil of smoke.

Alarm bells. I leaned on the railing, too, so I could devote less of my brain to keeping my balance.

Hiyam glanced at me coyly. "You have a crush on him."

"So do you."

"He's super hot."

I had no idea how I was supposed to react. Should I agree? Was it suspicious if I didn't? "Yeah, he is."

"I'd fuck the shit out of him."

Oh my god. How do I get out of here? "Not interested," I said. "I've got a boyfriend."

Hiyam's eyebrows rose. Then she smiled. "In college?"

"Older."

Her intrigue became genuine appreciation.

"What did you want to talk about?" I said.

She rolled her wrist, scrawling a spiral of smoke in the air. "I heard you can hook people up."

I was too drunk and unsettled to realize what she meant.

"I'm looking for some coke," she said bluntly.

Oh.

I opened my mouth, and then it hit me. The reason Hiyam invited us—me—to this stupid party. Because of my druggie mother. Because I could be a supplier. Not because we had one fucking thing in common, not even how we felt about our hot teacher.

My fingernails scraped against granite.

"I don't deal," I said.

Hiyam was accustomed to a certain degree of obedience. She didn't wheedle me. She looked at me icily, took a drag, and said, "Let me know if you change your mind. I can connect you with a lot of interested parties."

She walked away, trailing smoke.

My nails perched on the stone like bird claws. I thought I'd been reinventing myself, choosing who I wanted to be, but I was so naive. I'd always be my mother's daughter.

I went back in, looking for Wesley. The dancing crowd no longer seemed charming. They were just a bunch of stupid drunk kids who didn't know shit about the real world. Who wanted to buy coke with their rich parents' money while my mom gave blowjobs in her van to supplement our income.

I finally found Wesley outside, smoking one of his clove cigarettes on a bench beside a pool. A bare bulb shivered beneath the water, marbling his face with cyan light.

"These people suck," I said.

He glanced at me, then off into the shadows. I sat.

"What's your problem?"

"What's yours?"

"Hiyam thinks I'm a drug dealer. That's the only reason she invited us."

He turned halfway back to me. "Seriously? What a bitch."

"I don't know what I expected. We don't fit in with anyone, anyway."

I leaned back on my palms, looking at the Milky Way spilling in modest grandeur across the sky. A fountain of stars frothing over, surrounded by a mist of stardust. It looked like raw magic, like the glimmer I'd spy in a shadowy corner where the sun skimmed off invisible particles, reminding me there was a whole hidden world tucked inside this ordinary one. And it was up there every night, offering its mute beauty while we sat here with our heads down, tragically terrestrial. Not until I'd met Evan had I begun to open my eyes and really see this universe I was part of.

"You ever think the reason we're into filmmaking is because we're scared to be in front of the camera?" I said.

"No shit, Captain Obvious."

I smiled. The notes of an acoustic guitar floated into the

night, the beginning of "Wake Me Up When September Ends." We both laughed.

"How wonderfully cliché," I said.

"And the camera flies in for their close-up," he said.

I was still smiling at him, but his smile had fallen. I was so fucking naive. "Close-up for what?"

Wesley kissed me.

Your body sometimes automatically reacts to things, especially when that thing has been building up for a long time, especially when you're drunk and feeling like the only person who understands you at that moment is the person who was right beside you the whole time. So I kissed him back. I was stunned and responding on reflex and very, very slightly curious. Our kiss was gentle, sweet, almost pure. A boy and a girl kissing. I tasted bitter smoke on his lips and the clean metallic vodka we'd drunk.

Then my eyes opened, and reality came rushing back. I pushed him away.

Girl: shocked, bewildered. Boy: hopeful, anxious.

"What are you doing?" I whispered.

"I'm sorry," he said, breathing fast. "I've wanted—I thought—"

Neither of us were really looking at each other.

"Oh, god. Wesley—I'm with someone."

"Who? That guy you're sneaking around with?"

Now our eyes met.

"You wouldn't understand," I said.

He laughed, not nicely. "I wouldn't, huh? You act like you're so mature, but you're doing something you have to hide from everyone. Maybe I'm not as mature as you, but I know that's fucked-up."

I felt cold inside. "Don't judge me. You have no idea what you're talking about."

I stood and took a few aimless steps away, needing space. He followed.

"You know I'm your friend, right? Why don't you trust me?"

I whirled around. "Because of this. Because I had no fucking idea you were going to kiss me."

"You kissed me back."

"Oh my god. This is way too high school for me."

"God, you're stuck up."

"Fuck you," I said.

"No, fuck you, Maise. Why are you hiding all this shit from me and then acting like you're my friend?"

"I am your friend, you idiot."

At some point we'd progressed to yelling. My voice rang across the night. Shadows stirred, faces turning.

Wesley was close, looming over me. He lowered his voice. "Then who the hell is he?"

I shook my head.

"Why are you so ashamed of him? Who is he?"

"None of your fucking business," I spat.

Wesley laughed again. "You know, I should've listened the first time we met. You really meant it. You don't want friends."

He stalked off into the dark.

There's only one thing to do when your sole friend abandons you at a party full of people you hate.

Get shitfaced.

I found the Grey Goose guy and gave him another twenty

for the rest of a bottle, grabbed a cup of punch for a chaser, sat in the manicured grass beside a pool, and started drinking with steely determination.

Fucking Wesley. Ruining a good thing.

Idiot boys, never content with friendship.

Fucking cokehead Hiyam.

It occurred to me after five or seven sips that I no longer had a ride home. I couldn't call Siobhan, even though she'd probably sympathize. I took out my phone and instead of calling a cab, I looked at photos. Evan had taken one of me running into the rain. Dark doorframe, bright silver rectangle of water coming down like tinsel, a girl I barely recognized throwing her arms wide to the sky.

He answered on the second ring. "Hi," I said.

"Hi."

I lay back in the grass, my limbs all loose string. "I'm really drunk. I'm sorry for calling."

"Don't be sorry. Where are you?"

"Beverly Hills."

I pictured him frowning. "What?"

"My ride left. I'm stranded in paradise." I was very drunk. I knew this in a detached, clinical way, as if observing my body from behind glass. "Everyone hates me, Evan. Hiyam just wants drugs, Wesley wants to fuck me. My mom wants—she wants me to not exist. I can't give them anything they want."

His voice came through the phone like a warm breath on the side of my face. "Listen to me. It's okay. I'll come get you. Tell me where you are."

By the time he got there I'd finished the bottle and was temporarily happy again. I stood up and then immediately sat down, not prepared for gravity.

"When did everything get so heavy?" I said, but with fewer consonants than it needed to be intelligible.

Evan looked at the empty bottle with alarm. "Did you drink all of that yourself?"

"No. I think."

He started to lift me beneath the arms and a shadow wandered toward us from the bright blur of the house.

"Is she okay?" a small voice said.

It was Britt, from my history class. I hadn't even talked to her the whole night. I really was a stuck-up bitch.

"I think so," Evan said. "I'll take her home."

Once I was standing, I felt a million times worse. I leaned into him, arms around his waist for balance. The ground kept wanting to flip up and tumble me into the sky.

"Mr. Wilke," Britt said.

She handed him my phone.

He thanked her and said good night.

"Shit," I said as he walked me toward the gate. "She knows. They're all gonna know."

"It's okay."

"It's not okay. They'll take your job, they'll take my—" I couldn't think of what they'd take from me. Unknown privileges, vanishing in an instant.

"It's okay, Maise. If they know, they know. We'll deal with it. I'm going to make sure you get home safe."

"This is how it ends," I said mournfully. "I blew it. I'm a fucking idiot."

"You're not a fucking idiot," he said, squeezing my shoulders. "But you should probably stop talking about it."

I made it to his car in a sort of dream sequence, moments not fully connected to each other. Images jumbled like flotsam in my mind: my fevered forehead on the blessedly cool window; trying to tell him my address unsuccessfully until he found it in my phone. That detached part of me watched with loathing. *Child*, it said. *If you were trying to prove how unready you are for this, congrats. You nailed it.*

Somehow I communicated the existence of the spare key taped beneath the mailbox. Then I was on my couch in a living room that smelled like cigarettes and unsavory men. The hallway light slanted across Evan's face, an amber stripe showing stubble and soft lips. He smoothed my hair.

"You are really drunk," he said, almost wonderingly.

"Wesley kissed me."

His hand slowed. "Seriously?"

"He's in love with me. I didn't know. It's horrible."

Evan smiled. "I can see why."

I had enough wits to know he was making fun. "You—" I cut off, sitting up. A comet that had been accelerating inside my belly decided it was ready to crash to Earth. I clapped a hand to my mouth.

We made it to the bathroom just in time for the show.

Things I never expected to do my senior year: kiss my best friend, fuck my teacher, let said teacher hold my hair while I puked my guts out.

Thankfully, I was so drunk by then I barely knew what was happening. Cold linoleum, colder ceramic. Mouthwash, swirl and spit. Evan made me sip water that I promptly threw back up and he made me keep sipping until it stayed down. I felt a thousand years old, a set of bones wired together with rags and ancient sinew. He carried me back to the couch.

"Where's your mom?"

"Who fucking cares."

"I don't want to freak her out."

My eyes kept trying to drift shut. He was a fuzzy shadow against the warm hall light. "Are you staying?"

"Until I'm sure you don't have alcohol poisoning."

My eyes closed. "This isn't how . . ." I trailed off.

He stroked my hair again. "Sleep."

For a while, I did. Woke with my chest burning, the house dark. Evan sat on the end of the couch with my legs in his lap. I thought he was asleep but when I shifted, he looked at me. I was still pretty drunk.

"I kissed Wesley back," I whispered. "I don't know why. I'm sorry."

I caught the edge of his smile in the dark. "It's okay."

"It felt wrong. I'm not in love with him."

I couldn't make out Evan's face, but I heard his breath. His hand curled around mine, lifted it, brought it to his mouth.

"I'm—"

"Shhh," he said. "You're drunk."

"Not that drunk," I said, but my eyes had already closed, my brain slowly erasing itself into unconsciousness.

Later that night I woke again, and the hallway light was back on. A shadow stood in it.

"Who are you?" it said in my mother's voice.

"I'm her friend. My name is Evan."

"She okay?"

"Yeah. She is."

The shadow watched us for a moment longer. Then the light turned out.

I woke alone on the couch under a slab of late September sun. My head was a fireball, my body mummified. It took a while before I could think about anything except how much I wanted to die.

Then: panic.

What the hell had I said last night? I knew what I'd been *trying* to say while Evan hovered over me like a guardian angel, but had I actually said it?

I sat up, and the world took a good five seconds to recalibrate to our new viewing angle. I groaned.

On the coffee table before me, a folded piece of paper with my name on it. Inside, his handwriting, flowing and elegant, the letters not quite closed.

I haven't been fair to you, and I didn't realize how much stress I've been putting you under. Maybe I didn't want to realize it. You deserve better than this. You deserve better than being Harriet the fucking Spy. Sorry if this sounds dramatic—this isn't a breakup letter.

Jesus, I thought, my heart pounding, maybe you should've started with that.

This is me saying I'm going to do better. I want you to be happy, Maise. You mean more to me than you know. Seeing you miserable and drunk breaks my heart. I want to make you as happy as you were that first night when we got off that crazy death ride together. I want you to be that free again.

The paper trembled in my hands.

I have an old friend who owns some property in St. Louis. He might be willing to sublet us a loft for the weekends. If you're feeling better Sunday, I'd love to take you to the city.

My heart was going like mad again, but this time with joy.

You've done something to me, too. I can't get enough of you. "I dreamed that you bewitched me into bed and sung me moonstruck, kissed me quite insane." And before you think that's cheesy, that's Sylvia Plath. Google her, young Padawan.

I laughed and cringed at the same time.

Okay, I should probably go. I don't want to stop, though. I can't stop with you. Come with me to St. Louis. Let's find happiness.

I read it three times before I folded it up and stuck it in my bra. Not quite inside my heart, but that was okay. The words were already engraved there.

5

My bare feet propped on the dashboard, sun blazing in my heart-shaped glasses (I bought a pair before we left), singing along at the top of my lungs to Modest Mouse's "Float On" as we drove up I-55: this was going to be an awesome day.

Things I learned about my teacher:

He had pretty good taste in music, despite being born in 1980. He could cook and had been dying to cook for me. He was terrified of geese. ("Bad experience in a petting zoo." "How old were you?" "Twenty-six." I laughed.) He'd never been married but was briefly engaged. ("College mistake. She cheated on me with her psych professor." Awkward smile. Subject change.) He cried every time he watched *Casablanca*. ("We'll watch it sometime." He'd said that already. I think it made him nervous.)

Hot asphalt cut through woods so green they looked unreal. At the end of summer everything swelled with life, almost grotesque, bloated and overripe. The sky was so full and pregnant you could punch a hole in it and douse the world with blue paint. I'd been to St. Louis as a kid for a Cards game, but had only a vague memory of a giant pretzel I held with both hands and Mom letting me sip her beer, my nose wrinkling. I watched for the Arch like a hawk, occasionally sitting up at a silvery glint in the distance.

"Is that it?" I said.

Evan just smiled.

We followed I-55 up the Mississippi, through lazy suburbs rolling into city blocks. Finally the Arch appeared, like magic: a huge silver ribbon arcing over the skyline, stropped with white licks of sunlight. It looked like a handle on the world, as if God could reach down and pick us up and fling us into deep space.

Then we were in the city proper. St. Louis was a knot of rivers tied into a loose horseshoe heart. Sun baked the streets, everything glazed with light and soaking with color. Skyscrapers scaled in mirrored glass, tinted sky blue. Old red-brick factories. A boulevard with an artery of thick lush green running down the middle. People everywhere, wearing shades and drowsy smiles. I couldn't peel my face off the window.

"Hungry?" Evan said.

We found a restaurant with a patio. He took my hand when we got out of the car and I froze, instinct kicking in.

"No one knows us here," he said.

I relaxed, but a tiny live wire still vibrated somewhere in me.

We ordered scallops and a bottle of white wine and I had the most adult meal of my life. I savored the sweet buttery meat, the dry clarity of the wine. Evan fed me scallops by hand, his fingertips brushing my lips, my teeth lightly scraping his skin, goosebumps racing up the backs of my arms and legs, and then he leaned over and kissed me in front of everyone. My heart didn't know where to settle in my chest. It still felt like we held a secret, but at the same time I was beginning to accept this openness. I ran a hand over his thigh under the wrought-iron table and his muscle tensed. His eyes, usually so changeable, burned gas flame blue.

After lunch we walked around downtown, Evan's arm casually circling my waist. Another first in my adult life: window-shopping with my boyfriend.

Was he my boyfriend? Secret lover? Person abusing his position of authority or trust?

"You'd look amazing in that," he said, eyeing a diaphanous sundress, sheer and breezy.

A few stores down, I said, "You'd look amazing in that," nodding at a store clerk stripping a mannequin.

Evan gave me that sly smile that I felt as a warmth deep in my belly.

I glanced at our reflection in the plate glass as we walked on. If only you could see this, Wesley, I thought. I'm not ashamed at all.

We stopped to listen to a guy busking with an acoustic guitar and a voice like liquid velvet. His skin shone russet brown in the sun. He sang without seeming to care whether anyone listened, his eyes half-closed, his smile private and inward. I felt like a voyeur watching but couldn't look away. That's how I wanted to be. Creating something beautiful without caring who noticed. Doing it for myself, for sheer joy.

When the guy started singing the Yeah Yeah Yeahs' "Maps" I nearly lost it. I pulled out a bill without looking at it and dropped it into his guitar case. His smile flickered at me for a moment, then receded back into itself.

I walked away, trying to swallow the tightness in my throat.

"What was that about?" Evan said when he caught up.

I shook my head. How do you explain that everything is too beautiful for words?

If Wesley had been here, he would've filmed the moment, captured it. Raising the camera was his first impulse; mine was to feel, to let the world crash against my skin.

What if I was wrong about what I wanted to do with my life? What if I really just wanted to live, and hadn't truly come alive until I'd met Evan?

I stood in the middle of downtown St. Louis, staring at sun-beaten concrete.

"Maise."

I raised my face.

He didn't say anything else. We stood there as people streamed around us, like we had in the hallway at school. My brain simmered with wine and summer heat. I felt lost.

Evan did something he couldn't have done back home. He wrapped his arms around me, pressing his face against mine.

When we returned to the car I felt lighter, unburdened. We drove up to the Tivoli Theatre, an old-time movie house with a huge neon sign and a legit marquee. Stepping inside took us straight back to the Golden Age: velvet ropes and red carpet, classic Hollywood posters. The auditorium looked like a ballroom with chandeliers dripping from vaulted ceilings, rows of plush seats, even a curtain over the screen. I stared at everything, starry-eyed. Evan watched me.

"It's beautiful," I said.

He smiled. "Tell me about it."

Remember the roller coaster?

I zoned out during the film, which was a lot of vague, dreamy dialogue anyway. I was thinking about how far I'd come in five weeks, and how far I would go until I reached an ending of some kind, and Evan's hand, warm and solid, holding mine.

I was quiet in the car on the way to meet The Friend.

"He's sort of a douche," Evan said apologetically. "You won't miss anything."

Because they were going to meet in a club, where I couldn't go, because I was eighteen. Because I was pretending to be an adult in his world full of actual adults.

He left me with his car. "Two hours, I promise. Not a minute more."

Quick kiss. His hand on the side of my face. An earnest look into my eyes.

Then it was just me and the stuffed pony, alone in the city.

"You need a name," I said.

A hundred names leapt out from the streets of St. Louis.

"Louis," I said.

My creativity was legendary.

Louis and I drove around aimlessly for a while. Twilight came on faster here within the forest of steel and glass, neon signs popping out, streetlights searing cigarette burns into the darkness. The city smelled like hot asphalt and the weedy tang of the Mississippi. There was something melancholy and restless in me, magnified by seeing people together, laughing, holding hands, free with each other. I ditched the car in a parking garage, leaving Louis perched atop the wheel. I wasn't far from the river.

I walked past the Old Courthouse, the great dome lit up and the molding looking like a wedding cake, with the Arch shining behind it. The closer I got, the higher it seemed to rise into the sky. The city thrummed around me, a live passionate thing full of hearts and hands and desires, and all of it seemed to concentrate here in a collective defiance of gravity. I took a photo from a nearby park: a silver bend in the night sky, the trail of something that had tried to escape the Earth but not quite made it.

Okay, so I was being morose.

I sat on a bench in the park. A dad and his little girl walked by, the daughter gripping a handful of black-eyed Susans. She grinned at me shyly as if I'd seen a secret. Her dad smiled, too, but his smile dipped to the bare legs I crossed before he looked away.

For the first time in ages, I didn't feel good about that. I felt confused. I was eighteen, out in a big city doing whatever the fuck I wanted with an older man, but I was too young to go with him to a club, or to have my own real place, real job, real life. Wesleypedia told me once that human brains don't fully develop until age twenty-five. Seven more years until I was a full person.

What the hell am I? I thought. Too old to be a real teenager, too young to drink. Old enough to die in a war, fuck grown men, and be completely confused about what I was doing with my life.

You're right, Evan, I thought. No one knows us here. I don't even know myself.

I thought about the man with the guitar. A nobody on a street corner, but better than a million somebodies on TV. He didn't care—he did it for love. Love was what made it good and beautiful and ephemeral. And I thought about the man I was waiting for, the way my eyes had been gradually opening, sincerity replacing sarcasm, the way I felt I was constantly waking up and yet slipping deeper into a beautiful dream.

And it hit me—what my semester project was going to be about.

By the time Evan called, the night was heavy and complete. He asked where I was and said he'd meet me. I was nervous about seeing him again, because something inside me had changed. An acknowledgment of things forming and fitting together into definite shapes. I thought it would show on my face.

He got out of a cab and my heart pulsed in my throat.

"How did it go?" I said.

His hair looked messier now. His collar was open wider, his skin gleaming with a fine rime of sweat. He put his hands on my shoulders, his fingers flexing. "It's a deal. Two hundred a month and it's ours every weekend."

So we're doing this, I thought. We're going to move our affair across state lines. Was it legal in Missouri? Did it matter? We could be ourselves here the way we couldn't in Illinois. No worries about who would see us, recognize us. I felt my heart echoing through my whole body. Jesus, I am actually going to do this with him.

I let my breath out. "That's way cheaper than Lolita motels."

He laughed. "I don't care what it costs. I care that you get to be yourself. That we don't have to hide."

He was slightly drunk. I felt a twinge of—something—at the fact that he was drunk and I wasn't, but I let it go, because my giddiness was greater. This man didn't just want to fuck me. We were making plans for some kind of actual, lunatic life together.

You were so wrong, Wesley.

"Let's go look at this ridiculous thing," I said, taking Evan's hand. "I've been waiting for you."

The Arch was freakishly huge. Each leg was as large as a house, plated in sheets of stainless steel the length of cars. Looking up gave me instant vertigo. You had to admire this kind of pointless audacity, planting something so bold and stunning and utterly useless right in the navel of America. It was supposed to be a monument to going west, growing the country, Lewis and Clark and Manifest Destiny, but all I saw was a big gorgeous fuck-you to the universe. The steel was inscribed with graffiti from the ground to well over my head.

"Typical," I said. "Someone makes something saying 'I was here,' then a million people put their own 'I was here' on it. We're so vain."

Evan eyed me wryly. "You're so cynical."

"Not true."

"Prove it."

I took his face in my hands and pulled it down to me. Looked at him the way he'd looked at me earlier, my hands full of fire and my skin a veil of flame. Then I kissed him. There was alcohol on his breath and smoke and cologne on his clothes and I didn't care. He put his arms around me, pressing me against the steel. My eyes closed but I felt that knocked-over sense of vertigo again. My heart curved up into the sky just like the absurd beautiful thing behind us. I turned my face away, laughing, breathless.

"Did I prove it?"

He turned my face back to his and kissed me again, fiercely.

His hands slid to the small of my back. He pulled me into him. I kissed him like his lips were water and I could not get enough of it. We were part of this place, the blood thrashing inside the steel heart of this city, the crimson in its stone veins. We were the cells burning like stars. People like us. Passion like ours.

I didn't even realize there were other people around until I laid my head back against the metal. Two men strolled past, middle-aged, hand in hand, and one smiled at us. And I knew then that no one saw anything wrong. They only saw two people who were crazy about each other.

I could get used to this.

I asked a woman to take a picture of us beneath the Arch. I looked at the camera, but Evan looked at me.

"Two hours until we're home," I said as we walked out of the park, arm in arm.

Evan gave me an unreadable glance. He didn't say anything.

We kissed again in the garage, and when he leaned me against the driver's window and pressed his thigh between my legs, I gave serious consideration to another first: sex in a parking garage. I was wet and he knew it, and he was grinding his leg between mine and making me insane and sullen and miserable with want. My wiser self won out. We were doing things right. No need to risk everything now, on the cusp of . . . getting away with it.

Still there. The taboo. That kernel of wrongness. That thing I didn't entirely want to lose, because the nasty little Lolita in me liked it.

"I'll drive," I breathed against his ear.

We were quiet on the way back. A tense, moody quiet at first, almost hating each other for not consummating this awful desire. Then the miles smoothed it away, and the starlight and taillights soothed us. Evan had his eyes on me most of the ride. After a while he ran fingertips over my ear, my jaw, my collarbone. Not distractingly. Just enough to draw a pleasant shiver. To keep me awake.

It was late when I finally pulled into town. Before I could head for my house, he gave me directions to his.

My heart sped up. It didn't make sense to go there first. How would I get home?

Answer: I wasn't going home.

"Tomorrow's a school day," I said, staring at the windshield. "I have a class with you."

His hand circled the back of my neck. "I need you tonight."

Has there ever been a more effective line in the history of pickup lines than "I need you?"

My teacher lived in a second-floor apartment in a staple-shaped group of buildings bracketing a parking lot. There were other cars in the lot, other eyes in the windows. We walked inside without touching, but his stare was palpable. I followed him upstairs. My mind checked off every mistake I'd made since the beginning: kissing him in school, Wesley seeing the call from E, Britt handing Evan my phone as he took me home, and now this. Were we sabotaging it? Were we trying to heighten the danger to eke out some pathetic erotic thrill? Did we want someone to know, to stop us?

In retrospect, you know all the answers. You know the shadowy throes of your heart.

In the moment, you're a teenage girl walking into your teacher's apartment and your heart is beating like hummingbird wings, a wild red blur in your chest.

He opened the door.

When I stepped inside, my whole body tingled, as if I'd passed through an enchanted gate. The lights in the parking lot filled the rooms with a soft sepia wash. Smell of new paper and fresh laundry. Everything looked simple and clean and sedate. No messy effusion of emotion, no clash of warring desires like in my whirlwind-wrecked room, that spiral galaxy of torn-out magazine pages and printed quotes from the Internet and the random debris of my childhood, swirling around an explosive center. This place was fully formed, solid. I was a trespasser here. A girl spy in the land of adults. The crescent moon winked through balcony doors and I crept toward it, and there they were, those carnival lights he'd watched, thinking of other people's happiness, of me.

Wish you were here, I thought. And now I am.

Hands around my waist.

His body against mine, warm and hard. I turned my head to one side and his face grazed my cheek. The tickle of his stubble sent a charge through me, my nerves lighting up like neon. We kissed the corners of each other's mouths, his hands slipping under my shirt, running over my belly, the arch of my ribs. When he reached my breasts his fingers became possessive, rough. His body was rigid and unyielding behind me, his hands almost tearing at my flesh—it felt like he wanted to take me apart. That meanness I thought we'd left in St. Louis returned with a vengeance. I dragged my hand up the inside of his leg, grabbing his dick through his jeans, and he took my earlobe between his teeth, painfully. I felt the shock in every extremity, my toes, my nipples, my fingertips. I dug my nails into his thigh.

We made our way to the bedroom in fits and starts, stopping to tear clothes from each other. Even when I was naked he seemed to want more, wanted to strip me to the bone. He kissed me so hard it left my lips raw, the inside of my mouth bruised, and I couldn't get enough. I wanted it rougher, harder. Everything that had stewed in me all day came boiling to the surface. He was driving me back toward his bed when I grasped his face, making him look at me.

"Who am I to you?" I said, my voice hoarse. "Maise, or your student?"

The animal single-mindedness lifted for a moment. His chest heaved, but his eyes were clear and colorless in the moonlight. "Both," he whispered.

I felt chills.

"Then fuck me, Mr. Wilke."

He turned me around to face his bed. My heart hammered. I knew what to do. Got on my knees, palms splayed across the sheet. My hair fell around my face. The sheet wrinkled in my hands, moonlight scrawling over it in wet white ridges. I felt totally vulnerable and terrified and perfectly calm all at once. Noises behind me, a drawer sliding, something crinkling, then his weight and heat were pressing me down into the bed. He clutched my hips. I felt his stomach tighten against my back, his abs furrowing, and even though I knew it was coming I gasped when he thrust inside me, my hold on myself unraveling, my hands and feet instantly going numb. He held me tightly in place and fucked me and it felt like I was coming apart from the inside. My fingers curled in the sheet. His stubble rubbed against my shoulder blade, his breath hot on my skin. As soon as it evaporated, that spot turned cool until he breathed again. We'd been doing this to each other for weeks, but this was the first time we acknowledged that there was an element of wrongness in it. That we liked the wrongness. I finally understood what he meant when he said *wish you were here*—he wanted to do this to me, take me into his home as his student and fuck me on my hands and knees. No pretensions of goodness, of trying to do the right thing. We'd both wanted to embrace this fucked-up thing between us. His hands moved to my breasts and he pulled me against him and fucked me deeper and it almost hurt. So intense, too intense to feel directly, just a sensation of being full to my core, of my body wrapping itself with crazy anaconda strength around him, taking him in as deeply as I could until I thought I was going to scream, cry, cease to exist. At some point I became aware that I was saying, "Fuck me, Mr. Wilke, God, fuck me, fuck me," in a high pleading voice, an edge of my old accent bleeding through, and that the sharpness on my shoulder was his teeth. I couldn't come and I didn't want to. I just wanted to be dominated. So I called him by his teacher name and let my tense numb body slap against his and when he groaned and slowed down I said, "Please don't stop, please," and he didn't, and he didn't hold back, every muscle coiling, giving all of himself to me.

There's a very strange clarity when you get close but don't come. Your whole body feels like an exposed nerve, everything painful and grating but also miraculously clear. You don't have that sadness, the postcoital tristesse. The world is hard-edged and bright.

Evan held me, one arm around my hips, the other at my neck. His chest rose and fell against my back. Neither of us moved for a while. We knew what we were going to have to face when we looked at each other.

Our bodies separated. I sat on the bed, crossing my legs self-consciously. He sat beside me. We both faced the wall. The refrigerator buzzed in the kitchen. A man shouted unintelligibly outside.

"I'm sorry," Evan said.

"For not making me come, or for being my teacher?"

He was silent a long moment. "Both."

"Don't be."

He looked at me. I kept looking straight ahead.

"I've felt like this since the beginning," I said. We spoke in whispers, for some reason. Maybe truths weren't as harsh that way. "I wanted you because you were older. I don't feel anything for boys my age. And when I found out you were my teacher, something clicked in me. It felt wrong in the best possible way. Does that make sense?"

"Yes."

Now I looked at him. "You like me because I'm young."

"That's part of it."

"A big part."

"Yes," he said, and I smiled a little.

"Good," I said. "I like that you're kind of fucked-up, be-cause I'm kind of fucked-up." I uncrossed my legs, slipping one behind his. Ran my toes up the light hair on his calf. "I've been obsessed with you since that first night. Not just with you, but the way you make me feel."

"How do I make you feel?"

Alive. Real. Valuable. Whole.

"Like myself," I said. "More than I've ever been."

He touched my cheek. "Who are you?"

"Your student."

He shook his head. "No. You're the one teaching me."

My smile became full and genuine. I wrapped my arms around him, and we lay back on the bed together, quiet and calm, moonlight draping over our bare skin in a luminous sheet.

"Stay here tonight," he said after a while.

The first wrong note of the evening. It jangled inside me, discordant. Stop, I told myself. Why are you scared? Has he given you any indication he's going to leave you? What are you afraid of, being loved?

"I've been gone all day. My mom will freak out. I need to butter her up for St. Louis."

I need do no such thing. Mom hadn't cared where I spent the night when I was thirteen, and she sure as hell didn't care now.

Evan kissed my forehead, but I saw the disappointment in his eyes.

"Next weekend," I said, "we'll be doing this in a new city."

Waking up in the morning together. I had never woken up in the morning with anyone else.

"Are you nervous?" he said.

"No."

That's another thing about lies: if you convince yourself they're true, they become true. A lie is a discrepancy of belief, not fact.

———

Wesley skipped Film Studies on Monday. I looked for him in the cafeteria, but he wasn't there, either. Maybe he'd ditched the whole day.

It felt depressingly empty without him.

Britt and Hiyam didn't mention the party.

Mr. Wilke smiled at me, relaxed, peaceful. Beatific.

I hit the computer lab after school.

My phone took shitty video, but it wouldn't matter for this project. This was about impressions, experiences. The feeling of being there, the blurry bright overwhelming way real life looked as you lived it, not the surgical precision of HD after the fact. I scrubbed through my clips, looking for the bones of the story I knew was there.

Somehow the photos captured what I was looking for better. Receding taillights on a dark street. Evan's back, roped with muscle, his arms raised as he puts on his shirt in a motel. The little girl with the black-eyed Susans, walking with her dad beneath the Gateway Arch. A series of leavings, endings.

My old life ending. A new one beginning.

There was more to film than live action. I put headphones on, streaming music from my phone, and started scribbling.

you don't want friends
wise girl lovely too
i'm looking for some coke
just a trail of fire in my hands

I set the text over the photos in a video editing app. Each image flashed onscreen for a couple of seconds, then cut to the next. Taillights/trail of fire. Little girl/looking for some coke. Jarring. Weird. Kinda disturbingly beautiful. Closer to what I was trying to say, but I still wasn't quite sure what that was yet. Like Siobhan said, maybe it would emerge.

I missed Siobhan.

And her stupid, stupidly-in-love-with-me son.

———

"I'm cooking tomorrow night," Mom announced when I got home Thursday.

I flung my book bag at the couch. This week had been a trial. Evan and I thought it best not to see each other outside of school until the weekend, in case anyone had noticed our slip-ups. Wesley thought it best not to see me inside or outside of school until I dropped dead.

I was in no mood for Mom's tweaked-out bursts of chemical enthusiasm and trying to be a Real Mom.

"I've got plans this weekend," I said.

"I bought food already. Steak's marinating." She pronounced it *meer-uh-nay-ten.*

I looked at her dully. "The only thing you know how to cook is meth."

She did not find that amusing.

"What are you even cooking for?" I said, grabbing a jar of sweet pickles from the fridge.

"We're having company."

I froze. "Who?"

"Mr. Gary Rivero."

"Who is Mr. Gary Rivero?"

"A very important man. A very wealthy man."

I narrowed my eyes as I laid out bread for a sandwich. "That doesn't sound shady at all."

Mom sat at the kitchen table, sparking her lighter.

"Could you not smoke in the house, please?" I said.

"I ain't."

She stirred the ashes in a terra-cotta pot. I gave up trying to get her to quit smoking indoors; my only condition was she not do it while we breathed the same air. Sometimes I could not believe this woman and I shared DNA.

"Mr. Rivero is very interested in meeting you," she said.

"Stop calling him Mr. Rivero. That sounds like a teacher." I did not like that association attaching itself to her skeezeball friends. "Why does he want to meet me?"

"Because I told him what a smart, pretty girl you are. How you're going to college and all."

I paused in peanut-buttering my bread and glanced at her. That was almost a compliment. My mother's compliments were never without ulterior motive. "Why does he care if I'm smart?"

"I don't know, babe. Maybe you should talk to him and find out."

I had zero intention of doing that. "Like I said, I've got plans. I'll be gone all weekend."

"Where you going?"

"None of your business."

Mom scooted her chair back and loomed. She had a good three or four inches on me. Mentally, rationally, I knew this woman couldn't do shit to me. But I'd imprinted on her, and my brain remembered how to light up the fear circuits when she glowered.

"Long as you live under my roof, everything's my business."

I couldn't meet her stare. I addressed the peanut butter. "I'm going out of town with a friend."

"A friend? Your boyfriend?"

"Yeah."

"That man who was here the other night?"

"Yeah."

She mulled this over, her makeup almost moving in sync with her facial features.

"Well, I just need you here Friday night. You can go first thing Saturday."

God fucking dammit. This was not worth fighting over. Fighting with Mom tended to result in the molecular destabilization of household appliances. Lately, she had made threats against my laptop.

"Fine," I said, slapping pickles into the peanut butter.

Mom finally noticed what I was making. She frowned at the sandwich, then at me, and said with a dry, croaking laugh, "What are you, pregnant?"

Heart failure.

It only lasted a moment, and then I laughed back, right in her face. She couldn't tell the difference between sincerity and sarcasm anyway. Birth control was one thing I'd gotten right in my ridiculous life. I never missed a pill, and Evan was paranoid about protection for some reason I'd eventually cajole out of him. That, at least, would not be the drama that destroyed us.

Still smiling, I said, "What are you, a mom?"

———

By Friday afternoon I was utterly miserable. No one to talk to or sleep with or bother all week. Being miserable is even worse without an audience. I would've welcomed Wesley's senior citizen wisecracks right then. Go ahead and talk about how decrepit my mystery boyfriend is, I thought. The same one whose jokes you laughed at during third period. The same one Hiyam was imagining fucking in her head.

Wesley had found some clandestine place to eat lunch, so I stopped showing at the cafeteria, too. It was a bad idea, reckless, but I spent that lunch period in Evan's empty class, mostly talking and only kissing him for about five minutes out of forty.

"This is poor risk management," he said, pressing me against the whiteboard during those five minutes.

"I want to fuck you in this classroom," I said.

He exhaled slowly through his teeth.

"On this desk," I said. "While you're wearing your shirt and tie, and I'm wearing nothing but socks."

He kissed me to make me stop talking.

Before I left, he said, "This is torture."

"I could always drop out."

He looked horrified.

"Kidding," I said. "Relax, guy." But I ran my hand up his arm wistfully, adding, "I can't wait till tomorrow."

He embraced me, and said into my ear, "I'm going to fuck the shit out of you."

I lost my breath.

It was crude, it was unexpected, and it set me on fucking fire.

———

Mom insisted I wear the new clothes she'd bought. Suspiciously pleasant aromas leaked from the kitchen. It was possible she was concocting something actually edible in her cauldrons.

I was 99.98 percent sure Gary Rivero was a drug lord. The 0.02 percent was the possibility he was my father, reentering my life at the precise moment I'd cauterized the wound he left in me. Still, because I was forced into this and because fucking with middle-aged men was my favorite pastime, I put on a wispy skirt that showed generous thigh, a snug tank, and a brass locket from Nan. No makeup but a dash of eye shadow that made my eyes look feral, staring eerily from a shadowed cave. My hair decided to behave and do the milk chocolate waterfall thing. My body looked sleek and tight and new. I took a selfie and sent it to Evan.

Can I kidnap you? he texted.

Is it kidnapping if I give permission?

A delay before he responded. *Sometimes I can't believe you're real.*

I felt a weird, bittersweet sort of elation. Me either, I thought.

Mom didn't react when I came downstairs except to hand me a bowl of potatoes with the instruction, "Peel."

I hadn't bothered painting my nails, so I didn't care. I was not going to let *Mr. Rivero* think I gave more than the minimum Mom-mandated fuck about him. It irked me that she'd actually made an effort at cleaning. For once, the house smelled more like Pine Sol than smoke and despair.

"So how do you know this guy?" I said, shaving potato skins into a pile.

"Work associate."

"Does he run a cartel?"

Mom clanged a lid onto a steaming pot. "Rule number one: no business discussion unless Mr. Rivero brings it up first."

"He's not even here yet."

My logic did not move her.

"If this gets sketchy, I'm out of here," I warned, handing her the bowl. I watched her dirty up the ladles and dishes no one had touched in years. "Mom."

She glanced at me. Her makeup was understated tonight—she didn't quite look like a corpse who'd escaped from a funeral home.

"Thank you for the clothes."

Her eyebrows made a sad arrowhead pointing up. Jesus, please don't say you love me.

"You look beautiful, babe," she said, and dropped the potatoes in the pot.

I left the room, relieved and slightly queasy. I didn't want to hear her lie. I wanted her to actually love me, but I guess "you look beautiful" was about as close as I'd get. Some girls had mothers who never called them beautiful but swore their love up and down. It's all the same, really. All bullshit.

I answered the door when the bell rang.

Two men stood on our porch, both in suits, no ties. The

older one broke into an easy smile. I immediately pegged him as Mr. Rivero. Salt-and-pepper hair, dusky Italian complexion, aquiline nose, Mediterranean green eyes. Very Robert De Niro–ish. Handsome and slim for his age. He took my hand as he stepped inside, squeezing. I half expected him to kiss it.

"You must be Maise," he said.

"I must be."

Mr. Rivero's smile crinkled at the corners. "I'm Gary. This is my friend, Quinn."

I wasn't sure whether Quinn was a first or last name. He was built like a bear, more hair on his hands than his scalp. He nodded at me silently. Hired muscle.

I seated them in the dining room and poured drinks. Maker's Mark on the rocks for Gary. Water for Quinn. Mom was still busy in the kitchen, so I poured myself some Maker's, too. Quinn's eyes moved around the house, lingering on the windows. Gary's eyes lingered on me.

"So," I said. How the hell could you talk to a middle-aged man without mentioning business or sex? "Lovely weather."

Gary's smile said he knew exactly what I was thinking. "Your mother's told me a lot about you."

"Like what?"

"You want to go into the movie business."

"True. What else?"

"You're the smartest girl in school."

Had she actually said that? "Debatable. What else?"

"You're a stunning young lady."

I sipped my bourbon to mask the warmth in my face. I was aware of him watching every move, my hand setting the glass down, fingers poised on the rim. "Is it true?" I said.

"Very much so."

Pots clashed in the kitchen. I leaned toward Gary. Quinn's eyes darted to me.

"I don't do what my mother does," I said under my breath. "Any of it. Whatever you came for, you're wasting your time."

Gary didn't blink. His eyes were shrewd, intelligent. "I'm certainly not wasting my time," he said, and sipped.

The rib eyes were black outside, vivid pink inside. Perfect. There were three different vegetable dishes and a lemon custard pie. Quinn ate more than the rest of us combined and never stopped scanning the room. I stared at my mother, unsure if I was impressed or furious. She had the capacity for this and had let me grow up on microwave meals.

"What kind of movies do you make, Maise?" Gary said.

Plus one, Mr. Rivero. Thank you for not assuming beauty is my only asset.

"Experimental stuff. I'm interested in playing with the boundary between reality and fiction. True stories mixed with fantasy, in a way that makes both of them more true and more false at the same time."

I blushed. The alcohol had gone to my head.

Gary took a drink. "That reminds me of something I saw earlier this year. The one about killing bin Laden."

"*Zero Dark Thirty*," I said.

"That's it." He swirled the melted amber in his glass. "There's always controversy about things like that. You have all these people with their own version of the truth, trying to tell one story."

"And then we all interpret it our own way," I said, "and it becomes a million more truths."

Gary smiled. "What about you? What truths do you tell?"

"I haven't finished anything yet. I feel like I need more life experience before I can make something worthwhile."

Life experience that I was racking up rapidly with Evan.

"Quite a mature attitude." Gary tore the steak gently with his fork. He watched me as he chewed. It was like Mom and Quinn didn't exist. Mom was unusually quiet. "You show a lot of self-awareness for someone your age."

Backhanded compliment. "Thank you," I said. "You show a lot of cultural awareness, for someone your age."

Gary laughed. Mom pinched my knee under the table. I despised her. You don't even know what we're talking about, I thought. You're just reacting to tone. Like a dog.

"Anyone for pie?" she said.

Gary excused himself to smoke, brushing my wrist as he stood. "Join me," he said.

My pulse jumped. Whatever he'd come to ask, he was going to ask it now. I followed him to the back porch, Quinn behind us like a shadow on a leash. October had just started, a sharp, ice-toothed bite in the air, tearing the skin off the Earth. Leaves rustled in the yard, a sound I'd always thought of as dying. A thousand cells shivering, delicately giving up their ghosts.

Gary offered me a cigarette. I shook my head.

"Smart," he puffed.

You are some big-shot drug lord, I thought. You have a personal bodyguard who could rip a Bible in half with his hands. What the hell do you want with me?

"It's important to me that I understand all angles of a prob-lem," Gary said. "I don't like to make uninformed decisions."

He looked at me then, and I shivered, hard, understand-ing: I am an angle of the problem.

"What decision?" I said.

His gaze slid away from me, unhurried. He was not the kind of man to be rushed. "Raising a child alone is very difficult. I don't begrudge your mother her choices. But I do require her to be accountable."

A chill started to shimmy its way under my skin like a fine knife. *Require* had never sounded so ominous.

"Sweetheart," Gary said, "your mother owes someone a lot of money."

"I'm not part of her business," I said immediately.

"No, but you're part of her life. And when someone owes a lot of money, the people in their life become collateral."

I went cold all the way to my marrow. This was suddenly way too *Godfather*. I stared into the ghost-filled yard, seeing nothing.

"I've worked with her for several years. She's never disappointed me. I knew she had a daughter, and I knew she kept her daughter in the dark about certain things."

My eyes darted to Quinn. I wondered where the gun was on him. In his waistband? Strapped to his calf?

Gary put his hand on mine on the railing. It was warm and papery. He smelled like tobacco.

Holy shit, I thought. My life is a movie. A fucking drug thriller, happening right now, in my backyard.

"Please," I said, "I don't want anything to do with this."

"I understand. But she made you part of it without asking."

My mind filled with terrifying images. Having to sleep with this man. With Quinn. Being passed around a bunch of skeezy dealers. Snorting coke to numb myself to the horror. I was shaking.

I could call Evan. Let's run away tonight, I'd say. Let's start over in St. Louis. Or LA. As far as possible from this shit.

"What do you want from me?" I said, my voice like those rustling leaves.

Gary took his hand away. "As I said, you mother has never

disappointed me. I'm willing to help with her debts, smooth things over with some people. But I can't do things like that out of the goodness of my heart. That's not how a successful businessman stays successful."

"Okay," I said. "So answer my damn question."

When you realize you have nothing to lose, it's easy to be brash.

He merely smiled. Nothing I had said or done affected this man. He was a lizard, everything pinging off his scaly surface. "I don't want anything from you. I just wanted to meet you. Yvette's daughter."

He held my gaze, and I understood. *I don't want anything . . . for now.*

"Does this make you feel good about yourself?" I said quietly. "Scaring the shit out of little girls?"

"You're not a little girl."

He was wrong. At that moment, I absolutely was.

"How much does she owe?" I said.

His eyes got a shuttered, closed-down look. "That's business, sweetheart. Not for you to worry about." He stubbed out his cigarette and put an arm around my shoulder. It felt like a shackle. "Let's go in, before your mom gets the wrong idea."

I was too dazed to process the rest of the night. When they were gone and I was sitting in my room, my eyes full of water but not spilling, my entire body trembling, I suddenly remembered the squeaky bank teller.

I should have known what was coming. The foreshadowing was so obvious.

I logged into my bank account.

Balance: $0.00.

6

RAIN ran down the windows in rivulets thick and silvery as mercury. The world looked like an ashtray full of soft soggy grayness, headlights fizzling in it like cigarette cherries. All I heard was a crackling sound, rain and wet tires, as if one long strip of Velcro was endlessly peeling.

Evan had seen how somber I was and let me brood in peace. I put on music for a bit, then turned it off and listened to the rain. I should have told him before we left. I shouldn't have left with him, dragging him into my doomed orbit, toward this black hole I was slowly circling. The seat was cool and I pressed the bare backs of my legs against it. I felt like I needed to shiver from a place deep inside of me, one not connected to my nerves.

Traffic slowed as people tried not to die in the rain. Evan took a hand off the wheel and laid it atop mine. He didn't speak.

We reached St. Louis well past noon. The Arch was a faint

shadow in the downpour, almost frightening, a shape without context. It could have been the leg of an alien ship touching down. Rain washed the color out of everything. We hunted the hot blurs of traffic lights, hitting every red. Even the universe was telling me to stop.

Evan pulled into an underground garage. I got out, leaving my bag in the car. He looked at me with concern but remained silent, and I appreciated this.

We took a haunted freight elevator up six stories. It rattled as if possessed, screeching when the gate opened and closed.

"Nothing says 'Welcome home' like poltergeists," I said.

Evan smiled nervously. He seemed relieved I'd finally spoken.

We walked down a dim brick hallway to a steel door, and when he opened it my bleak mood lifted for a moment.

The Friend's loft was huge, a couple thousand square feet of bare concrete and brick. One entire wall was windows, flooding the space with pearly gray light. The open floor was divided into groupings of furniture: leather couches arrayed around a TV, a dining table and bar, a bed framed by bookcases. Stairs led to a walled area above the kitchen—bathroom, probably. There were canvases everywhere, big, messy abstract paintings, all motion and color, no form.

"This is really nice," I said, feeling infinitely small. I didn't even notice my voice crack.

Evan's hands on my shoulders. "Maise."

He turned me around. I felt a dangerous rearrangement of my facial features in preparation for tears.

"What's wrong?" he said. His face was doing that big-eyed, furrowed-brow thing that I could not lie to.

I started to cry. "I'm sorry I made fun of the elevator."

He laughed a little, helplessly, and pulled me close. "That's not why you're upset. Is it?"

"No."

"Can you talk, or do you need to cry?"

"Need to cry," I said like a child, and did.

At first I tried to retain my dignity, but once I started it became a runaway train, and the best I could manage was to hold on while an unstoppable force moved through me. I got the worst out standing there in Evan's arms, the loft as blurry as the rainy world outside. Mother. Witch. Whore. Devil. Stealing my money, the money her own mother had given me as compensation for being part of this fucking family. Putting my life in jeopardy. Ruining my future and the happiness I had with this man. All because she refused to get a real job, because she was forty and still thought she could cheat the world and get ahead without working as hard as all the other suckers.

Evan led me to the kitchen. Wiped my face with a warm washcloth, listened to me blow my nose and mumble semi-coherently.

"I shouldn't have come here," I said. The tears never stopped, merely waned. "I have to—we have to stop."

He looked frightened until I explained that it was because of Mom.

"I'm sorry I didn't tell you before, but I never found the right moment. 'Hey, by the way, my mom's a drug dealer.' Is there a greeting card for that?"

"Tell me everything," he said, sitting with me at the counter.

After an hour he knew the gist of my sordid family. He listened without comment, handing me tissues, stroking my hair, staring sadly at my swollen, ruddy, childish face.

When I quieted, he said, "I can't believe you've been dealing with this your whole life."

"Well, now you know." I wasn't crying anymore. My voice was raw, husky. Like Mom's. "I'm sorry about all of this."

"You have nothing to apologize for."

"Yes, I do." I made myself look at him. "We can't keep doing this, Evan. It's not going to work."

"Why?"

"Because I might be on a hit list somewhere? Because my life just became a low-budget version of *The Sopranos*?"

He took my hands. "I'm worried, okay? No, I'm terrified. This is some seriously fucked-up shit, and I have no idea how to handle it. But it doesn't change how I feel about you."

"Oh my god," I said. "You're the mob wife. You won't leave me, even though there's a price on my head."

He stared at me for a second. Then we both burst out laughing. Wild, brittle laughter, on the edge of hysteria. He pulled me close, pressing my forehead to his chin.

"You're crazy," I said. "You should run away."

"If I ran away, I would be crazy."

Somewhere in my cavernous chest, another sliver of light chipped into my heart.

I leaned back. "Maybe I should run from you again. For your own good."

He looked at me with that sweet pout and I knew I couldn't. Though he never mentioned it, leaving him that first night had shaped the way he saw me. The shooting star he couldn't hold. Sometimes he'd touch my hands and my face as if to check whether I was really there.

God, if I could only go back to that night and tell myself to stay. Tell her, *There's something so beautiful waiting for you. Don't run from it. Run toward it.*

"What would your mother think," I said, "if she knew what kind of girl you got mixed up with?"

His eyes tightened. He looked through me for a split second. Then he focused on my face, a mask sliding over his with a smile painted on it. "She'd think, 'I am not surprised.' Now, if you're done trying to break up with me, I'd like to cook for you. You can reevaluate whether you still want to break up afterward."

There's another hidden story about your past, I thought. Now you owe me two.

———

Things I did for the first time in my life that day: shopped for groceries with my boyfriend (we spent an hour walking around a fish market in our sunglasses, calling each other Mr. and Mrs. Smith and pretending to be undercover assassins); made out in an elevator (haunted or not haunted—both firsts); took a shower and shaved my legs while my boyfriend watched, spellbound ("I've been fantasizing about this." "No touching. Is something burning?").

When I stepped out of the bathroom there was a trail of lit candles leading down the stairs.

Oh sweet Jesus, I thought.

I followed the light and the smell of tomato and thyme. Evan moved around the kitchen like a maestro, lifting a lid, stirring, gliding over to the oven just as it dinged. I watched him with an awed, goofy gape until he enlisted me to chop fresh basil.

"What are we making?" I said.

Besides an insane love story, obviously.

"Pine-nut-crusted flounder, roasted vegetable medley in herb and butter sauce, and tomato bisque." He paused behind me, raised my hair, and kissed the nape of my neck, all while taking a dish out of the cabinet above me. I stared at my hand, wondering what would happen if I put the blade to my skin. I didn't think it would cut. I didn't think I was awake.

Whose life is this? I thought. How did I sneak into it?

"Who taught you to cook?" I said as we set the table. "Your mom?"

Again, that millisecond flicker in his eyes. "My dad, actually."

"What's your dad like?"

He looked at me for a moment like he couldn't remember who I was. Because I was young. Because the concept of dead parents hadn't yet occurred to me. I had only two concepts for parents: Gone, and Wish You Were Dead.

"He was better than we gave him credit for," Evan said.

I stared at a fork, wondering how to take back my question.

"He was a mechanic," Evan continued, his good humor returning. "Strongest man in town. A car fell on a guy he worked with, and he lifted it by himself till they pulled the guy out. It messed up my dad's back, so he had to stop working. He started taking cooking classes out of boredom. Imagine the Hulk in an apron, but less green. Same approximate radius of destruction."

I smiled. "Who's 'we'?"

"What?"

"You said, 'better than we gave him credit for.' "

Evan's gaze shifted away. "Me and my sister."

Another mystery sister. First Wesley, now him. It was like every XY I knew didn't want me to know he was related to an XX.

We stood there with our secrets and mistakes, a beautiful dinner waiting for us.

"Let's forget all the bad stuff for tonight," Evan said.

"Deal."

We ate by candlelight in the sepulchral loft. Storm clouds obscured the real stars, but the city came alive, a horoscope of earthbound constellations spreading below us: meteoric taillights, neon pulsars, twinkling and shimmering all the way to the horizon. It made my heart ache. The city at night gave me the same melancholy twinge I'd felt as a kid watching Mom plug in the Christmas tree. Something beautiful and full of promise, but something you knew you could never touch.

The food made me feel good and strange, too. Light, sweet flounder broke apart and dissolved on my tongue, and the bisque was so creamy and savory I wanted to drink it straight from the bowl. It was overwhelming. He'd done this for me. All of this. I watched him carry our plates to the sink, thinking, All of this came from one night. If I hadn't gone to the carnival, you would've looked at me like any other student when I walked into your class. And that made my heart ache, too—the thought of how much happiness lay scattered across the universe, unrealized, in fragments, waiting for the right twist of fate to bring it together.

"If we hadn't met, where would you be right now?" I said.

Candlelight danced over his face. His eyes were embers. "Watching the lights."

We stood at the windows, looking out over the rainy city. He held me to the cold glass and kissed me, slow and intent. Our mouths tasted like pinot grigio. We moved to the couch, him atop me, crushing the leather, but after a while we ended up simply lying there.

"I'm sorry," I said. "My mind is all over the place."

His arms tightened around me. "Don't be sorry."

I watched the dark, glittering city.

"Did your dad love you?" I said.

"In his way."

"Did you feel loved, when you were a kid?"

"Not really."

"What about your mom?"

His body went rigid. I breathed as shallowly as I could, not wanting to disturb whatever was happening inside of him.

"My mom is an alcoholic. She pretty much ruined our family."

I glanced at him. He had that lost, X-ray-through-the-world look again.

"How?"

Evan sat up. He laid a hand on my leg to show me it was okay, then let it fall.

"My dad hit her, and she drank. I never knew which came first, but they fed each other. My mom was a nasty drunk. She'd say horrible stuff, call my dad stupid and worthless, call us all names. She was miserable and abused and clinically depressed and never got the help she needed. She'd drink herself into blackouts."

I thought of Mom and her gray-outs. "Jesus," I said.

"One day, she was in the backyard with Elizabeth, my little sister. I was in the garage so I didn't see it, but I've thought about it so much I feel like I was there. Beth was in the pool, in the shallow end. She had water wings on. Mom was drinking at ten in the fucking morning, guzzling gin. I hate gin, by the way. The smell of it makes me sick. So Mom was drinking, and she passed out, and Beth was playing by herself when her foot got too close to a drain. It sucked her down and the wings couldn't keep her above water. She kicked and splashed and screamed, and then she drowned. In three feet of water, in bright sunlight on a summer morning. And the whole time my mother was lying right there, five feet away, while Beth screamed for her."

I stared at him, my mouth open, eyes wide. I didn't know what to say.

He looked at my knee. "For years, I hated my mom. I wished I could've switched places with Beth. That any of us had died instead, because we all deserved it. She was innocent." He sighed, his frame sagging, succumbing to gravity. "It changed my mother. She finally stopped drinking. She went to church, though she was only looking for forgiveness, not faith. She cried all the time. She said she'd do anything to make sure I was happy, because now I was her only child."

"Did she?"

"I don't know. I left when I was sixteen, and I've never been back."

We sat there in the shadows, full of unspeakable things.

"Now I know," he said, touching me again, "why I was drawn to you. We have the same darkness inside."

"Our fucked-up parents?"

"Our lost childhood."

I curled against him, running my hands over his arms, his chest, lightly, reverently, as if I'd just discovered he was breakable. How bizarre, I thought. Mr. Wilke has a psycho mom and a shattered family, too, and that's why we understand each other. Why did everything beautiful come from pain?

"You don't seem that much older than me," I said. "Do I seem young to you?"

He kept stroking the same lock of my hair absently. "In school, you seem older than everyone. With me, you seem young. But I feel young with you, too."

"We have no age. We exist outside of time. We're timeless."

Evan smiled. "Like Jack and Rose."

"Or Lady and the Tramp."

He laughed. "The nurse and the English patient."

"Louis and Lestat."

He took my face in his hands. "You are the bravest girl I've ever met. You've been living with this crazy family shit and never said a word."

I shrugged. "Or maybe Louis and Claudia. I'm the little girl you've frozen in time because you plucked me like a rose and made me a vampire. We live together for a hundred years and I hate you and yet I'm in love with you."

Oh my god. I had actually said it. As a joke, but those were the words, in the proper order and everything.

"Maise."

"You've been living with a dead sister and never said a word. Is it brave, or just how things are?"

His hand moved against my face. "You are so worldly," he said, and it was both a compliment and a regret.

We kissed again, and his body lay over me and pushed me into the cloudy vagueness of the couch and I thought, Do what you want, I relinquish myself to you. But I guess he saw the disconnection in my eyes, because he stopped, and breathed against my throat, holding me. Just holding.

"It's okay," I whispered. "I want you to."

He looked into my face. "That's not what I want."

"What do you want?"

"All of you."

It seemed like such an incredible thing to ask of a person.

"I don't know where all of me is right now," I said, feeling silly and young.

He kissed my temple, my eyelids. "It's all right. I'm happy. I could spend this whole weekend just talking to you and be perfectly happy."

"Me too," I said. My voice was strained. "So if we're both so happy, why are we sad?"

Evan laughed, and we kissed again, without expectations.

———

Going to bed was awkward. I didn't know the protocol. Should we brush our teeth together? Little kids brushed their teeth with an adult. Just pretend you're alone at home, I told myself. I took everything off but my underwear and a T-shirt. He stood on the other side of the bed in pajama pants. We stared at each other.

Then we both laughed.

"This is so weird," I said, echoing Wesley at homecoming. Where was he? Was Siobhan kissing him good night? Did she do that?

"Weird because I'm your teacher, or because you've never done it before?"

Good question. "I can't even tell."

We sat on opposite sides of the bed.

"Oh my god," I said. "Is this how it is for married people?"

"Awkward and distant? Probably."

I grinned. "Let's pretend we're a troubled married couple."

"I feel like you're trying to test if I can actually act."

"I hate how you do that, John. You always think I'm testing you. I guess our kids are just a test, too."

He looked at me, trying not to laugh. "Well, Martha, maybe if you didn't hand me a questionnaire every time I want sex."

"And when is that, John? At midnight, after I've spent

all day babysitting your spawn? Or when your secretary isn't available to blow you on the weekend?"

"Come here."

"I think we should see a marriage counselor."

"Maise, come here."

My heart skipped. I sat beside him, our backs to the brick wall. In the darkness the loft reverted to a factory, mysterious machines hulking all around us, sitting in abandoned silence. The sadness of factories, I thought. Once upon a time they'd made things. Now they were all slowly decaying, like used-up mothers. My eyes traced the maze of pipes and beams that made up the ceiling, all the messy guts shoved together. Evan put his arm around me. I felt the contours of his muscle and bone through my shirt, the hard lines of this body I had taken into mine.

"Are you scared?" he said into my hair.

"Yeah."

"What scares you?"

I kept my eyes on the ceiling. "That this is too good. That it won't last. That you'll leave."

Fingertips ran up the smooth plane of my thigh. Goose-bumps, everywhere.

"And you?" I said.

"Same exact thing, but about you."

I turned to him. That boyish face, scruffy with stubble, almost like two different people looking at me. He wasn't perfect. His lips were a touch too full, too sulky, his forehead a little too tall, and there was a permanent trace of mourning stamped into his features that sometimes made him look helpless, but all his imperfections fit him perfectly. I adore this face, I thought. How is it possible he's scared of losing me? Never in my life had I considered I might be something someone worried about losing.

"Statistically," I said, "we're doomed, you know."

"Statistically, everyone is doomed."

"Right, but we are specifically doomed. Wesleypedia told me that at the beginning of a relationship, your brain releases tons of dopamine. You literally make yourself high. But after a few months it stops, and then you're basically going through withdrawal while trying to figure out why you're in bed with this person and sharing germs."

Evan wore a rueful smile. "What made you so grim?"

Life, I thought.

His hand moved up the back of my knee to the inside of my thigh. He looked at my face as he touched me, watching each layer of irony and cynicism splinter, crack, fall away. I didn't move. I let every cord in me tighten, slowly pulling into a knot in my center. I was so finely tuned I felt my nipples graze my shirt as I breathed, the hair on his arm tickling my thigh. He pushed my legs apart and I bit my lip.

"Look at me," he said.

I did.

His voice was soft and gritty. "This is what I think about in class."

His fingers rose to the crease of my thigh. He dragged a nail along the edge of my underwear, and I shivered and couldn't stop, as if a low electric current ran through me. He didn't touch me directly, but traced every boundary until I couldn't sit still. My mouth was open, my breath spilling wildly. All the electricity in me surged to predict where his fingertips would brush, like one of those glass balls full of plasma that shoots to the surface when a hand gets near.

Every subtle shift of fabric was unbearable. My skin was too hot, too ripe with blood, a summer creature full of too much life and lust and desperately in need of release.

"Please," I said.

His hand spread across my thigh and squeezed. "I think about you saying that, too."

My breath was still out of control, but I said, "And what else?"

"I think about undressing you."

I leaned forward and shrugged out of my T-shirt. My body felt elastic and sinuous, like a snake. His hand ran up my belly, between my breasts, never quite touching the places I ached to be touched.

"I think about your skin," he said, his thumb moving over my collarbone. "Your mouth." He opened it, put his index finger between my teeth. "The inside of you."

I closed my lips over his finger, looking at him. I felt so womanish, suddenly. You think you're the one corrupting me, I thought, but I'm corrupting you, too. My eyelids lowered. The power was all mine now. I took him deeper, almost to the knuckle, curling my tongue around his finger, scraping my teeth over it lightly as he withdrew. When he pulled away I took him into my mouth again. He groaned. So I did it again, and again, enthralled at how his body responded, leaning closer, softening, giving itself up to me. God, it felt so good, having all the power. I could get used to being the teacher.

He withdrew his hand finally and pressed his face to my shoulder. "What are you doing to me?" he said, his voice far away. "This is all I think about. I'm obsessed."

I swallowed. I could still taste his skin, clean and warm and faintly salty. I put my arms around him, and we lay down together, and were lost in each other until morning.

The day was half gone when I woke. Evan was up already, working on school stuff. He called me sleepyhead and kissed me and sat on the bed to watch me dress. Funny, how even clothes going *on* my body was absolutely mesmerizing to him.

We walked around the neighborhood in search of food. The city looked like an old-time photograph tinted the colors of coins, silver and nickel, its edges blurred with mist. Headlights made bright lighthouse beacons in the fog. We walked close and slow, arms around each other's waists. Trees still saturated with rain from last night seemed to glow a hyperpigmented green. The streets were a dizzying brew of wet concrete and brick and asphalt. On one side of my body, Evan's heat; on the other, the cool lick of rain-dampened air.

We bought coffee and almond croissants at a café and sat on the patio, watching the world flow past.

"I got you something," Evan said.

He took his hand from his pocket, something small and shiny in his fingers.

My body went into slow motion. I looked up at him slowly, breathed slowly, felt the long, slow strokes of my heart ticking like a close-up clock in a movie.

"I was going to give it to you yesterday, but the timing wasn't right." He turned the ring in his fingers. "I keep pretending I'm okay, looking at you in class and playing Mr. Good Teacher, when all I want to do is take you in my arms. And I want you to know that even though we have to do this, the hiding and pretending, there's not a moment that goes by when I'm not thinking of you, wishing it was different. So I thought maybe this would remind you. That this could hold you when I couldn't."

He finally raised his eyes. He looked so young right then.
"Do you know how to wear this?" he said.

I laughed, part disbelief, part giddy wonder. "I'm fucking Irish, Evan. Of course I know."

He smiled. He knew I did.

It was a silver Claddagh ring: two hands clasping a heart with a crown atop it. Every part of it was symbolic: the heart stood for love; the hands, friendship; the crown, loyalty. Depending on how you wore it, it meant different things. On your left hand, heart pointing out, it meant you were engaged; heart in, married. On your right hand, heart out meant you were looking for love; heart in, you were in love.

He held the ring out to me, and I took it, swallowing. My skin flashed hot and cold at the same time. This, I thought, is going to become a memory: the way I'm shivering but so warm inside, the way the sky is trembling above us, threatening rain, and the way your eyes are bluer than I've ever seen. I slid the ring onto my right ring finger, its heart pointing inward, toward mine.

Our gazes met across the table. There were a million things I wanted to say at the same time, so I said nothing.

Evan opened his mouth.

A huge stiletto of rain hit the table, splashing onto my half-eaten croissant.

"Oh, shit," I said.

In three seconds flat, it was pouring.

I was so surprised and happy and overwhelmed by everything, the whole weekend, the craziness of my life, the ring on my finger, that I stood up and shrieked, joyously. Evan tried to save the food, but it was destroyed in moments. We took off running down the block, him laughing and me still screaming happily, like a kid. I was drenched and blissful and ran across a street where a car sat at the red light, and I kissed my hand and slapped it on the hood. The driver gave me a funny little frown and I beamed at her. I fucking love you, lady, I thought. I love this entire world and everyone in it.

We reached the old factory building completely out of breath, our hair plastered to our skulls, clothes heavy as iron with water. Evan started to unlock the entrance and I snatched the keys away and he pushed me against the door, kissing me. A wild, rough, messy kiss that tasted like rainwater and rust. It was elemental, a force as raw as the one that tore the sky apart over us. We went in finally but stopped outside the elevator, and he lifted me under the legs and held me against the wall, kissing me viciously, his tongue thrusting hard into my mouth. Rain darkened his hair from gold to brown. I ran my hands beneath his wet shirt, his skin searing. I would have fucked him right there. I didn't care. But we got on the elevator, and it took forever to get to the loft because we stood there with the door open, kissing madly. I took his shirt off and dropped it. He took off my shorts. We left our shoes and socks strewn across the hallway. My bra at the front door. His jeans and everything else on the stairs up to the bathroom.

My skin was clammy, hair stringy, and I turned on the shower, but we didn't get that far. He lifted me onto the bathroom counter, my ass on the freezing tile, and I decided that that was far enough. That was where I wanted to be fucked. I wrapped my hand around the back of his neck, the ring cool against his burning skin. He didn't stop for a condom and when he entered me the heat was a shock. I leaned back, arching my spine. In the harsh halogen lights his body looked carved out of stone, his skin polished with rain and sweat, every muscle rigid. We'd had no sex for a week and the tension was insane. The veins in his arms stood out. My own body felt hard and brutal, my breasts bouncing every time he thrust into me, and it didn't feel so much like sex as smashing my nerves with a hammer, blunt and savage, primitive. He held my hips and fucked me roughly and fast and I felt a heavy wave of lava surging up my thighs and could not. Hold on. To myself. And I said, "Please, come. Please, please, come in me."

His hands tightened, painfully, and he pulled out and clutched my body to his, gasping.

I stared at the wall behind him, bewildered.

"Evan?" I whispered.

His body heaved against me, frantic, breathless.

I pulled back, trying to look at his face. His head was down. He wouldn't look at me. The white noise of the shower crackled between us.

"Evan," I said again, my voice sharper than I'd intended. I'd been so close to coming, and after the week of no sex, I couldn't help my frustration. "What's wrong?"

"I'm so sorry," he said.

I managed to lever him away so I could look at him. My skin was flushed, tight as a drumhead. He was still hard but his face was pained. God, what the fuck? So awkward. So fucking awkward.

"You can't keep doing this," I said. "Tell me why it freaks you out so much."

He winced at my words, turned his head away. Please, I thought. Don't be like this. Don't be another high school boy who can't handle his own feelings. You're supposed to be a grown man.

He leaned against the wall. Raked a hand through his hair, propped his forehead in his palm. We looked like two crazy people, naked and covered in rain and sweat. I slapped my hand down on the counter and the ring rapped loudly, startling us both, making us look at each other.

"Talk to me," I said, gentler now.

"I am terrified for you," he said. His voice was low and hoarse.

"Why?"

"Because I don't ever want to put your future at risk. Even in the slightest way."

I sighed, my tension uncoiling. "I won't let that happen. I'm not careless, you know that. I'm going to college, and I'm going to get a real job, and I'm not even going to think about having a family until I'm like, thirty." I looked him full in the face, willing him to understand. "I've had to take care of myself most of my life, and I won't let that go to waste by getting knocked up at eighteen. So you don't need to safeguard my future. I've got it covered."

The anxiety drained from him. He looked defeated, embarrassed. "Here I thought I was being responsible, but you're way ahead of me."

"Well, it means a lot, that you care about my future." I turned off the shower and sat on the edge of the counter, stretching out my hand. "Come over here and be awkward with me."

He did, wrapping his arms around me, sighing. He'd gone soft, and the edge of my frustration had dulled. This was just an embrace, tender, tired. I rubbed my finger over the silver band.

"You gave me a ring," I said.

"I did."

I leaned back, a small, cocky smile on my face. "Who else have you given a ring to?"

"No one."

"Not even your fiancée?"

He shook his head. "Broke up before we went ring shopping."

I stared at him, my heart beating fast. "I'm the first?"

He put his hands to either side of my face. His eyelashes were matted, sparkling with water. He looked like a little boy who'd been playing in the rain. "You're the first. You're the first of so many things."

My gaze shifted from his eyes to his mouth, his lips red and full, and I kissed him, delicately, a girl kissing a boy. It was all lightness, softness. His hands drifted airily over my back. I pressed myself against him as if I weighed nothing, as if we floated underwater. None of the savagery of earlier. But somehow that tenderness grew and he hardened against me and I took him inside without my breath or pulse changing at all, as if this was no different from that. I wrapped my legs around his waist. He kissed me as he moved inside of me, his eyes closed, his eyebrows raised in bliss. I was still a little numb but something gentle and sweet collected in my belly, a warm rain building up. Both of us got close to coming and looked at each other and didn't say anything, and when I let my eyes roll back and all my being condense to the line of pure heaven shooting up my spinal cord, he came, too, cupping my body against himself like something precious, breathing his rapture in my ear.

He held me like that for a while. Eventually I felt the counter again, the cool imprint of tile. There was a whole world full of ticking clocks and calendar days out there. I kissed Evan's shoulder, his neck, his throat flecked with fine stubble, drinking in the smell of him. He straightened and pulled out and the soft hot rush of wetness between my legs made my heart stammer. This was completely, completely real.

He stroked my jaw, giving me a sleepy smile.

Something went very tight and sharp in my chest. God, this is happening, I thought. You're taking over my heart and I can't stop it. I don't want to.

"Will you tell me why?" he said.

"Why what?"

"Why you were so insistent."

I ran my hand over the downy hair on his belly and up to the place above his heart. I listened to it beating through my skin. "Because I want all of you," I said. "Every part."

He whispered back, "It's yours."

Evan decided my film education should work backward from when I was born, going through movies decade by decade.

First up: the 1980s.

"I can't believe I was a little kid watching this shit," he said as we sat down with *The Lost Boys*. The Friend had a huge, expensive TV, and we'd made popcorn and drinks and everything. Legit date night. "This whole decade was so dark. Everything now is safe and colorful and sanitized. Everyone's scared of giving kids psychological scars."

"That's not true," I said. "I grew up with the Internet pumping filth into my brain."

He laughed. "Good point."

I saw what he meant about the darkness. Even in a campy vampire film full of mullets and feathered hair, there was an undertone of ugly, almost chthonic horror. Not the ultrareal yet somehow ultraclean gore of the *Saw* generation. This was a sleazy, leering, scummy feeling, a glimpse of a time when adults weren't so terrified of terrifying kids. There was something refreshing about it. Life without the shrink-wrap.

As I sat there with his arm around me, his easy laugh in my ear, I thought, How different are we? We came from such different times, his era murky and analog, mine bright and digital, and yet we got each other's jokes, had a similar way of looking at the absurdity of the world and laughing. How much of it was real, and how much the chemical honeymoon my brain was on?

I twisted the ring on my finger.

Next up was *The Breakfast Club*. I fell in love with it immediately. The cheesy eighties clothes, Molly Ringwald and a hot young Emilio Estevez, the razor-sharp dialogue, everything. Change the clothes and hair and add cell phones and you had any modern high school.

"Oh my god," I said when it was over. "I'm Allison."

"You're a compulsive liar?" Evan said.

"No, I'm a total weirdo. But maybe I'm lying about that."

"I had the biggest crush on Ally Sheedy."

I grinned. "Which one were you, in high school?"

"Guess."

"The bad boy."

"Nope."

"The jock?"

"Nope."

I frowned. "The nerd?"

"Is that such a shock?"

I climbed across his lap, pushing him back against the couch. Popcorn spilled out of the bowl beside us.

"No," I said, wrapping my hands in his shirt. "It's fucking hot."

He smiled that Hollywood smile and gave me a drowsy,

knowing look, all smoky desire, and I kissed him and we had sex again right there on the couch, using a condom out of consideration for The Friend, my knees sinking into the cushion, my head thrown back, and Evan gazing up at me, entranced. This is mine, I thought. This body, this act, this man, all mine. This belongs to my heart and my skin and no one can take it from me because it is etched there, indelibly. I laid my hands on his shoulders, a woman in total control. It felt—*right*. When we stood up afterward I saw the silhouette of our bodies in sweat on the espresso leather, evaporating in the chill.

I took my sweet time getting in the car. Reality intruded on my thoughts like war flashbacks, depressing images of Mom and Gary Rivero and my big fat zero bank balance.

"Why even go back?" I said. "Let's start over here."

Evan looked at me across the roof of the car in the underground garage. He almost seemed to consider it.

"Running never works," he said finally.

Tell me about it.

I flipped open the glove box to toss my sunglasses in, and a pile of papers cascaded onto my feet. Evan was backing out of the parking space and slammed on the brakes. That made the rest of the junk fall out.

"Sorry," I laughed. "I'll get it."

He helped me stuff everything back in hurriedly, but something caught my eye. The car was registered to Eric Wilke of Westchester, Illinois.

"Who's Eric?"

Evan took the paper and slipped it inside a folio. "My brother."

"You have a brother, too? Jesus." I sat back. "Evan, Eric, and Elizabeth. Am I missing anyone?"

His eyes were cloudy. He didn't look at me. God, another dead sibling? Or just another sad story he didn't want to tell?

"I'm sorry," I said, feeling like an idiot.

"Don't be. I'll tell you about him sometime."

But not tonight, apparently.

The highway at night looked like a movie flashing past us in fast forward, all the lights receding, out of reach. Autumn spread its golden disease through the woods, Midas trailing his fingers over the treetops. Dying things became extraordinarily beautiful at the very end. I pressed my hand against the window, the ring gleaming. Where was the lens between me and the world? Was it my eyes, my skin, my mind? Where did reality stop and my perception of it begin? Suddenly, horribly, I missed Wesley. I felt too embarrassed to talk to Evan about shit like this. Wesley was just a boy. I didn't care what he thought of me.

"Maise," Evan said.

I turned to him.

"If things don't work out with your mom, and you need somewhere to go, you can stay with me."

Cardiac arrest.

"You have options. Bad ones, maybe. Maybe they're kind of like the premise of an after-school special. But they're options."

I stared at him, every muscle in me slack.

"What are you thinking?" he said.

"What is an after-school special?"

He laughed. He knew I was trying to make him feel old.

"I'm also thinking the night I met you was like someone

handed me a winning lottery ticket and said, 'You can only have it if you don't tell anyone.'"

He gave me a sad smile. "I feel like that, too."

"Do you start to wonder if it's even real?"

"All the time. Like maybe I made you up on that roller coaster."

I thought of the Sylvia Plath poem from his letter, "Mad Girl's Love Song." *I shut my eyes and all the world drops dead. I think I made you up inside my head.*

"You could've imagined me with fewer problems," I said.

"You must be real, then."

I tapped my fingers on the window. "Can we stop somewhere? I need to pick up some rat poison to feed Mom."

It was actually getting close to my period, and I was out of tampons. We pulled up at a Walgreens when we got into town, parking in the far corner of the lot, just in case. Back to the espionage game. I swallowed my pride and asked to borrow money.

"Just until I get a job," I said. "I'll keep track of every cent."

"You don't have to worry about it."

"I want to worry about it. I want to be equal in this with you."

"You are."

We stared at each other in the dark car. Why did this bother me so much? Because I didn't want to give him any excuse to see me as a teenager? But I *was* a teenager. Maybe I was the first girl he'd given a ring to, but he was my first everything.

He handed me some bills.

"Besides," I said, "if you're going to insist on protection, I at least get to pick."

I jumped out before he could respond.

The store was deserted, bright lights blasting, some swoony radio singer pouring her heart out to the emptiness. No one at the register. I dawdled in the aisles, not wanting the night to end yet. It felt ridiculously erotic to browse through the condom section. A man turned into the aisle, saw me, and turned right around. I laughed. That's right, I thought. I'm a gorgeous teenage girl buying condoms for my boyfriend to fuck me with. Can you handle that? Guess not.

I dumped my stuff on the counter at the register. Still no cashier.

"Hello!" I yelled. "I would like to exchange money for goods and services."

There was someone back there after all. He'd been kneeling, shelving cigarettes. At the sound of my voice he stood up, all six foot three of him.

Wesley Brown.

Our eyes locked, wide with surprise.

"Hi," I said.

"Hey."

We stood there like morons.

"You work here," I said stupidly.

"Well done, Captain Obvious." His words were mocking, but his voice was gentle. He cleared his throat. Mine was dry and twisted.

I missed you like crazy, I wanted to say. *Why aren't we friends? This is stupid.*

Instead I just stood there.

Wesley glanced at the counter. So did I. We both looked at the box of condoms, then back at each other. This time his mouth hung open a little while my face turned traffic light red.

He scanned the box. I stared at his hands, mortified.

He said some numbers.

"What?" I shook myself. "Sorry."

Our skin brushed when I handed him a bill. My ring flashed so brightly I swear it made a little *ping* sound. Wesley stared at it, then shoved the money into the till. He laid my change on the counter.

"Wesley," I said, not knowing where to go after that.

"Have a nice night," he deadpanned.

I walked out of the store. It felt twenty degrees colder outside.

When I reached the car, I opened my door and leaned on it, not getting in.

"What's wrong?" Evan said.

I grabbed my backpack, stuffing the shopping bag inside. "Wesley works here. I'm going to wait until his shift's over and ambush him."

Evan raised his eyebrows dubiously.

"He's ambushed me enough times. Turnabout's fair play." I knelt on the seat. "I'll get a ride home, okay?"

"You sure about this?"

I kissed him. "Nope. But I have to try."

"Text me when you get home."

"I will."

We looked at each other in the weak, watery car light. This is the part in the script where three words go.

"I'll miss you," I said.

Not the right three words.

He brushed my cheek with his knuckles. "I'll see you to-morrow morning."

"I'll still miss you."

He kissed me again, pulling me farther in, and I climbed across the seat to kiss him like I had when he drove me home in the rain, urgent, desperate, losing myself in him. This will be different now, I thought. I'll see you in class and remember what you told me, how every time you look at me you imagine everything we've done and everything we're going to do. How am I supposed to get through the week? How am I supposed to sit still with this supernova inside me?

We pulled away from each other.

Say it, I thought. You have to say it first.

But he already had. It was on my finger, saying itself constantly.

Cheater.

"Good night, Mr. Wilke," I said.

I sat on a curb in a pool of whiskey-colored light, skipping gravel and shards of broken glass across the asphalt. The storm front had finally broken, tatters of cloud pulling apart like cotton candy and sprinkling the sky with the bright sugar grains of stars. It felt like one of those timeless nights, not any season or year in particular, simply a snapshot of twenty-first-century loneliness. Far away a train horn wailed, a sound out of a postapocalyptic landscape. I felt like the last person alive on Earth.

Half an hour later, Wesley exited from a side door and immediately froze. We faced each other across the lot. He started toward me, and I stood.

"What are you doing here?" he called.

"Saving our friendship."

He snorted. "There's nothing to save."

"Don't be an asshole."

He reached me and stopped, shaking his head. In the harsh orange light his features looked stark, masklike. "What do you want, Maise? You want to taunt me some more about your awesome love life?"

"I never taunted you."

"Whatever."

I took a step toward him. "Look, shit got weird. It's not the end of the world. I miss you, okay?"

"You miss having an audience."

"That's completely un—"

"You know what I realized?" He pointed a finger at me, damning. "I'm not your fanboy. I'm not some sycophant who follows you around and pets your ego when you need it. If you really want to be friends, it has to be equal."

My mouth dropped.

"Okay," I said. "You're right."

Wesley's eyes narrowed beneath his fringe of dark hair.

"I wasn't treating you like an equal. I'm a jerk. I'm sorry."

He shrugged and glanced away, uncomfortable with winning. We stood there awkwardly.

"I'm on my way home," he said.

"Is Siobhan picking you up?"

"I think I'll just walk."

Then he looked at me with a tiny glint of hopefulness in his eyes, and my heart lifted.

"I think I'll just walk, too," I said. "It's a free country."

We didn't go home but headed for the water tower. We walked on the dirt shoulders of roads, past fields shredded to flinders from the harvest, a billion matchsticks strewn across the earth. In the cold starlight they looked like scenes of massacre. I was shivering, and when I stopped to pull a sweater out of my bag, Wesley crouched beside me.

"Did he give you that ring?"

"Yes."

He flicked a pebble into the road. "Is it E?"

"Yes."

I swallowed as the silence stretched. If he'd asked me right then, *Is it Mr. Wilke?*, I would have told him the truth. But he didn't ask anything else.

"When did you get the job?" I said as we walked on.

"I started Wednesday."

"Do you like it?"

"I can feel my neurons dying. This week was boring as shit."

I laughed. "Trade you my week."

He glanced at me guardedly. "What happened?"

I told him about Mom and Mr. Rivero, and his eyes got progressively bigger until he looked like an anime character. When I got to the part about St. Louis, I told him that, too. Not the details, but the gist. I'm seeing an older man. I'm ecstatic and terrified at the same time. I'm sorry I didn't tell you, because the truth is, I wasn't ready to accept it myself. It's only now starting to feel real.

We reached the reservoir then, which gave us an excuse to let the conversation die. I dropped my bag and followed Wesley up the ladder. Our legs dangled off the platform, and when he lit up the familiar smell of sulfur and cloves made my throat sting.

"Fair's closing soon," he said.

"Maybe I have time to die on a roller coaster before I get shot." I paused. "Maybe they'll shoot me *on* a roller coaster."

"That would actually be kind of awesome."

"The end of my life would be 'kind of awesome'?"

Wesley ashed an arc of sparks into the night. "You really think they're coming for you?"

"I don't know. Sometimes I overdramatize."

"You? No."

I stabbed a finger into his ribs. "Seriously, though. I think Gary's going to ask me to do something I don't want to do."

"What if he does?"

"I don't know. Maybe there's an after-school special that says what to do when a drug lord propositions you."

Wesley frowned. "What's an after-school special?"

I started laughing, and it caught like wildfire, sweeping through me. God, what a ridiculous world. I lay back, giddy, laughing at the sky. Wesley raised his eyebrows, but a grin crept over his mouth.

"Are you in love with me?" I said impulsively.

The grin fell. He managed to maintain eye contact, but he looked like he was staring at a wild dog, hoping it wouldn't bite. "I don't know. I just like you."

"Still?"

"I dunno. Yeah."

I sat up. "I can deal with that, if you can. And if you can respect me being in a relationship."

He averted his face.

I touched his hand, carefully. Not too intimate, but not some half-assed there-there pat, either. Would he understand? Usually the thought process of a seventeen-year-old boy went *girl touching me → omg → boner*. But if he wanted me to treat him as an equal, he'd need to deal with complicated, uncomfortable adult feelings, too.

"I like you," I said, "as a friend. And I kind of like flirting with you, too, but I like flirting with everyone. That's who I am. You get it, right? Because that stuff about filming me—it weirds me out. I can't be your manic pixie dream girl. I can't be the girl who teaches you how to open your heart and embrace life and all that bullshit, because I'm trying to figure out how to do that myself. I need a manic pixie dream boy of my own."

I let go of his hand and he stared at me, and I worried

that this was pointless, that I was trying to explain quantum mechanics to someone who thought gravity was just apples falling. But then he nodded, slowly.

"That actually makes a lot of sense," he said. "I never thought about it like that."

"That girls are human, too?"

"That you're human."

I flicked his ear. He chuckled. And just like that, we were friends again.

We stayed up in the crow's nest for a while, shooting the shit. I texted Evan so he wouldn't think I'd run into an ax murderer, and Wesley watched. Not my phone, but my face, my body language.

"What's it like with him?" he said quietly.

I lay back on the planks, bouncing my heels on the edge. "Intense," I finally said.

"Good or bad?"

"Good. Amazingly good. And also weird, and scary, and beautiful. All at the same time, in equal measure."

"Are you in love with him?"

I rolled my head on the plank to look at Wesley. "I don't think I know what being in love is yet. But this is different than anything I've ever felt."

"What's it feel like?"

"Remember when you thought I was jumping off to kill myself?"

He winced.

"It's like that," I said. "But no one catches you. You're just hanging over infinity."

7

OCTOBER was the longest month. Not in days, but in the way the hours dragged as we tilted farther away from the sun, the shadows stretching longer and longer, curving thin blue fingers over the Earth. There was an Indian summer, a blush of heat and warm wind stirring the gold-foil leaves. One hot afternoon I jumped into Wesley's pool with all my clothes on, the water deliciously cool beneath the skin of sunlight on the surface. He took his shirt off and jumped in after me, particolored leaves swirling around us like kaleidoscope pieces. Siobhan stopped by to laugh and offer towels. Wesley tried to pull her in, and she casually threatened to remove him from her will. When we climbed out there was the obligatory pause when we saw each other soaking wet, his long hairless torso glazed with water, my shirt molded to my boobs. I smiled; he didn't. Siobhan helped dry my hair and caught my hand, raising the ring to the falling sun. I couldn't read the look she gave me. It seemed deeply knowing.

At first Evan and I were careful, saving everything for the weekends. No making out between classes. No trysts in motels. He called every night, and when I wasn't talking to him I sent him the absolute filthiest texts I'd ever sent in my life. That second weekend at the loft, we only ventured outdoors once. We spent two days straight having sex and watching movies and talking and laughing and kissing in a hazy, dreamy montage, until finally we stumbled out into the indigo twilight, delirious and exhausted, blinking at the lights and cars and the speed of life as if we'd just come out of a hundred-year sleep. We bought Italian ice and walked along the riverfront, watching the boat lights drift like floating candles, marveling at the bridges stretching across that thick, strong vein of water. The Mississippi was calm but the calm was snakelike, a vast power momentarily relaxed.

October nineteenth was Evan's birthday. The night he turned thirty-three, we ate sushi at a place near the Cathedral Basilica. The cathedral looked like an illustration from a storybook, almost every inch of it lined with mosaic tiles scintillating in the candlelight. I wore the sundress he'd seen in that shop window, and eye shadow, and flat little-girl shoes, refusing to be pigeonholed into an age group. He wore his pinstriped shirt and tie, looking more like Mr. Wilke than Evan. It was the first time I'd had sushi, and the only real conclusion I drew was that it was very sensual. Like eating something still alive. When we staggered into the haunted elevator later, tipsy on sake, I did something else for the first time: I gave him a blowjob. His body melted in my hands, his fingers running through my hair softly, so softly, every part of him boyish and submissive except for the hard dick in my mouth. Another experience that was purely sensual. I swallowed when he came, warm saltiness in the back of my throat, the faint taste of the sea. He pulled me up and kissed me, and I said, "Happy birthday, Mr. Wilke."

I told Wesley I wanted to work on my own project for Film Studies, and he agreed. But we shot videos together, too, just for the fuck of it: Hiyam holding court with the Mean Girls, causing one of them to run off in tears. Two boys, both in varsity football, kissing under the bleachers, muscular silhouettes merging against the deep purple sky. I wasn't the only one with a secret. In the grand scheme of things, my secret wasn't even as dangerous as some of theirs. One day at lunch, half the cafeteria ran out into the hall, and we caught the tail end of a fight in front of a locker where someone had scrawled COCK SUCKING FAG in Sharpie.

Some days I lied to Wesley and skipped lunch. I locked Evan's classroom door so I could touch him. Only touch. We never had sex in school—that would be too insane, obviously. I had standards for my insanity. But I kissed him and ran my hands over his body, the hardness against his leg, until he said, "Don't make me do this." "Do what?" I said, and he answered, "Something I'll regret." So I started over, touching his face, his lips, kissing him, and we tormented each other until the bell rang.

Some nights he called me and I biked to his apartment, let myself in with the key he gave me, darting quick glances over my shoulder, and met him in his dark bedroom where we took our clothes off without speaking and fucked like it was the last time, quiet and desperate, breathing in each other's ears as we exorcised the demons inside us. When it was done I would kiss him and leave without a word, looking over my shoulder again as I biked home, my brain on high alert but my heart calm. In my own bed I lay staring at the monster shadows on the ceiling, clawing, seething.

Sometimes I saw watchers in them. Sometimes I saw myself.

"Do you still have a crush on Mr. Wilke?" Wesley asked, and I just looked at him, expressionless.

In mirrors, I saw someone new. A feral girl with electric eyes. She was beautiful, her mouth lush and maroon, her skin glowing like moonlit alabaster, but there was something a little off about her. At certain angles, her bones showed through the skin. Shadows made hollows in her ribs and cheeks. She was starving for something, and the more she ate of it, the thinner she became.

"What if you're wrong?" I asked Wesley. "What if the dopamine rush doesn't end? What if it keeps coming and coming until—"

What? What came next? I thought of Mom lying on the living room floor.

The more you took, the more you needed. And you'd keep taking more and more and more until you overdosed.

I'd failed my promise to confront a fear during September, unless starting a relationship with someone I actually cared about counted. If not, October was going to count double.

So I sat at the kitchen table, waiting for Mom.

I'd come prepared: bank statement, printout of the trust paperwork, and my house keys, all neatly arranged before me. Upstairs, my bags were packed. I'd left the new clothes in the closet.

Turned out I needn't have bothered. As soon as she walked in on me wearing my Very Special Episode face, she dropped her purse on the floor, sank into a chair, and started bawling.

For god's sake, I thought.

I stared at the laminate tabletop, counting the cigarette

burns. Something slithery twisted in my chest. Look at the cabinet doors. Picture what's behind them: stale soda crackers, peanut butter, marijuana. I was probably the only kid at school completely uninterested in drugs. Jesus, her face looked like a wax dummy melting. Don't give in. Don't give in.

I gritted my teeth, scooted my chair back, and fetched the paper towels.

"I'm so sorry, babe," she blubbered. The paper towel took half her face with it: magenta clown mouth, centipede eyelashes. "I fucked up. I really did."

Be hard and cold as steel, I told myself. "You knew why Mr. Rivero wanted to see me."

She mewled some kind of denial.

"You were trying to pimp me out to him," I said. Flinty, brittle steel. "Do you have any idea how disgusting you are?"

She had the nerve to raise her face with indignation. "Gary has money. Lots of money. He could take care of us. Of you."

"I don't need taking care of."

"That why you're running around with older men?"

"Don't even," I said. I couldn't finish the sentence.

"I seen that man you're with. Drives an old beater. You can do better."

"Oh my god," I said. "I cannot believe how fucking clueless you are."

"You ain't so smart yourself, babe. You're giving it away for free like a stupid milk cow."

I slammed my hand on the table, the ring pinging like crystal. Ashes puffed out of the terra-cotta pot.

"Shut your mouth," I said.

She stood, making me back up. "Or what? What you gonna do?"

There was fire in me, and for the moment, that fire was stronger than the fear.

"I'll walk out that door and you'll never see me again. I'm eighteen. I don't have to put up with your shit."

Mom laughed, a throaty, ugly sound. "Yeah, you're eighteen. That means I don't got to put up with your shit, either."

"So don't," I yelled. My hands were tingling. My accent slipped out, and I didn't care. "Throw me on the street. Then you can finally have your empty house, and your gross men, and your fucking drugs. And when the police come, no one's gonna bail you out. No one's gonna sit at home waiting for you, because no one else cares about you, you stupid bitch."

The windows seemed to rattle from my voice. The kitchen light dimmed, a flux in the current, but it felt like it was in response to me. I'd never stood up to her like this.

"You know the worst thing?" I said, stepping closer. "It's not that you put my life in danger. You did that the day I was born. No, the worst thing was stealing my money. The money Nan gave me for college, so I could make a future for myself instead of turning out like you."

I saw the precise moment her pride cracked. The moment she stopped being my forty-year-old mother and became a teenage girl, screaming *I don't want to turn out like you* at her own mother. Her bloodshot eyes widened, lucid green finally showing. The leathery folds of her face smoothed out with shock. For a moment we probably looked more like each other than we had in years.

My body trembled. I scrubbed a hand across my eyes, smearing hot tears. So much for cold steel.

"Oh, babe," she said. Her head was nodding slightly, repeatedly, the way you'd rock yourself for comfort. "It's been real hard for me, too."

"I don't care," I said, crying. "You were supposed to take care of me. Be the adult. For once, be the fucking adult, Mom."

"You don't know what it was like." Her breath stuttered. Jesus, I thought. If we both start crying, I am really going to lose it. "I put myself through shit I never want to think about again, all to make sure you had food to eat and a place to sleep and clothes to wear."

"It wasn't all for me. Half your money goes to buy the drugs you're supposed to be selling."

"You think it's easy, living like this? You think I want to live this kind of life sober?"

I thought of the men she'd installed on our living room couch. The kind of men who'd touch a twelve-year-old. If they were that brazen with me, what kind of shit had they done to her? I'd seen some of her scars. There was a long sharktooth ripple just below her collarbone. *Car door caught me,* she'd said. And a puckered dimple on one thigh. *Dropped a cigarette lighter.* Sometimes she came home with shiners. *Got mixed up in a bar brawl.*

Key to making your mother the villain: believing the lies she told to spare you.

"You could've been normal," I said. "Plenty of single moms work at McDonald's and don't smoke crystal."

"It ain't that simple. You don't know what being addicted is like."

Instinctively, unthinkingly, I said, "Yes, I do."

And I stared at her, my mouth hanging open, thinking, Yes, I do.

"Well, then, I pray you don't turn out like me," she said, sniffling. "I pray you get away from here and start a new life and do something good."

My tears had stopped, but my face was still wet. "You can't get the money you owe, can you?"

"I'm trying, babe. But it don't look good."

"So it's up to me to bail us both out. Again."

We stared at each other in our dismal little kitchen where no one cooked and no friends came to visit and meth was cut on the table late at night.

"You must really hate me, huh?" she said.

"No." I took a deep breath, wiped my face with my hand. "If I thought you could change, I'd hate you for not trying." I looked her dead in the eye. "But this is who you are. You're a liar, and a thief, and a junkie. I don't hate you, Mom. I'm disappointed in you."

I unpacked my bags and stayed up until two a.m. responding to job ads on Craigslist. In the back of my mind, I knew I could stay with Evan, or maybe Wesley and Siobhan. But Mom's shamelessness and weakness of will had led me to become the opposite: stubborn and proud. Too proud to ask for help, even when I needed it most. Especially when I needed it most.

I'll do this on my own, I told myself. I'll stay here till she throws me out and make back every penny she stole and work something out with Mr. Rivero. I'm smart, I'm resilient—I had to be, to raise myself without functional parents. I'll figure it out.

And when I do, I'll leave and never look back.

Of course, in my eighteen-year-old brain, leaving implicitly entailed bringing Evan and Wesley and even Siobhan, as if I could transplant everything I still loved about this place to a new one, where only the bad things would be erased. I didn't think, How will I hold on to them? I only thought, I have to get away from her.

A few days before Halloween, I skipped lunch with Wesley to see Evan. The minute I locked his door, he pushed me against the wall and put his mouth to my neck. It wasn't so much a kiss as a display of hunger, his stubble scraping my skin, his teeth nipping, not gently. I leaned my head back and looked out the windows at the world deconstructing, leaves coming off the trees in flurries, everything baring itself to be ravished by winter.

Hello, visual metaphor.

Later, I would understand what drove us to screw up that day. That the more complicated and fucked-up my life became, the more I wanted to push away reality and lose myself in him. *I shut my eyes and all the world drops dead.* He was doing the same with me, for reasons I didn't yet know.

But in that moment, I just wanted to be ravished.

Evan took my jaw in one hand and made me look at him. His body was close, the scent of suede and faint smoke, like a snuffed candlewick, flooding over me. The mere smell of him made something in me unlace, opening itself.

"Come over tonight," he said.

I laid my palm on his chest as if to push him away but let it slide down instead, over his tensed abdomen, to his fly.

"That's so far away," I said languorously, drawing the words out.

His eyes focused on my mouth.

I unbuttoned his jeans. We were both breathing fast. We'd never done anything more than make out in school. Being discovered here was death.

But there he stood, rock-hard, not stopping me.

"Shouldn't you tell me this is a bad idea?" I whispered, cupping my hand over his erection. "I thought you were a responsible adult."

"I thought you were."

I felt a little out-of-body right then. Like things weren't entirely in my control, including my own skin. When I smiled, it felt like someone else smiling with my face. My voice seemed to come from somewhere outside of me, like ventriloquism.

I brushed my lips ever so lightly over his ear and said, "I'm a girl who wants to be fucked by her teacher."

His dick strained against his fly.

"Is the door locked?" he said.

"Yes."

He slipped his hand between my legs. I wore jeans, too, and his heat radiated through the tight denim and seeped into my blood. We'd done this so many times now it shouldn't have felt so new. It shouldn't have made my heart go haywire, fluttering wildly, erratically, as if he'd never touched me before. But he hadn't. Not as Mr. Wilke, not here. This was the inescapable truth. No matter who we were outside, in here we were teacher and student.

His other hand slid inside the waist of my jeans. Where our skin met felt like nerves short-circuiting, fuses popping. It filled my belly with static and made me lift up onto my toes, my back arching against the whiteboard. The class was dark, but all someone had to do was peer through the pane in the door and see Mr. Wilke pressing a student to the board. He unbuttoned my fly and his thumb rubbed firmly against the crotch of my jeans and I clutched his collar, gasping. No wrapping myself around him. Avoid anything identifiable from this angle. He pulled my zipper down slowly and it felt like he was opening my skin.

Then he stopped. His palm rested atop my belly.

"We do this every day and no one notices," I said. "No one will notice if we go a little further."

I started to unzip him and he grabbed my hand. Moved it to my side, held it there, and put his other hand inside my underwear. My pulse trilled. I looked up at him and his face was blurry with shadow.

"Let me touch you," I said.

"Shut your mouth."

My eyes widened. My breath was coming so, so fast. Hot fingers glided over the smooth coolness of my skin, slipping lower until they reached the part of me that burned, too. He put his mouth near my ear.

"Spread your legs."

I did, my heart wild. He was telling me what to do, like a teacher. My teacher.

He traced me, light and soft, sending ribbons of electricity up into my belly. My jeans were so tight that his palm rubbed against my clit every time he moved. God, fucking sweet agony. When his finger finally parted my lips I was so wet it slid along the inner edge effortlessly, and I sighed, half miserable, half blissful. Adrenaline sizzled in my veins. I was waiting for footsteps in the hall, a knock at the door, a gasping face. It felt so fucking wrong to be doing this, so gloriously fucking wrong. I tried to move my arm and his grip tightened, pinning me to the board. He was so slow, so meticulous it drove me crazy, tracing, teasing, until I realized I'd bared my teeth and was grimacing at him, and when he slid his finger inside of me it felt like a pain being soothed, a raw place being pressed closed. I almost told him to stop.

Anxiety and tension and want were mixing in an unpleasant way. But as his finger fucked me the anxiety sweetened, and I wrapped a fist in his shirt and raised my hips toward his hand, and he lowered his face and said, "You feel so fucking good," but didn't kiss me, just shared my breath. He went in to the knuckle, and then he slid another finger inside, and I put my palms against the whiteboard and tried not to cry out. I thought of the class that had been here fifteen minutes ago, Wesley and Hiyam and the rest of them sitting ten feet from where we stood now, not knowing Mr. Wilke and I fucked the shit out of each other almost every day, not knowing he was going to fuck me right here while their chairs were still warm, that I was going to come in the same place he'd stood and lectured, that I was going to come all over that big, gentle hand inside of me.

And then it happened.

The knock.

We both froze. I was so close to coming I didn't care, I just wanted to finish, but he pulled out and for a moment I was fully capable of murdering the person at the door. We didn't move, our breath grotesquely loud in the silence. God, had I been making noise? I wasn't even sure.

"Maybe they'll go," I whispered.

The knock came again, slower. Almost mocking.

I shivered.

Evan buttoned up, wiped his hand on his jeans, and I did the same. I smoothed his shirt and he straightened my hair.

"Don't be afraid," he said.

The knock again.

He turned and walked to the door. There was nowhere I could hide—everything was open, revealed. I stood beside his desk, my chin up. I felt the radiant flush emanating from my skin and knew there was no masking it. Own it, I told myself. They're less likely to suspect if you act like you've done nothing wrong.

The door opened, and even in the dimness I could make her out.

"Hiyam," Evan said clearly, for my benefit. "What do you need?"

Her eyes darted past him straight to me. Not a flicker of surprise.

"I didn't know you were in here," she said.

"I'm with another student."

It shouldn't have stung, but I was still jacked and frazzled and suddenly I hated those words. I was not just *another student*.

"With the lights out," Hiyam. "And the door locked."

Not questions.

"We were just on our way out," Evan said calmly.

Hiyam stepped into the room. "Good thing I caught you, then." Neither of us missed the double entendre. "I need to talk to you, Mr. Wilke."

"It's not really a great time. How about—"

"Oh," she said with faux coyness, "am I interrupting something?"

My jaw hardened. This bitch. She fucking knew, though she probably couldn't guess how far it had gone. Probably thought she'd interrupted a chaste little kiss. Whispered words of self-denial. Smell his hand, I wanted to tell her.

"We were discussing the semester project. Maise had some questions."

Hiyam strolled up a row of desks toward me, trailing her hand over them. "I thought we weren't allowed to ask you any questions about it."

Evan caught my eye from across the room. He finally looked alarmed. I understood. Leave. Give her less ammunition.

"I'll be going," I said flatly. "Thanks for the help, Mr. Wilke."

Hiyam paused, watching us with cool amusement.

"Anytime," he said. His voice and face were vacant.

I walked past him and out of the room, wishing I could scream.

———

"Tell me again who knows," he said.

He stood at his bedroom window, blinds shut. He looked like Harrison Ford in *The Fugitive*. Just add prison jumpsuit and oncoming train. A lamp cast a brooding glow over us, flickering fretfully. I'd had to argue for five minutes before he let me turn it on. I leaned my palms on the bed, sighing. We'd been over this a hundred times.

"No one," I said.

"Britt saw us at the party."

"She saw you taking a drunk student home."

"Wesley knows about 'E.'"

"Wesley can barely focus on anything but my tits. And he's my friend. He won't say anything."

Evan rocked on his toes, not looking at me. "Hiyam saw. She was taunting us."

I stood and moved toward him. "Hiyam's had a crush on you since the first day of school. She told me at homecoming. Besides, she has a filthy mind." I touched his forearm, ran my fingers over the soft gold hair. "Even if we weren't sleeping together, she'd think we were."

It was terrible, but now that the immediate danger had

passed, the idea of people knowing excited me. Without proof, they couldn't do shit. It was right there under their noses and they couldn't pin anything on us.

He never touched me, Principal Boyle. That's a filthy lie.

No, Principal Boyle, I never had sex in school with a teacher.

Mr. Wilke is a great teacher, Principal Boyle. He's taught me so much about cinema, and life, and myself. About my body. About how amazing he can make it feel.

Of course, if I seriously thought we might be exposed, I'd have cooled everything off. I never wanted Evan to lose his job and get branded with the student-seducer stigma. But Hiyam was all talk. She still thought she could use me for a drug connection. She wouldn't out us.

Evan wasn't convinced.

"What are we doing?" he whispered, looking at me with a worryingly tragic face.

"No one's going to say anything. We just have to be a little more careful."

"Maybe we should wait, Maise. Until you're out of school."

He had never, ever said this before. The idea cut through me like a guillotine blade, splitting everything into cold halves.

"You cannot be serious," I said.

That pained look deepened.

I stepped closer, my body hovering against his, not quite making contact. "If you think you can stand looking and not touching for eight more months, you're welcome to try."

"*Try* being the operative word," he said, sighing. "No, I can't. And I don't want to try."

"But you've thought of stopping this? Of waiting?"

He sat in a chair near the lamp, his shoulders bowed. "What if I lost my job? What kind of life could I offer you?"

"Your part-time job teaching an art class? You didn't even want it. You can do better, Evan. You could be an actor."

"That's a pipe dream."

"Every dream is a pipe dream before someone achieves it." I leaned beside the blinds, looking up at the ceiling. "What if we went to LA?" I glanced at him without turning my head. "Together?"

He didn't answer, but his posture became alert, attentive.

"I know it's expensive as hell. But Wesley's sister lives out there, and he wants to go, too, after graduation." I bit my lip. "We could all rent a house together. Me and Wesley will get jobs and go to college. You could teach. Or you could audition for roles. Or—god, you're fucking gorgeous, maybe you could model. I'm sure some catalog needs hot guys to stand around in V-necks."

He laughed, softly.

"And if it doesn't work, if we run out of money and suck at everything, then we can always come back. Or go somewhere else. Or never see each other again."

"Come here," he said.

I went to him. I sat in his lap, straddling his legs, his arms around my waist. His hair had a reddish-bronze gleam in the lamplight. Those boyish features looked delicate sitting inside the hard, square lines of his jaw.

"How long have we known each other?" he said.

"A little over two months."

Sixty-eight days. Sixteen-hundred-odd hours. My entire life.

"It feels like a lot longer," he said.

"We did more with our time than most people do."

That Polaroid smile. "I'm crazy about you, Maise O'Malley."

Another rift of light chiseled into the blood-red gem in my chest.

"Why do I think you're about to say something I won't like?" I said.

His smile turned tender, suspiciously regretful. "I want this to work. But we can't do it like this."

"What?"

"We have to stop seeing each other in school."

My throat tightened. "I can't. I have a class with you."

"That can change."

Was it just me, or did time stop for everybody?

"You want me to drop your class?" I said in a small voice.

"You can switch to another elective—"

"I can't, Evan. I need that class on my transcript."

"You don't need it. You can get in without it."

"To a state school, maybe," I muttered. Something sharp and thin curled in my chest, like peeled metal. It felt horrible. I could not believe he was saying this.

"I can write you a letter of recommendation," he said. "I *am* your teacher."

Uncomfortable pause. It had never felt so awkward before.

I twisted away, swallowing the prickly burr in my throat. "I feel like you're punishing me for something we both did."

"It's not punishment. If I had my way, I'd lock us in that classroom and throw away the key. You're right, Maise. I can't look without touching." He stroked my face. "If they found out they'd call you a victim and they'd call me a predator, and those labels would stick. And I hate the thought of people pitying you and telling you how to feel. They don't know you like I do. They don't know what you've been through, how strong you are. I won't let them reduce all of that to some checkbox on a police report." He breathed in, held it, breathed out slowly. "If it makes it easier, I'll resign. You have to be in that school. I don't."

My eyes were full of water. It took superhuman willpower to keep from letting it go. "How would that make it easier? I'd just miss you and feel like shit all the time. And it's not even about the credit, Evan. I like your class. I'm actually fucking learning."

We stared at each other for a moment, wearing our absurdly pained tragedy masks. Then I started to laugh and cry at the same goddamn time.

Evan touched my face again, kissing away my tears, laughing in a gentle, commiserating way. And once he started kissing me he couldn't stop. He kissed my cheeks, my mouth, tilting my head, opening my jaw with his hand. I tasted hot saline, the salt of my own tears. All of my tension unraveled into beautiful chaos, a mess of sorrow and hurt and desire and tenderness, completely mixed up and completely mixing me up. His tongue curled around mine and he kissed me like he wanted to draw out something deep, the breath from the bottom of my lungs, the blood from the innermost crypts of my heart, the essence of me. When I pulled away, his arms tightened relentlessly around my back.

"Why do I need you like this?" he said, his voice rasping.

I looked at his glassy, mercurial eyes, the haggard lines of want etched into his face, and said, "Because you're addicted."

———

In the tranquil moments after sex, I hatched my plan.

"Let me finish the semester with you," I said.

I was sitting on the edge of the bed, naked, while Evan lay tangled in the sheets.

"I don't know."

"It's only fair. I need to finish my film for college apps. You would never jeopardize my future."

His eyes narrowed. "You're trying to manipulate me."

"*Try* being the operative word," I said, and he grabbed me around the waist and pulled me down while I squawked, indignant. I failed to free myself and gave in, letting him pin my arms to the bed, and then his humor faded. His expression became pensive.

"Maise," he said. "I'm worried about the kind of relationship we're developing."

"What do you mean?"

"I don't want to be your teacher if it's all that's driving this."

"It's not," I said immediately, but his hands tightened on my wrists.

"It is, to some degree. Be honest."

"Don't act like it's all me. You liked telling me what to do when you were fucking me in class."

He breathed deeply. Lamplight ran up one side of his body, gilding the rungs of muscle over his ribs, his roped arms. "I did. And that scares me a little. We had something real before we became teacher and student."

"This isn't real?" I said.

"It is. Of course it is." He squeezed my hand, pressing the ring. "But even if everything goes perfectly, it won't last forever. It's over in June, one way or another. And I don't want it to end. I want to keep you. I want to hold on and never let you go."

No one in my life had ever said anything like this to me. I felt disembodied again, but this time because my body was too full to contain me, too crowded with light and stars and shimmering galaxies like pinwheels studded with diamonds, spinning their brilliance into the void without caring whether it would ever be seen, just needing to shine. The bed beneath me was cloud, my skin a sheet of moonlight lying atop it. And this man, this amazing, impossible man, was the sun.

"You can't, though," I said, trying to defuse the intensity. "Remember? You can't hold on to a shooting star."

He smiled, looked away. Released me.

"Besides," I said in as light a voice as I could manage, "you can't dump me as your student yet. You still haven't shown me *Casablanca*."

"Promise not to mock me if I cry?"

"Nope."

"Heartless."

I blew on my nails and rubbed them on the sheet.

Evan laughed, and tackled me, and wrestled me still and kissed me and started the entire cycle all over again, my numb and tired body somehow rekindling, quickening, giving itself up to him.

And the whole time I wondered, If you weren't my teacher, who would you be?

In his class on Halloween that Thursday, I felt hot, feverish. Not in a good way, but with a curl of nausea in my stomach, a feeling like my body was moving too fast, about to slam into something. I couldn't look at him. I couldn't look at the whiteboard where he'd held me and put his fingers inside of me. I couldn't look at Hiyam, her smug eyes glazed with knowing. So I spent the period staring out the windows. Everything was flame shades of tangerine and pomegranate, ripeness on the brink of decay, and when the wind rippled the leaves they looked like a mosaic of fire, like the walls of the Cathedral Basilica. The bell rang and I sighed in relief, following Wesley out.

"You're actually coming to lunch?" he said.

Cortana and Master Chief walked past, stopping for a group pic with Spock and Kirk. We were allowed to wear costumes as long as they weren't "disruptive."

I held Wesley's gaze. For a moment I could imagine not being in Evan's class anymore as a good thing. As freedom. "What are you doing tonight?" I said.

He shrugged. "There's a party I'm thinking of hitting up."

"Where?"

He glanced at me briefly, then away.

"Hiyam's?" I said, my voice rising.

"So?" He looked so ridiculous when he was embarrassed. Too much landmass to be self-effacing. "She invited me."

"She invited you," I repeated. "She didn't invite me."

"I guess you pissed her off."

"Well, have fun," I said, turning away.

He followed me down the hall. "Maise, come on. I just thought, since you're always busy at night . . ."

He trailed off. Neither of us looked at each other.

"What are you doing tonight?" he said.

"I don't know."

"This is the last night of the fair. Want to go?"

My turn to shrug.

"You should," he said. "And I'll show up and accidentally run into you. We can do a meet-cute."

I glanced at him, amused, and also feeling a cold frisson of unease. Paranoia. Secrecy. It was bleeding into every part of my life, staining everything.

"You'd ditch the Princess of Persia for me?" I said.

He grinned his friendly wolf grin, and I thought, You are a better friend than I am.

It was cold that night, the sky layered with clouds, sheets of cirrus shifting and moving in parallax and occasionally opening like a lens to expose the stars. Siobhan drove us and I insisted she come with, which almost killed Wesley. The truth was that seeing the carnival up close again set off demolition charges in my chest, and I needed all the distraction I could get from the crumbling, collapsing feeling inside me.

It should have been us coming back here. Me and Evan.

In the autumn chill, there was less drunken glee. The laughter that rang around us was crisp and dry. I wore skinny jeans and a hoodie, and whether I was too covered up or because they thought Siobhan was my mom, no man tried to eye-fuck me. I felt very young. We rode the merry-go-round together, and I halfheartedly played tag with Wesley while Siobhan sat on a white tiger, laughing her chiming, melodious laugh. I could see a glimpse of the girl she'd been, savvy and self-possessed, full of mysterious humor. She caught me staring at her and smiled.

"Let's ride the roller coaster," Wesley said as he leapt off the platform.

I froze in my tracks. "No way."

"Why not?" Then he saw my face. "Is the fearless Maise O'Malley actually scared?"

I'm not scared, I thought. It's sacred.

"Bullying is grounds for disinheritance," Siobhan said.

"Mom, this is not bullying. It's friendly concern."

"I'm afraid of heights," I lied. It was the easiest way to shut him up.

But he gave me a funny look, and I thought of swinging out from the crow's nest. Shit.

Siobhan came to my rescue. "I feel a strong desire to be used as a human canvas. You're welcome to join me."

We all sat down, mercifully spared from talking as the face painters worked on us. Wesley got snake fangs at the corners of his mouth, and a freckling of scales. I got a feline rim of kohl around my eyes and abstract whiskery scrolls on my cheeks. But Siobhan went full out: a feathered mask across the bridge of her nose, complete with stick-on rhinestones and black lipstick. Wesley shook his head, embarrassed, but I beamed at her.

"You're beautiful," I said sincerely.

Her fingers grazed my ear. "Sweet child."

As we walked through the game stalls, Wesley leaned close and whispered, "Do you have a crush on my mom?"

I elbowed him in the ribs, hard. But after a moment I whispered back, "Platonically. You're so lucky, and you don't even appreciate it."

He scowled and walked ahead. But he knew I was right.

The distraction didn't work as well as I'd hoped. In the funhouse, my reflection stretched out like taffy, a pale girl with haunted black-rimmed eyes and long empty hands. I thought about how I was pulled between two selves: the normal one who went to school and hung out with her friend and his mom, and the secret one who conspired with drug dealers and slept with her teacher. I found a broken mirror that split my face into Picasso shards and lingered there, unable to look away. He'd warned me. He'd said it would be hard to deal with the secrecy. And it wasn't the secrecy itself that was difficult—it was that not talking about it made me question whether it was even real. I was still a teenager, and part of being a teenager was constantly checking your answers against everyone else's. What did you get for number four? Is falling in love with someone twice your age gross, weird, amazing, or all of the above? The secrecy insulated me in a vacuum-sealed bubble. I could only ask myself, How does this feel? Is this good? Is this right? And the only answer I ever got was my own echo.

Sometimes when I couldn't sleep, I'd google things. *Is it wrong to have sex with your teacher?* The answers were useless to me. I wasn't a minor. I wasn't being abused. It had started before we ever set foot in school together, and it was technically legal. What I really wanted was to read other people's stories. Other girls and boys who'd fallen for a teacher, and how it ended. Depressingly common tropes: power imbalance, surrogate parent figure, midlife crisis. Worse were the ones that ended when the parties realized taboo was all that held them together. That was what we'd finally been forced to confront: if our relationship was based on forbiddenness, what would happen when it was no longer forbidden?

Wesley and Siobhan bought hot dogs loaded with onions and relish, and I told them I had to hit the restroom. Really what I needed was a moment alone. I wandered toward Deathsnake, leaning on the railing and watching the cars click-clack up the track, hair whipping off the sides, voices carrying on the wind. I hadn't felt this lonely since the night I first met him.

"Maise," a warm voice said.

At first I thought I was hallucinating. How the hell could he be here? But he walked up to me, squinting, smiling in surprise, a beautiful thing emerging from the blur of neon and smoke. He wore a sweater with the sleeves rolled up, his hair raking messily above his forehead.

"What are you doing here?" Evan said.

"What are *you* doing here?"

We stared at each other. His surprise was brightening into happiness.

"It's the last night," he said. "I had to come."

"Me too."

We couldn't have shown up together, but here we were anyway. It was in the script.

Evan peered at me strangely. "What is on your face? Are those whiskers?"

"I'm a lion."

He laughed. "You are, aren't you? My little lioness."

All the loneliness and confusion I'd felt minutes ago evaporated. "Well, I *am* a Leo."

"You're adorable." He put a hand against my neck, slid it through my hair. His voice dropped. "I missed you so much today."

Too late, I said, "Evan, Wesley's here."

Siobhan stepped up to the railing a few feet down from us, gorgeous and enigmatic in her painted mask, her dark crepe dress flowing around her like an extension of the night. What was that expression? Surprise? Intrigue? "Hello," she said pleasantly. "Maise, who's your friend?"

Evan turned, not knowing who she was, not getting enough distance from me. And Wesley appeared right on cue, gnawing on a giant pretzel and raising his eyebrows.

"Mr. Wilke. What are you doing here?"

I took a step away from him and knelt smoothly to tie a shoe that didn't need tying.

Siobhan glided forward, smiling. "So this is the famous Mr. Wilke."

"Famous?" Evan said.

Wesley groaned. "Mom."

I stood up and her eyes swiveled from Evan to me. They paused on me a moment. I wasn't imagining it. Fuck.

"I'm Siobhan Brown," she said, lifting her hand. "Wesley's mother, much to his dismay."

Evan laughed graciously and took her hand. "Evan Wilke. Wesley's teacher."

"Maise's teacher, too," Wesley said.

Evan glanced at me and said, "Right."

Oh my god. I should just make a run for it.

"It's so weird seeing you here," Wesley said.

I felt I needed to say something, or my silence would become noticeable. "What, teachers can't have real lives?"

They all looked at me, and suddenly I wondered whether I'd just blurted out the whole sordid confession. *We're sleeping together. He's E. Stop fucking staring.*

"It's not much of one," Evan said, and smiled. The incredible thing was that he could smile like I was just some student, some girl, and yet I saw the brief flare of warmth in his eyes, a secret message just for me.

You really are an actor, I thought.

"Good to see you guys," he said. "And so nice to meet you, Ms. Brown."

"Wait," Wesley said, brandishing the stub of his pretzel, "you're leaving already?"

I could have decked him.

Siobhan wore an appraising half smile, the painted mask making it slightly sinister, and for the first time I realized how dangerous a woman she was. "If you don't have much of a life, you'll fit right in with us."

"Oh my god," I said.

"Seriously," Wesley agreed.

She raised an eyebrow at us. "These two think I'm preventing them from having fun because I'm the parent. Such failure of imagination." Her look turned sly. "A handsome bachelor will remedy my appalling wholesomeness."

"Mom," Wesley said, "please do not flirt with our teacher."

Evan laughed, genuinely, a little shyly. "I'm flattered, really, but I've got papers to grade."

I darted him a warning look. You don't give out papers, Mr. Wilke. You think papers are bullshit.

"Another time, then," Siobhan murmured.

Evan smiled at each of us, and when he looked at me his eyes flickered to my hand, then back to my face. You could have clocked him with a stopwatch. He didn't spend a single extra millisecond on me, yet he'd told me everything. I clenched the ring in my fist.

He walked away. Wesley jammed the end of his pretzel into his mouth and said, "Kinda sad that he comes here for fun."

"We come here for fun," I said.

"Yeah, but we're losers."

Siobhan clucked her tongue. "One percent of your share is going to your sister."

"Mom," he said. "You already said that like five times this week."

I laughed. "Your sister's going to be rich, Wesley. Better start being nice to her."

Siobhan smiled at me. But as we turned back to the carnival, her eyes held mine, and I knew that she knew. Everything.

8

THE only way to cure an obsession is to become obsessed with something else. So I did: my semester project.

I was infatuated with Terrence Malick in those days, especially his latest stuff: *Tree of Life* and *To the Wonder*, films that evoked the old silent era of storytelling. They were fragmented, visual, more stream-of-consciousness than stories with clear dramatic arcs. Watching them wasn't so much like watching a movie as dipping yourself into someone's memories. Wisps of dialogue floating atop swirling, too-close images. Music drifting in and out like something heard from a passing car. Echoes and shadows.

I'd built up a library of clips now, mostly from St. Louis, visual mementos that only held meaning for two people. Sunlight rolling off the striped awning at the chocolatier where Evan bought me pralines that he fed to me by hand. The velvet ropes at the Tivoli where I'd kissed him in a crowd, no longer self-conscious. Our bare feet, side by side, after we'd walked across the stepping stones in the Citygarden downtown, the water shockingly cold, drying in the pale autumn sun.

I strung them together without stopping too long to cut or trim. I wanted it to be messy, overlapping, spontaneous. I pasted bits of text here and there, faded in a verse of one song, then another. I was trying to speak in several different languages at once, visual and verbal and musical, and what came out was a babel of color and sound that eventually became incomprehensible, smearing into impressions of feeling, mood.

It was exhausting. I pulled off my headphones and rubbed my sore ears.

You're so quiet, I messaged Wesley, who sat across the computer lab. We'd decided not to show each other our projects so we wouldn't cross-pollinate. *Are you watching porn?*

Ha ha ha, he responded.

How's it going?

Okay. A pause, then, *Want to see? IDK if I like it.*

Believe in yourself, I said, *and surprise me.*

October had felt slow, but November ran through my fingers like sand. The only tedious parts were, ironically, in Evan's class, where I sat watching him act like a teacher, watched the fine spiderweb of cracks growing at the edges of his facade. I ate lunch with Wesley and made myself smile and laugh, no matter how robotic it felt. The weekends weren't enough. I showed up at Evan's apartment on school nights and he told me it was too dangerous and let me inside anyway, taking me in his arms as if we hadn't seen each other in months. Those nights were almost too intense, edged with hysterical urgency, my fists crumpling his bedsheets, his hands pulling me close to fuck me deeper, none of it ever giving us more than a few hours of respite. The weekends in St. Louis were sweeter, more relaxed, the rapid city paradoxically slowing us down, but every Sunday a gradual dread would build, a coil in my chest tightening and choking until it felt like my life was ending when we got in the car. Melodramatic, but in a way, it really was. The life I had with him felt more real than the one I'd lived on my own.

There was one day when it became more real than I wanted.

We were standing on a street corner downtown, waiting to cross, the wind sharp and peppery with ice, and Evan had said something that made me laugh and when I turned to smile at him, I locked gazes with the driver of a sleek gray Benz idling beside us. Face like wood hacked with a blunt hatchet, eyes that never blinked. Quinn. He looked right at me and recognized me instantly, even in my coat and scarf, and he nodded, once, and drove away.

I didn't say a word about it to Evan. But it ticked in the back of my mind, a clock that would eventually run out.

Looking back, I can barely remember what we did in those weeks. I have videos and photos to prove they happened. I remember the last leaves falling. Rain turning to needles of sleet. The world tinting to gray scale. But when I think of what we did together, all I remember is how I ached. With anxiety, with want, and with loneliness. Even when I was with Evan, I'd think of how little time we had left before we had to go back to town or school and pretend to be normal, not miserable and apart. I'd think of the semester ending and switching classes and seeing him even less. I'd think, I hate this. I hate that we can't be together like normal people. I just want to be with you. And then I'd start thinking about what I was willing to give up for that.

I spent Thanksgiving with the Browns.

Natalie came home to visit, an intimidating girl with pin-sharp blue eyes and Wesley's long, canine grin and her mom's acerbic wit. She was nice to me, though, and we ganged up on Wesley and took him to task for the assorted Evils of Men until he threatened to call his dad. Then alliances shifted, and Wesley and Nat turned against Siobhan. I sat on the sidelines and listened to family stories. Siobhan taught them not to break curfew by waiting for them in the dark kitchen one night in a white gown, holding a chef's knife. Nat got arrested for shoplifting a bottle of vodka, which Siobhan said was doubly stupid because they had way nicer stuff to steal at home. Wesley fractured his collarbone when he made a DIY helmet cam and recorded himself trying to jump his bike over a truck (also ruined a five-hundred-dollar camera) (also the reason he never rode bikes).

The house was full of candlelight and the smell of cinnamon and sweet potatoes. Wesley flicked my ear, and Siobhan put her arm around my shoulder, and Nat joked with me like she'd known me for years, and I thought, You are my real family. I made up a fantasy that they'd accidentally lost me as a baby, and I'd been raised by a scheming witch addicted to her own potions, and the truth of my parentage only came to light on my eighteenth birthday, when the curse masking my identity lifted. Now we were finally together again. I drank too much rum punch and got teary and excused myself for some fresh air.

Siobhan followed me onto the back deck, closing the glass door behind her. She tugged an afghan around her shoulders. "Cold?"

I shook my head. The alcohol sent my blood rushing to the surface. I felt like all of me was gathered on the outside of my skin.

Siobhan sat beside me on the wooden rocker. The sky was so clear it made a deep cobalt matte behind the trees, dusted with a scattering of silver stars. The moon was a thin white fang. We hadn't really been alone since Halloween, and a sober corner of my mind worried about this.

"I'm glad you came tonight," she said.

"I'm glad you invited me."

She smiled, her eyes moving frankly over my face. "There's something I've been meaning to talk to you about."

Oh, shit.

Siobhan turned away. "I love my children more than anything in this world. Even more than I love the alimony payments. And you're starting to feel like a daughter to me."

Heart palpitations.

"I know there are things you keep private from everyone." She glanced at me. "And I want you to know that I will never tell anyone unless you ask me to."

I exhaled. A weight slid off my shoulders that I hadn't realized was there.

"Do you want to talk about it?" she said.

"I can't. It's not bad. It's just—I can't."

She nodded, as if that was the answer she'd expected. Her heavy-lidded eyes caught tiny sickles of moonlight. "Did Wesley ever tell you about his father?"

"No."

Siobhan smiled, tilting her face to the sky. "When I was twenty, and very stupid, and very pretty, I was utterly in love with my economics professor. It is one of the most unsexy subjects, but the way this man talked about numbers was obscene. It helped that he was fucking gorgeous, too."

I laughed.

"There was a boy in econ who always sat next to me and found excuses to talk. He'd share his notes if I daydreamed during class—and I did a lot of daydreaming about that professor." Her smile deepened. "This boy was persistent, so I made a deal with him. If he could ask the professor a question which he answered incorrectly, I'd agree to one date."

I pulled my knees up and rested my chin atop them, waiting eagerly.

"The boy thought about it for a while, and then he asked, 'Will Siobhan go out with me tonight?' And the professor said, decisively, 'No.' So the boy, thinking himself clever, asked me where I'd like to have dinner, and I said I'd tell him later." Her teeth flashed as she spoke. "After class, I asked the professor why he'd answered no with such certainty. Do you know what he said?"

"What?"

"He said, 'Because you're having dinner with me.' And that was the night I started dating Professor Brown."

My jaw dropped.

Siobhan laughed, those low, dulcet tones dropping into the night like orchid petals. She looked me right in the eyes. "Perhaps I understand more than you think."

Formula for honesty: alcohol + loneliness.

"How long were you with him?" I said.

"Five years."

"How old was he?"

"Forty-one to my twenty."

My eyebrows rose. "How was it, being together?"

Siobhan tilted her head up again, remembering. "Exquisite," she said in a throaty voice, and I shivered. "Not perfect, but something that could only happen once in a lifetime. Most people fumble through young adulthood with idiots of equal age and naivete. Youth wasted reinventing the wheel. Being with an older man changed all of that. It shaped me in many, many ways."

"Good ways?"

Her eyes fixed on me again. "Some good. Some not. There are times when I wonder who I would've been if I had gone out with that boy instead. If I had discovered life through trial and error, rather than through Jack."

"But you're amazing," I said, earnest with rum and adoration. "You're so smart and wise and beautiful. You're perfect."

Siobhan gave me a funny look. Then she leaned in and kissed my cheek, her lips warm and dry.

"You are a dear thing," she said. "You deserve happiness."

I stayed there for a while after she went inside, my palm pressed to my cheek where she'd kissed me, trying to hold in the feeling of being loved.

———

We were in St. Louis for the first snow.

We walked through the white fleece lying over downtown, Evan in a wool coat, me in fur boots and knit stockings, like a little girl. I felt like a little girl, laughing at the snowflakes colliding gently with my face. They collected in my eyelashes and when I looked at Evan he said, "You've got stars in your eyes," and I kissed him, his lips warm and sweet in the cold. Our breath wrapped around us in scarves of steam. On the smooth white cloth spread before us, pastel lights rippled in soft, diaphanous waves, like auroras.

I refused to let myself worry about expensive cars pulling up, men with guns. My heart was too full of beauty to admit fear.

The loft was freezing in winter, so we curled up on the couch with blankets and mugs of peppermint tea. My nose was always cold, and Evan kept kissing it. He'd let his beard grow out a little and I ran my fingers over the bristles, blond and auburn and a few isolated silvers.

"Almost Christmas break," I said.

We hadn't decided where to go yet. Chicago, maybe. I'd never been up there. All that really mattered was we'd have two solid weeks together, no school, no sad Sunday good-byes. It'd be like living together. I was nervous, even after all of this. The removal of all boundaries, all distractions, leaving us with nothing but each other—scary. What kind of people would we be without secrecy and desperation?

"I want to show you something," Evan said.

I watched him fetch his laptop. The snow falling outside cast shadows over us like rain, and I remembered the rain-drops running down the windows of his car a million years ago. Everything had a gunmetal tint, the shadows cool and misty, drifting, filling the loft like a sunken ship. All day I'd had Lana del Rey's "Young and Beautiful" in my head, and now I heard it again and something hot twisted in my throat.

Evan sat beside me and ran a hand over my knee. "I haven't shown anyone this in a long time. It's old, and it's not who I am anymore, but I want you to see it because it was part of me, once."

He played a video.

There he was, a twenty-something college guy, baby-faced, higher-pitched, skinnier. His acting demo reel. The clips were mostly from student films, overly Serious and Meaningful, everyone trying too hard to Act except for him. He didn't look like he was acting at all. He looked like a sad, lost boy who'd wandered into a shot and knew it was all fake and absurd and embraced it with fatalistic humor. The camera focused magnetically on his eyes, his mouth, the way he conveyed so much in the subtle flicker and shift of a lip, an eyebrow. But the thing that struck me most was how absolutely alone he looked. Even in a group of people, he was apart from them. He'd smile, but his eyes would go elsewhere, to some place inside himself.

I looked up from his laptop.

"Did that lower your opinion of me?" he said.

I shook my head.

"Is it weird seeing me when I was your age?"

"A little." Would I be so different in ten years? "Evan, you are actually good. Seriously good. Why did you stop?"

He stared off into space. The light waned, the snowfall turning opaque, a muslin sheet flecked with stars.

"It didn't make me happy," he said.

"That's it?"

"That's everything."

I put my hand on his wrist, feeling the broad bones, the veins spiraling up his arm. Startling, how real he was. "What makes you happy?"

I wasn't fishing for compliments. I really wanted to know. But he touched my face and I knew what he was going to say, and suddenly I didn't want him to say it. I averted my eyes.

"I don't get you sometimes," I said.

"What don't you get?"

"Why me?"

I thought of Siobhan and her professor and all the men who'd been drawn to me, who I'd used and discarded and never felt a twinge of regret over. What did they see in us? Did they see us as girls they could teach about all the things they couldn't share in their classes or jobs or wherever? Did they just see pretty faces, smooth young bodies? Were they less intimidated because we were young and dumb and not yet hardened by disappointment? Maybe it was more about themselves, about getting a second chance to be the men they hadn't been when they were young. It hurt when I thought about that. That I might merely be a lesson for Evan to learn something about himself. That I might just be schooling the teacher.

"It could have been anyone," I said. "All the women who look at you when we go out. Ms. Bisette at school. God, even Hiyam. Why me?"

He stared at the coffee table, the reflection of snow like confectioner's sugar sifting down.

"It couldn't have been anyone," he said softly. "For a long time before I met you, I felt my life was this kind of test. I was in deep, cold water, swimming for shore, and my arms were getting tired, my skin numb. On the shore was everything I thought I wanted: a better job, a house, a family." He swallowed, his throat cording with tension. "But I could barely keep my head above water. Eventually I stopped seeing the shore. Only cold dark blue, in all directions. I know it's cliché, but when I met you, my eyes opened. I looked around and realized I could stand up whenever I wanted. There was firm ground under my feet. That shore in the distance was an illusion. I was already somewhere beautiful."

I stared at him, my lungs not seeming to be doing anything vital to my survival.

"You are so alive, Maise. You are so *here*, so present in the moment. You've taught me that happiness is possible now, not in some distant future. You'll scale a mountain without a second thought, face your fears, throw yourself into danger, and you're not reckless but bold, proud. You have a lion's heart. You're not afraid to live."

I was shivering, even under the blanket. Wesley had called it self-destructive. Evan understood. It wasn't about flirting with death, like Mom. It was about wanting to live all the way to the seams of life.

But how could he feel that way, when he'd made *me* feel that way? How could two zombies bring each other to life? I wasn't brave before I met him, and I definitely wasn't happy. Cockiness and not caring aren't boldness or pride—they're coping mechanisms. When you're a wounded animal in the company of jackals, you can either cower and submit, or feign strength. Wear your blood like a red badge of courage. That's all I was doing.

"Let's watch something," I said finally.

Evan glanced at me.

"Show me *Casablanca*."

He was quiet as he turned on the TV. A nervous energy buzzed between us, a revelation building up. It hummed in my marrow, the roots of my teeth, electric and tense, and I knew something was coming, something that would change me.

He sat beside me on the couch and seemed about to speak. Then he hit play.

Bandshell orchestra blares. Credits come up over a map of Africa. The countries are bigger and simpler, before all our modern wars and genocides. It's a complicated story: two refugees from Nazi Germany are trying to book passage to Lisbon via Casablanca, which is part of Vichy France. The Nazis want to prevent resistance leader Victor Laszlo and his wife, Ilsa, from leaving. At the heart of Casablanca is Rick's

Café, where Rick himself makes money off desperate refugees and corrupt authorities alike, playing everyone. Rick's friend scores some priceless letters of transit that will get anyone out of Casablanca, no questions asked. Even a resistance leader wanted by the Nazis. The friend entrusts the letters with Rick and is then assassinated by the cops, which sends Laszlo and Ilsa looking for help from Rick, now the only guy who can get them out of the country. Of course, it turns out that Rick knows Ilsa. They were lovers in Paris. She left him on a train platform with a broken heart and a good-bye letter, the ink bleeding in the rain.

I was intrigued at first, and as the story went on I got totally caught up in it, grabbing Evan's arm at tense moments, laughing at the whip-smart dialogue, becoming completely absorbed against all of my twenty-first-century ironic instincts. I disdained the moral simplicity of old movies, the clear-cut villainy and heroics. But this movie was all about gray areas and moral ambiguity. Rick helped people, but he profited from their desperation, too. Ilsa tried to use Rick's love to save herself and her husband. The French police captain took advantage of powerless girls yet let Rick shepherd them to freedom. There was good and evil in everyone.

When Rick remembered his days with Ilsa in Paris, that humming in me became keening, sharp and poignant. I couldn't help seeing the parallels. A forbidden love blossoming while dark forces surrounded them. The dread of the encroaching end. I knew what was coming, the inevitable parting—the repercussions of that parting had been rippling through cinema for decades. But when it happened on the runway at night, Ilsa getting onto that plane with Laszlo as Rick stayed behind, I started to cry. Jesus Christ, I had not cried at a movie since I was a kid. But I couldn't stop.

Evan turned the TV off. "Are you okay?"

"No," I said, laughing at myself. "I don't know what's wrong with me."

I couldn't see him too clearly, but his eyes shone in the snow-shrouded gloom, and his voice was thick. "What are you feeling?"

"I don't know." I cleared my throat. "Why didn't he ask her to stay? He still loved her."

"That's why. He let her go because he loved her."

Stupidly, this made me cry harder. My tears were so bewildering that I kept laughing, too, and I probably seemed like a total head case, my nerves wound so tightly I felt like I was tearing apart from the inside, and over what? A stupid old movie? If I'd watched it a year ago I would have had intelligent things to say about the lighting, the cinematography, the pacing. Instead I was dissolving into human goo. Evan looked at me with wonder, the way he had when I got dead drunk on homecoming.

"This is ridiculous," I said, trying to laugh it off. "I never cry at movies."

"Because you've never been in love," he said.

The keening in my blood reached its highest point, and then it stopped. I felt every beat of my heart tolling in the silence. I blinked until my eyes were clear and I could see him, looking at me steadily, his lips parted and his warm breath reaching me, the wonder still in his face. The snow globe world spun outside, all glittering crystal and frost. I felt a thrill run along my skin, the sense of a shiver coming, and I knew as I saw him swallow and breathe and shape the words I'd been waiting for that this was something that could only happen once in my life and it was happening here, right here, right now.

"Maise," he said, "I love you."

The shiver came, and everything in me turned to the same sparkling whiteness that fell outside and drifted, weightless, evanescent, catching the light for a heartbeat and melting the instant it landed. I couldn't speak. My head was full of snow and static. He touched my face and I touched his and we didn't kiss, just looked at each other. I love you, I thought. If I was the only person truly alive that night, it was because of you. You made the world come alive for me and I love you, I love you, I love you. But it was so hard to get the air out of my lungs, and then he kissed me, and I stopped trying.

I didn't feel completely corporeal. My body felt like layers of tulle, gauzy approximations of a girl. Air moved through me and drenched me with oxygen. I kissed him, the roughness of his face making mine tingle. And as I kissed him the icy tissue of my body flooded with fire and blood and then I was the one cupping his face, looking down at him, taking his hand in mine and pulling him across the cold concrete. I was the one pushing him to the bed and holding his face still so I could kiss him, my tongue in his mouth. I unbuttoned his shirt and took it off and he sat there, letting me touch him, the heavy bone yoke of his shoulders, his light gold skin, the softly chiseled slabs of muscle fitting over him like breathing stone, solid and warm. I pressed my face to his collarbone, inhaling the smell of him like a drug. I'm in love with this man, I thought. I'm in love with my teacher. I'm in love with Evan Wilke. It felt so crazily good to think it, accept it at last. But my mouth wouldn't say it. I could only put my lips to his skin, heat to heat, and imagine that somehow it was communicated through our blood. I closed my eyes. Pushed my senses to the tips of my fingers and toes, and felt as if I held the world in my hands, a luminous sapphire veined with light and revolving slowly in the sun, ludicrously, absurdly beautiful.

This is what being in love feels like, Wesley. Gratitude. Gratitude that you exist in this fucked-up, beautiful universe.

—————

Movies tend to follow classical Greek dramatic structure. You begin with Exposition: who, when, where. Then you're off, and it's Rising Action (plans, hijinks, search for MacGuffin) until you get to the Climax (explosions, bad guys die, acquire MacGuffin) and then you coast through Denouement (girl gets guy, MacGuffin restored) to the ending credits (terrible pop song). The basic shape of drama is a pyramid.

Greek tragedies take it one step farther. The Climax can also contain a moment called *peripeteia*. A tragic reversal. A sudden change of circumstance or fortune. This reversal is often precipitated by *anagnorisis*, a critical revelation. Everything seems to be heading in a certain direction until *boom*, a plot IED detonates and it's all thrown off course. Aristotle's famous example is Oedipus discovering he's murdered his father and married his mother. My famous example is Donnie Darko realizing he must let the jet engine crush him to save the world and everyone he loves.

Revelation. Reversal. The essence of tragedy.

These concepts will be important, class.

—————

It snowed all during the last week of school. I pelted Wesley with snowballs in the parking lot and walked around wearing fingerless gloves and a big dopey smile and when I saw Evan in class I was calm, content, simply happy. In love. The town turned into the tiny plastic village inside a snow globe, the sky full of glitter and the streets layered with cake frosting. It was too snowy to ride my bike, so Evan would pick me up and take me to his apartment, where we'd set up a small Christmas tree and hung rainbow lights on the balcony, the air sweet with cranberry potpourri. The snow and our winter coats were camouflage, emboldening us. I didn't glance over my shoulder constantly. I saved my glances for him. Mom left town for a few days and I brought him over to see my room. We made out on my bed but he didn't want to have sex in the house because I'd grown up there, been a little girl there. I told him that made it even hotter and ran my tongue in the seashell of his ear, but he just laughed and called me incorrigible. "How do I become corrigible?" I said. "Teach me." He laughed again and said he couldn't, because I was also unteachable.

Wesley and I were scheduled to show our films on the last Friday before break, so we got to see everyone else's first. Some of them were surprisingly good. Hiyam's was a documentary on her Iranian parents and the discrimination they faced here. Another girl did an amazing stop-motion animation with Lego about a boy who decided to become a superhero. And one group made a sci-fi murder mystery that took place in 2030 on Mars, among the first colonists. I was impressed at the breadth of imagination.

"Are you nervous?" I asked Wesley at lunch on Thursday.

He shrugged. He was uncharacteristically quiet that week, and I figured it was about his project.

I flicked his ear. "Don't be so glum. I'm still coming for your birthday. And tell your mom *not* to get me anything for Christmas. Seriously."

Wesley stared at his mashed potatoes, raking them into a wispy mountain. "Maise."

"What?"

He raised his face. "You're my best friend. Did you know that?"

My heart gave a little hiccup, but I said, cockily, "No shit, Captain Obvious. I'm your only friend."

He locked eyes with me, not saying anything. Wesley was so infrequently emotional that I had no idea what I was looking at. Being a boy, he probably didn't know what he was feeling, either. The silence stretched.

"You're my best friend, too," I said quietly.

He dropped his gaze to his plate. I glanced out the window, feeling inexplicable unease. The snow came down in a soft rush, erasing the world over and over, struggling to wipe out all our mistakes.

Don't treat me any differently than the others, I'd told Evan, and on Friday, he didn't.

"Maise O'Malley," he called.

My hands shook as I plugged my USB stick into the laptop near the projector. When we showed our films, we got to sit in the back of the room like we were the teacher. Evan was down in the audience with the rest of the class. Good, because facing him now was something I wasn't sure I could do.

I'd skipped my fear confrontation in November. December was going to count double. Actually, it was going to count for the whole fucking year.

We weren't allowed to explain or qualify our films before we showed them. We could only give a brief intro.

"I'm Maise O'Malley," I said, my voice surprising me with its steadiness, "and my film is titled *Dear You.*"

Evan's head turned ever so slightly. I clicked play.

We begin facing a roller-coaster track, a steel spine arcing up into the night, its vertebrae painted neon red and moon white. The camera lurches forward with a metallic squeal. We're moving up the track. My voice says, *I'm not going to do the whole roller-coaster-slash-falling-in-love metaphor. I didn't fall in love with you up there.* It's Halloween and I'm sitting next to Wesley, pretending to be terrified, while he films this for me, an unknowing aide. The shot jumps to golden lights in a parking lot and a little boy kicking pebbles. Then to the carnival from the crow's nest at the water tower, a cloud of fireflies. Then to the derelict gas station, where my shadow kicks her leg off the side of the cooler, waiting. As we move from scene to scene, I tell the story that I've been telling you. The songs I mentioned swirl in and out. These words pop up, type themselves, backspace, vanish. You didn't always see the camera in my hand, but it was there. People are so used to cell phones that they don't even notice when they're being filmed anymore—or when they're filming. Paul's scarecrow shadow looming across the porch. Gary's hand on my wrist as I pretend to text someone. Wesley's silhouette by the illuminated pool, waiting to kiss me. And Evan, over and over, his hands moving hungrily over my skin, the boyish way he rocks on his toes, his wonder at life filling me with wonder, too. Never anything identifiable. No faces or voices, just allusions, obliquities. I caught all these little moments while I was pretending to live them. I did live them, but I'm not sure where I was when they happened, if I was the lens watching or the skin being touched. That's the whole point. We don't know anymore. And there are scenes from my private education spliced in with my real life. Hal 9000's eerie unblinking red eye (paranoia). Velociraptors stalking through a kitchen, their claws clicking on the tile, while kids hide under a counter (secrecy). Rick drunkenly yelling at Sam to play "As Time Goes By" (obsession).

As the stream-of-consciousness goes on, it grows more crowded and chaotic. Images and words flash past too fast to parse, like the cliché dying moment in film, when life flashes before someone's eyes. Except that isn't what happens when you die—it's what happens when you live. It all flashes past. You barely have time to feel it before it's gone. The images slow down toward the end and we're back at the top of the roller-coaster track, the world below a pinball machine full of noise and light, and my voice says, *I guess I'm trying to say what I couldn't say that night. You can call it love, or you can call it free fall. They're pretty much the same thing. And I love you.*

Car drops. Lights rush up. Cut to black. Roll credits.

Mr. Wilke didn't move. Someone got up and switched on the light. Heads turned to look at me. Not Wesley, I noticed.

Evan cleared his throat. "Class? Thoughts?"

"That was really intense," Rebecca, the stop-motion girl, said.

"I don't get it," a boy said.

"It's a love letter," someone else said.

"Oh."

"I thought it was like, she was dying, and her life flashed before her eyes."

Laughter.

"She died on the roller coaster?"

"Maybe it crashed."

"It's a metaphor, genius."

"It had parts of other movies in it. Is that even legal?"

"Fair use. Like a remix."

"I think those parts were what she was feeling. Like, the dinosaurs were about being afraid."

"Afraid of what?"

"Being found out." This from Hiyam.

"Found out about what?"

Hiyam glanced at me and didn't say anything.

"What do you think about the collage technique?" Evan said.

"It was kind of like a music video," Rebecca said.

"Yeah," someone agreed. "It made me think how when I walk around with headphones on, my whole life becomes this music video."

Laughter again, appreciative.

"I'm in a band," a skater guy said. "If you ever want to do one for real, we'll pay."

I shrugged and smiled coolly. Translation: hell yes.

The discussion continued for a while, but I lost track. I couldn't stop staring at Evan and Wesley. Neither had looked my way even once, and Wesley hadn't said a word about my project. Did he think it was awful? Was he jealous of what I'd confessed? Jesus, what?

Evan stood up and went to the board. He graded tougher than I expected, but as long as you showed a modicum of understanding about something he'd taught, you passed. There were only two As so far: Hiyam's *Yellow Dust* and Rebecca's *When I Learn to Fly*. I watched Evan write *Dear You* and pause with the marker hovering and then write something fast, decisively. He turned around and finally looked at me.

Grade: A.

"Beautiful work, Ms. O'Malley," he said. "You have a true passion for this. Hold on to it, cultivate it, and it'll take you far."

His voice only quavered slightly, not enough for anyone else to notice. But I glowed ultraviolet inside.

I took my seat in a daze and so did he. For the first time since this crazy thing between us started, I felt okay about it. Yeah, we were sitting five feet apart and didn't dare glance at each other, and I could practically hear Hiyam swishing her tail with nefarious intent, but it was all okay. I was in love with him. And he knew. And he was in love with me.

That was enough.

"Time for our final victim," Evan said. "Wesley Brown."

Someone hit the lights. Evan was two empty desks away from me, and when the lights dropped he flashed me a small smile. I smiled back. The ring on my finger seemed to pulse in time with my heart.

Wesley didn't introduce his film. He just clicked play.

A black-and-white shot, extreme bokeh, blurry overlapping discs of light. The camera slowly focuses on a girl sitting at a picnic table with a—

Oh my god. It was me. The night of the carnival, the first night, before I'd even met Wesley Brown. You couldn't see my face, but I knew those clothes, that body, that dark hair flying when the girl threw her head back to drain the last of her beer, the can winking with moonlight.

Evan recognized me, too. His shoulders stiffened in my peripheral vision.

The title comes up on a black frame, with some austere, brooding piano music:

Obsession.

Jesus Christ, I thought. Okay, yes, I'd just declared my love for somebody with my own film, but that was reciprocal. Wesley shouldn't be doing this. We'd talked about it. And how the hell did he get that shot?

Cut to the interior of the carnival. The camera hovers at the back of the roller coaster, watching it fill up. All the seats are taken except the front car. The girl walks toward it, turns around for a moment, then gets in. A man joins her. You can't see their faces.

Cut to the water gun race, the girl's foot running up an old fat guy's leg.

Cut to silhouettes kissing in a Chevy Monte Carlo.

(Cut to me in class, my heart a fist of ice, realizing this is not about Wesley's obsession with me.)

Cut to the girl disappearing down the road on her bike in a blur of moon-pale skin and night-flower hair.

Cut to—

I stopped processing it at some point. I stared at the screen, my insides churning like broken glass. He never showed our faces. Every frame was artfully cropped, focusing on hands, legs, the backs of our heads. Mostly on my hands. It was a whole fucking film about sign language, really. The tension, worry, and desire I expressed with my hands. And it continued into the school year. Me waiting on the hood of Evan's car. Our hands clasping briefly in the hall. Both of us leaving his class together after fourth-period make-out sessions. You couldn't read any incriminating details—Wesley was oh so careful to edit those out—but if you went to this school, you knew it was here. And you knew it was a teacher and student. And you knew that the student was obsessed with the teacher, always waiting, wanting, twisting herself into knots with it. There were scenes I didn't even remember: me seeming forlorn and angry, kicking my bike over, flinging crab apples at a brick wall, sitting on a curb with my head in my hands. When did that happen? It was like watching a stranger.

Final shot: Halloween night in Siobhan's car. I stare out the window, compulsively twisting the ring on my finger, over and over and over and over.

Piano trails off. Hard cut to black. Credits.

Someone flipped the lights on and I imagined myself standing up with a gun.

Evan didn't even get a chance to prompt discussion.

"Whoa," a guy said.

"Yeah," said someone else.

"So, like," a girl said, "what is your genre? Because that looked really, really . . . real."

"Docudrama," Wesley answered in monotone.

You fucking liar, I thought.

"So it's made up?"

"Reenactment."

"That's going on? At Riverland?"

"They're actors."

Other voices chimed in.

"But it's based on something real."

"Oh my god. Did that actually happen here?"

"Man, that happens all the time. Don't be naive."

I had not looked at Evan. I couldn't. But his voice sounded perturbingly calm when he said, "Let's focus on theme. Aside from the title, what kind of themes did you notice?"

I almost laughed. How can you even discuss this? I thought. Throw him out of class. Let us out early. Let me beat the shit out of him.

"Loneliness," someone answered immediately.

"Depression."

"Lust?"

Giggles.

"Sex."

Every single word went through me like a voodoo pin. This is my fucking life you're talking about, you idiots. It does not have a fucking theme.

"I think it's about love," Rebecca said tentatively, "but . . . kind of messed up."

"You know that's a teacher, right?" a guy said.

"So?"

"So, that's like, pedo."

Rebecca made a sound of disgust.

"No it's not," someone else said. "At my old school this girl was seeing a teacher, and when she turned eighteen they got married."

"Gross."

"I'd totally do it with a hot teacher," a guy said, and a girl said, "Ms. Bisette?"

People laughed.

I felt like I was going to vomit. I started to stand and Evan shot me a warning glance. Drawing attention to myself was probably a bad idea.

"Class," he said in that smooth actor's voice, "let's focus on the work." He turned to Wesley then, and my heart pounded. "Wesley has told a story very effectively without any dialogue, or even seeing the actors' faces. Why do you think he chose that direction?"

Because he's a fucking coward, I thought.

"To show it could be anyone."

"To hide their identities."

"I think it's so we focus on the emotions," Rebecca said.

"What emotions? It's about infatuation."

"You can still feel things when you're infatuated."

"I don't think she's infatuated," Rebecca said. "I think she really loves him."

"How do you know?" a guy said. "Have you been with a teacher?"

Laughter.

"Focus," Evan said.

"She's right."

Hiyam's voice. Icicle straight to my heart.

"I think it is about love," Hiyam said. "I'd like to know what Maise thinks, since hers was about being in love with a teacher, too."

I turned to her. The whole class was looking at me. I couldn't speak. Suddenly I was aware of the ring, the fucking ring right there on my hand. I couldn't hide it now, they were all staring. God, don't see it, I prayed. Don't see this thing I've been waving right under your fucking noses.

"Well?" Hiyam said.

"Hiyam," Evan said. "Bullying."

"It's an honest question."

"She doesn't have to answer."

"I'll answer her fucking question," I said.

No one gasped, but there was a sudden, reverberating silence.

"I think it's easy to judge someone you don't know anything about," I said. "Like before I saw your film, I thought you were nothing but a spoiled cokehead. Now I know it's not your parents' fault."

"Maise," Evan breathed behind me, low and alarmed.

I turned to Wesley, who sat on the dais at the back of the room, in shadow.

"And I thought you were a good person. But now I know you're a fucking psycho."

"Maise," Evan said sharply, like a whip crack.

No one moved. It was dead still.

"Leave the class."

It was as if I'd been struck. I turned to him, numb, furious, hurt. He met my eyes for a moment and then looked away.

I stood up and walked out. I didn't slam the door, but I stalked straight across the hall and kicked open the boys' bathroom, and when a guy at a urinal looked at me in shock, I growled, "Get out."

I paced. I stood with my palms on either side of a sink, feeling like I could rip it out of the wall. I turned on the cold water and splashed it on my face. Tried to drink some but ended up spitting it at the mirror. Then I paced some more.

I didn't have long to wait. The bell rang, and I stepped out and watched the kids leaving, flocking into small groups, whispering frantically.

When I saw Wesley I walked up to him, grabbed his shirt in my fist, and twisted as hard as I could.

"What the hell?" he said.

"You want to do this here, or you want to do it in private?" I barely recognized my voice. It was flat and gritty, sulfurous. The drag of a match head before it burst into flame. Other kids were staring.

Wesley eyed me anxiously for a second. Then he followed me to the boys' bathroom. When he walked in I kicked the garbage can in front of the door and spun around fast, swinging. He caught my arm. He was bigger and stronger than me and I hated him for that.

"Let me hit you," I said.

"You're crazy."

"You're a fucking traitor. You stupid asshole. How could you do this to me?"

He stared at me wide-eyed, as if surprised. "You're blowing it way out of proportion."

"You fucking stalked me, Wesley. You're sick. And you knew this whole time it was him. I can't believe I trusted you."

"I can't believe I trusted *you*," he snapped. "You've been lying your ass off to me about everything."

I let go of him so I could stab a finger at his chest. "It's my fucking prerogative to lie about this. If anyone knew, he'd lose his job. But now he's going to anyway. Great fucking work, Wesley. A-plus. Gold fucking star."

"God, stop yelling. Nobody knows it's you."

"Hiyam saw us, you idiot. And now you gave her proof."

"What?" he said.

"She. Fucking. Saw. Us."

"Where?"

"Where do you think?" I slashed my hands through the air, wishing it was his face. "In there. In his fucking class."

"What did she see?"

I took a step closer to him, my chest touching his. "What do you think she saw? Us. Together."

Wesley stepped back. "You were with him in class?"

"Jesus," I muttered.

"You did it in *our class*?"

"Don't you dare judge me. You have no right—"

"I can't believe this," he said, his pitch climbing. "You did it with him in our class. That's so fucking sick, Maise. What the fuck is wrong with you?"

"What the fuck is wrong with *you*?" I screamed. "You fucking stalker. You traitor. 'You're my best friend. Did you know that?' Go to fucking hell."

His voice was cold. "You're the traitor."

I laughed. "Why, because I popped your precious cherry, you naive little boy? Grow up. This is real. The world is ugly and nasty and fucked-up, and so are we."

He didn't flinch. His jaw jutted out, but he faced me eye to eye. "Listen to what you just said. That's how you see yourself with him. 'Ugly and nasty and fucked-up.' That's exactly why I did this."

If I'd had any sort of loose object, I would have flung it at him. Instead I raked my hands through my hair and pulled. "God," I said, trying not to scream again. "You seriously think you're teaching me something, you arrogant piece of shit."

"Yeah," he said huskily. "But you're too stupid to get it. You're the one who's naive. You don't even see what he's doing to you."

I spread my hands, laughing. "Please. Enlighten me, Professor Brown."

"He's not who you think he is."

"Then who the fuck is he?"

"I don't know. But I know it's bizarre as hell that there's nothing online about him before twenty eleven. He's a ghost. He came out of nowhere."

I felt nauseated. My fury was cooling, hardening into hate. "You don't know anything about him. I know about his past."

"Yeah? Where did he come from?"

"I'm not telling you that."

"Where did he teach before this?"

"Shut up."

"Where does he go on his days off and why does he sit in his car for hours, talking to himself?"

I stared at him. "What?"

The bathroom door scraped against the garbage can and a boy stuck his head in. We both yelled, "Get out!" The head disappeared.

I looked at Wesley again, my breath heavy and dry and tasting of bile, as if I'd run for miles, worn myself down to acid and bone.

"I saw him," Wesley said. "Yeah, I stalked him. Fucking sue me. I thought you were in danger, Maise. He's using you. I was trying to protect you."

"Ruining my life is how you protect me?" I shook my head. "You're sick, and you're obsessed. That's what your film is about, Wesley. That's the irony you don't get."

"Get over yourself." He stepped closer, and I had to tilt my head up to look up at him. "Yeah, I am kinda obsessed. I'm fucking sorry. But this is not about me. You don't even see what he's done to you. You put on these rose-colored glasses and think you're in love, but you're not. Open your eyes, Maise. I see how miserable you are every day and now you've seen it, too. It was the only way I could make you see what he really is."

I stood on my toes and spoke in a whisper, viperously soft. "You betrayed me in the worst possible way. You make me sick. Do not ever talk to me again."

And I shoved the can aside and stormed out and didn't see a thing through the brilliant bokeh of my tears.

9

*M*EET *me at home after school.*

I stared at Evan's text, wanting to smash my phone to pieces. No fucking point in secrecy anymore, was there? The raptors had found us. I'd spent the entire day in a black haze, seeing nothing but blood and bones and a trail of my own guts leading back to his classroom.

Please, he added, and something plucked sharply in my chest, a plangent, dissonant note.

I didn't respond. I slammed my locker closed.

Hiyam was waiting behind the door.

Myocardial infarction.

"O'Malley," she purred. "I've been looking for you."

I'd had my Revelation. This could only be Reversal.

"Let's walk," she said.

I still had World Lit, but no one went to the last period before vacation. The building was quiet, most classes dark. My locker slam echoed too long. This place was already a tomb.

"I've got class," I said. "What do you want?"

"I want to help you keep Evan Wilke from going to jail."

My body stilled, my entire cellular metabolism pausing. Her face was flawlessly composed, those high, upward-raked cheekbones and teardrop eyes like a mask. I couldn't read her. She raised a pencil-thin eyebrow at me and walked away.

I followed, like the stupid kid sister.

"So," she said when I caught up, "what do you call him when you're alone? Evan, or Mr. Wilke?"

I swallowed. Admit nothing.

She propped open a stairwell door, ushering me in. I felt like I was walking to my own execution. I leaned against the cold concrete wall, staring at the caged bulb opposite us as if it could open fire any moment.

"Up," Hiyam said.

We climbed to the roof door, which was unlocked.

"We're on camera," I said.

"Didn't stop you with Mr. Wilke."

If I gritted my teeth any harder, my face would shatter.

Freezing air blasted over us when she opened the door. The roof slates had become a diamondback of ice, slick scales twinkling in the sun. Cloudless periwinkle stretched from forever to nowhere. Hiyam went to the ledge and I followed, calculating the chance of death from a four-story drop.

She lit a cigarette. The smoke and her breath hung in the air, gossamer snakeskins.

"This is what I've been wondering," she said. "Why you?"

I stood beside her, arms crossed. I wore a man's flannel shirt and tight leggings and the cold cut right through, but I kept my chin up, refusing to cower.

"I mean," Hiyam said, "he could have had anyone. If he took me home, I would've blown him in his car. Actually,

I would've had my driver pick us up and blown him in my father's car."

"So why me?" I said dryly. "Why not one of you pathetic little girls with daddy issues? Good question."

She laughed. Her smoke scribbled arabesques that looked like the Persian alphabet.

"There's something about you," she said. "You don't give a fuck. It's kind of hot."

"Save the flirting. You're not my type."

Hiyam laughed again. "Such a bitch. I like it, O'Malley. Now let me tell you how this is going to work." She sat on the ledge. "You are going to supply me. Anything I want, any quantity, and I'll pay street price. No haggling. My *baba joon* would be so disappointed if he knew I didn't haggle." Something hard flashed in her eyes. "In return, I won't tell the principal or the police that you've been fucking Mr. Wilke. I also won't tell them that he fucked me."

I stared at her. "What?"

"Because that would be a felony. Since I'm seventeen."

I uncrossed my arms and stepped toward her. "What the hell are you talking about?"

"I'm talking about the fact that I can lie."

"You're insane," I said. "It'll never hold up. There's no evidence."

"Isn't there?" she said. "Mr. Wilke has been seen in many compromising situations. Like showing up at my party. And being in a locked classroom with both of us. Which Wesley conveniently preserved on film. My *baba* will hire the best lawyers. His poor little girl, taken advantage of." She laughed smoke into my face. "I see you thinking about pushing me. But you won't. You'll do exactly what I say. Because you belong to me now. You're my toy."

If there is a God, or an Allah, or anything, I thought, strike this bitch down. Please.

"This is nonnegotiable," Hiyam said. "If you work with me, it can be a mutually beneficial partnership. If you fuck me, it will be a master-slave arrangement. Up to you."

She flicked her cigarette off the roof.

"I've got big plans for New Year's. I'll be in touch before then."

She left me there, and I stared at the cherry burning on the wet asphalt far below, thinking, There I am. Down there. That's me.

After a minute, the fire went out.

My frozen hand wouldn't turn the key properly, but it didn't matter. As soon as he heard me at the door, Evan opened it, took one look at me, and pulled me inside, crushing me to his chest.

"I thought you wouldn't come," he said.

It was dusk, the sky striped pink and baby blue, all gentle annihilation. I could see the gibbous moon, a milky eye peering through a pastel curtain. His apartment was dark, Christmas lights off. Tinsel glinted in the gloom like tiny cuts in the air.

I had walked there and I was chilled to the core and he took off my coat, settled me on the couch with a blanket, started water for tea. I let him fuss, trying to steel myself inside. But when he knelt before me and took my hands in his, looking up with wet eyes, I couldn't hold it anymore.

"I'm sorry," I said, starting to cry. "I was so careless. This is my fault."

"We were both careless. It's no one's fault."

The teakettle whistled. He waited until my tears slowed before he got it.

Harden up, I told myself. Don't manipulate him. Do the right fucking thing, for once.

I took a few sips of hot tea and said, "Need something stronger."

He came back with two tumblers and a bottle of Old Forester.

"I can't believe Wesley would do this," I said as I drank. Oak and vanilla, burning in the back of my throat.

Evan sat on the floor on the other side of the coffee table. He peered into the thick syrup in his glass. "I talked to him after school."

I went still.

"I told him no matter what he thought of me, it was wrong to do this to you. You're innocent. I'll have other jobs, other opportunities to not fuck up fantastically, but this is your one and only senior year."

"What did he say?"

"Nothing. But I think he understood." Evan sighed. "I know you don't want to hear it right now, but I think he really does care about you."

"He's a stalker and a traitor. He can go fuck himself."

Evan raised his face. He looked so exhausted. He looked, for the first time, *old*. "Well, for what it's worth, he promised not to say anything."

Not that it mattered, thanks to Hiyam.

"You know what's been bothering me most?" Evan said. "This is a measure of how fucked-up my reality is right now."

"What?"

"Telling you to leave class."

I swallowed, not looking at him. The fumes in my throat

mellowed into burnt sugar. "I get it. I was disruptive. You had to be the teacher."

"It felt wrong."

It was comforting, that it had also made him uncomfortable.

I took another long sip, filling my chest with fire. When I breathed I tasted all the winter decay, the sweet rotten leaves and pulped wood that lay under the ice outside. I was suffused with a sense of things ending. Louis the pony sat on the couch beside me, and I wrapped my arms around him.

"I can't believe I fucked this up," I said.

So cocky. So sure of myself. Not realizing—not in a visceral, gut-twisting way—how much danger Evan was in. How could I let this happen? I should have guarded him. I should have been the one protecting him.

He kicked my foot beneath the table. "You didn't fuck it up. We're here, aren't we? It may sound weird, but it's almost relieving. We couldn't have kept doing this. And I don't like what it was doing to us."

"What was it doing to us?"

"Making us feel like something good was wrong."

I swallowed. The burn in my throat wasn't entirely from the drink.

"Listen." In the dark all I could make out was glass and shine. Moonlight filtered through the whiskey, casting eerie maple stains on the carpet. "I made a decision today. One way or another, I'm quitting."

"What?" I said. "No."

"Yes." His socked feet bounced against mine. "They need a permanent sub at Carbondale Community. One of the teachers was diagnosed with cancer. Tragic, of course, but life must go on. Go Terriers."

I put my glass down. "Which class?"

"Who cares?"

"Which class?"

"Speech."

I wrinkled my nose.

"The point is," he said, "I won't be your teacher anymore. No more fucked-up power imbalance. No more hiding."

"And what, we'll see each other on weekends? Carbondale's like an hour from here. Your commute will suck. You should stay and I'll just—"

"Move in," he said, touching my hand on the table.

Flatline.

Neither of us spoke. Then we both did at the same time.

"I know it's kind of soon—" he said, while I said, "Are you fucking serious—"

He laughed. I didn't.

"I am serious," he said.

"No, you're not. You're insane."

"Insanely serious."

I stood up, Louis and the blanket slipping to the floor. I started to walk—not toward the door, necessarily; I just needed to move. Evan was up and after me in a heartbeat. He grabbed my shoulders. I wrestled away. Now I *was* heading for the door.

"Maise," he said. "Wait. Please."

I waited.

"Did I freak you out? Too much, too soon?"

"No," I said. "Jesus. God. I don't know."

He stood behind me, pressed his body against mine. Slid his hands around my waist. His touch was light, tender. I could have easily stepped out of it.

He didn't prompt me. He didn't say teacherly things:

What do you think? (This is a mistake.) *What do you feel?* (Terrified.) *What's the theme of this conversation?* (Bad decisions.) He just held me. Supported me. Loved me.

And I started talking.

"I'm afraid," I said to the shadows. "I'm fucking terrified. Other people know about us. Even if you leave Riverland, they can still come after you."

"Who else knows?" he said against my hair.

I shook my head, unwilling to explain. "It doesn't matter. Even if they didn't, I'd still be afraid." Okay. Here it comes. Here is the hardest thing I am going to say. Be a fucking lion. One two three roar. "I love you, Evan. I know I've already said it a million ways, but it's really hard for me to accept and actually say out loud like this. I love you. God, I love you, I love you, and it's scary and overwhelming and when you say you're quitting your job and want me to move in, I panic. Because I've never grown up. I'm stuck, like Peter Pan. I don't know how to have a grown-up relationship, I don't know how to live with someone, I don't know how to be with you outside of this teacher-student thing, and today proved how much I fail at that. I pretend to be this person I'm not when inside I'm a scared little girl, waiting for someone to tell me it's okay."

He turned me around and I wouldn't look at him. He touched my jaw.

"It's okay," he said.

"I'm fucking terrified. I'm just a kid inside, Evan."

"So am I." He stroked my hair. "Maise, so am I. Nobody knows how to be a grown-up. We're all just pretending for each other. It takes some people their entire lives to figure out what you already know."

Out of everything I ever learned from Evan Wilke, I

think that lesson was the most important: that none of us actually grow up. We get bigger, and older, but part of us always retains that small rabbit heart, trembling furiously, secretively, with wonder and fear. There's no irony in it. No semantics or subtext. Only red blood and green grass and silver stars.

"Don't be afraid," Evan said. "We're in this together, hand in hand, against the world."

He was holding mine, and I thought of that moment in August when we teetered a hundred feet above oblivion, my fear spread out across the night, waiting to devour me. The way I'd held his hand and laughed in its face.

"Here's looking at you, kid," he said.

And he kissed me.

And we lived happily ever after.

———

Until the next morning.

I woke early, told him I had errands to run, and left the warm haven of his bed for the rough cold world outside. I didn't mention Hiyam. How I couldn't trust her to keep mum even if I did her bidding. How the thought of him ever having to step into a courtroom because of me made me sick. I'd put him in enough danger.

The right thing to do now was to walk away. Sever it cleanly.

I didn't let myself think of it as the last time, or I never would've been able to step through the door. When Ilsa got on that plane, I don't think she thought of it as the last time, either. We never do. If we did, the airlines would go out of business. It's always *good-bye* with the mouth and *until we meet again* with the heart.

I walked home, my chest feeling weird, heavy and light at the same time. I stood in the living room doorway where Mom had stood homecoming night, looking at the couch. I'd known I was in love with him that night, but he wouldn't let me say it. People know their feelings much sooner than they consciously accept them.

When did you realize you were in love with me, Mr. Wilke?

Mom's bedroom door opened soundlessly. I had years of practicing my ninja skills on her. She lay facedown on the pillow, her snore like a saw going at aged oak even through three inches of cotton. I padded over to the nightstand and picked up her phone.

Five minutes later, I had a brunch date.

———

"Pleasure to see you again, Maise," Gary Rivero said.

I let him take my hand and squeeze. Cool bluish light fell over us, bright but heatless. The white tablecloth glowed like snow. Quinn sat at an adjacent table and nodded at me, his scalp shining through his crew cut.

"Thanks for sending a cab," I said.

Gary gave a gracious shrug. He wore a charcoal gray suit and pink shirt today, his hair a wave of brushed metal. His seawater eyes always seemed to be smiling even when his mouth wasn't.

"I was surprised, and delighted, to hear from you," he said.

Silverware clinked musically across the restaurant. Rich aromas of frying butter and bacon grease drifted from the kitchen. We'd been seated in an empty area; Gary had some understanding with the staff.

"I've been thinking about our talk," I said. I knew I

shouldn't be too specific. Discussing business with these people was an art of subtlety and doublespeak. "And I may have a solution to that problem you mentioned."

"That's fine," Gary said, sipping his coffee. "But we can talk about that later." He smiled, put his cup down, and peered at my face searchingly. "I'd like to know more about you, Maise."

I stirred sugar into my cup. "What is it you'd like to know, Mr. Rivero? What I look like naked? How much it'll cost you to sleep with me?" I tapped my spoon, set it down. "Those things are never going to happen. That's where my boundaries are. Are we clear?"

"I don't think you understand. If I wanted those things, they *would* happen, sweetheart. But I don't. All I want is to get to know you as a person."

I hoped he couldn't see me swallow. I took a sip of my sugar-and-cream coffee.

"So," he said, "let's talk to each other like human beings. What kind of person are you?"

"Trustworthy."

Gary's mouth quirked wryly. "Everyone says they're trustworthy. You may as well tell me you're breathing."

I thought of Wesley betraying me, the sinking weight it had left in my stomach. "In my case, it's true. I can prove it."

"And how is that?" Gary said, signaling for the waiter.

"By showing you I can keep a secret." I took a breath. "I've been keeping a big one for the past few months. A dangerous one. It could send someone to jail."

Gary lifted his hand again, this time telling the waiter to back off. His eyes stayed laser-focused on me. "What secret is that, sweetheart?"

I could not believe the first person I would legitimately

tell about this was a fucking drug lord, but exactly which part of my life so far has been anything near normal?

"I'm having an affair with my teacher," I said.

And I told him the whole thing. It just spilled out of me, as if I'd been waiting, dying, to tell someone, and although I was slightly horrified at myself, it felt so fucking relieving to finally get it out. This man had no actual interest in my life. It was like talking to a psychiatrist, or a priest. A blessed unburdening. I omitted Wesley and Hiyam, of course, and when I was done Gary drank his now-cold coffee and sat back with a new look in his eyes.

"I have a daughter your age," he said. "If any man did that to her, I'd kill him."

Some dads make threats to prove they're doing their job of caring. In Mr. Rivero's case, I'm pretty sure he meant it literally.

"Do you believe me now?" I said.

"Do I believe you're trustworthy? No." He tapped a finger on the table. "Trust is something you earn by actions, not words. But I do believe you can keep your mouth shut, and that suits me." He signaled the waiter again, and said, "I never talk business while I'm hungry, Maise. So let's eat."

———

I made it through the entire day without reading Evan's texts. But that night in bed, I felt like a million wires were hooked into my skin, pulling me in every direction. I slipped a hoodie on and climbed onto the gentle slope of the roof outside my window, laying back on the shingles, Garbage's "Beloved Freak" on repeat in my earbuds. Ice at the base of my neck, exploding hydrogen and new galaxies being born a hundred billion miles above me.

Hiyam won. It was over with Evan, just like that, in one apocalyptic afternoon.

My fist hit the shingles and fire shot up my nerves. I raised my hand: blood welled black in the starlight. Then I screamed at the sky, wordless, meaningless, raw animal pain, and the stars shook with light.

Fuck all of this, I thought. Fuck how I've lost everything good in my life. Fuck how everyone uses me, abandons me, throws me away. Fuck how I use them and abandon them because I don't know any better.

Tonight we were supposed to be in Chicago, in the great silver city by the lake.

Fuck you, Wesley. And fuck you, Mom, and fuck you, Dad, and fuck you, Hiyam.

Fuck you, Siobhan, for not teaching your son better.

And fuck you, Evan. Fuck you for being my teacher. Fuck you for letting me fall in love with you. Fuck you for existing.

I couldn't lie still any longer. I stood, balancing precariously in my socks on the freezing shingles, and crept to the edge to look at the starlit yard below, a duotone landscape of blue shadow and white frost, my ghost-bodied breath swirling over the emptiness. The grass looked soft, like dark velvet. The odds of dying from a twenty-foot fall were pretty low. Why not? I thought. Why not just let go, trust the Earth to catch me? Why not take the risk of getting a subdural hematoma and dying in my sleep? Sweet dreams forever, little girl.

You have a lion's heart. You're not afraid to live.

Goddamn him. He was right.

I sat on the roof's edge, my legs dangling over the yard, my heart hanging over infinity, and sang to myself and the silent night.

That week, I buried myself in college apps and ignored my phone. The only person I planned to answer was Gary. Evan texted, called, emailed, and on Wednesday finally showed up at the house. I walked onto the porch in my socks and pajamas and told him, without crying, that I couldn't see him anymore. He asked in a soft, heartbreaking voice if I wanted to go talk somewhere and I declined in what might have been coherent English and closed the door. I made it all the way to my room, to my desk, shaking the whole time, before I lost it.

Wednesday and Thursday were a blur. I was a quantum haze of probability. The likeliness of a girl crying her heart out.

On Friday I broke down and walked to his apartment, but his car was gone. I waited for hours in the cold, refusing to call, at first very Serious and Stoic but eventually so bored I made snow angels and threw slushballs at his balcony. For some reason I was fixated on the idea of explaining everything to him in person. Calling seemed too needy.

This was the kind of logic I was operating on: none.

I went back Saturday morning and his car was still gone. He had to be in St. Louis.

Gary had given me a small stipend for "business expenses." I took a cab to Carbondale and spent the day in the mall, watching the ashen, dead-eyed Christmas shoppers with my headphones on, waiting for the midnight Greyhound.

I kept falling asleep on the bus, drifting in and out of a reverie of reunion, apologizing, telling him about the blackmail, figuring out some brilliant plan where we could still be together. Mostly I focused on how it would feel to touch him again, to be held by warm solid smoke. I tried to think of his face but it was all shadow and fog. When I got off in STL I felt like I was walking on the moon, everything freezing and too bright, my body floating over the pavement. I shivered the entire taxi ride. I could see the loft lights from the street, and a huge weight rolled off me.

Thank you, Jesus.

I ran to the elevator, my breath clouding inside the cage. My heart beat wildly as I opened the front door.

Movie cliché: I walk in on him with another woman.

Reality: I walk in on a stranger with another woman.

A guy I'd never seen before looked up at me in shock from the couch. Behind him, a woman turned away, straightening her dress.

"Oh," I said, standing there like an idiot. "I'm sorry."

The guy got up and moved toward me swiftly. Short, around my height. He was Asian, tanned, spiky black hair, light goatee. And totally ripped, muscle bulging beneath his tight silk shirt and jeans.

"Can I help you?" he said with strained politeness.

"I'm sorry," I repeated. "I was looking for Evan."

The man frowned. "Who?"

"It's the weekend," I said helplessly, starting to back up. "We're usually here. I thought—"

A light went on in the guy's eyes. "Oh, shit. You're Eric's girlfriend. Right?"

I stopped backing up. In my head, every single neuron swiveled a spotlight on that word.

Eric.

"Right," I said slowly. "Eric Wilke."

And I heard Evan's voice in my head saying, *Now I was her only child.*

The guy's posture relaxed. "He said he was going out of town this weekend. I didn't know you'd be here."

"We must have miscommunicated," I said glibly, amazed at my poise when my brain was screeching with static. "I'm sorry to interrupt your evening."

The woman came up behind the guy, touching his arm. "Park?"

"It's okay, honey," Asian Guy said. "Just a mix-up. This is my buddy's girlfriend . . ."

He raised his eyebrows at me.

"Maise," I said. "I'm sorry, I—"

"Come in," he said, stepping aside. "Please. I'm Park. Jun-yeong, but everyone calls me Park. This is Kara."

Kara, bleach-blond and tan, her boobs squeezing out of her tube dress like toothpaste, kept her eyes on me. I must have looked pitiful, shivering and bedraggled, drained from days of weeping and bone-breaking angst like some consumptive Victorian heroine, but still she stared at me as if I might run off with her boyfriend any minute.

Focus on Kara and her ridiculous boobs. Focus on anything but the horror building in me.

Park led me to the kitchen. "Cocoa," he said, "tea, coffee? Or there's some bourbon—" He turned around and gave me a funny look. "Are you old enough to drink?"

"Twenty-one," I said smoothly.

Kara raised her eyebrows. Kara didn't look much older than twenty-one herself.

"What's your poison?" Park said.

"Tea, please." I desperately wanted alcohol, but getting drunk around strangers was never smart.

Kara's phone rang. She left the kitchen to answer it.

"I'm really sorry," I told Park. My voice sounded like a

recording, tinny and small. "I didn't mean to ruin your evening."

"Actually," he whispered, "let's hope that's a 'friend' who has an 'emergency.'" He widened his eyes.

Kara called him over. He set a mug on the counter.

"Excuse me."

I warmed my hands on the cup. My head felt like a shattered mug that had been inexpertly glued back together, and now it was leaking something scalding.

"I've got to go," Kara hissed, loud enough for me to hear. "Jen's having an emergency. And I'm not into babysitting teenagers."

"Okay, honey. I'm sorry about this. I'll call."

Kissing sounds. Kara moaned—for my benefit, I thought. The door closed, and Park reappeared in the kitchen, rolling his eyes in relief.

"You don't like your girlfriend?" I said.

"I've been trying to break it off for, like, three weeks."

"How long have you been seeing her?"

"Three weeks."

I laughed, maybe too harshly.

Park poured himself a rum and Coke and sat one stool away from me. "Things going bad with you and Eric?"

God, it was like a bullet in the chest every time. "What makes you say that?"

"Well, you showed up without him. And you didn't know he's in Chicago this weekend."

Chicago. Chicago.

"I don't know what's going on," I said emptily.

Park took a drink, looked at me, took another drink, and then said, "How old are you really?"

"Eighteen."

"Shit," he said. "High school?"

This gave me a feeling of mortal dread. "Does it matter?"

He rubbed a hand over the back of his neck. "What did you call him, when you came in?"

"Who?" I said. "Eric?" Maybe he'd forget.

"You called him something else."

I turned to face this stranger. I could smell his cologne, hard and clean and slightly alcoholic. Despite being built like a brick shithouse, there was something innocent and soft in his face. It made me not want to lie to him.

"I called him Evan," I said.

Park's eyes scanned me rapidly. "Are you in trouble?"

"What trouble?"

"Are you pregnant?"

I'm pretty sure my eyebrows briefly touched the roof. "No. Jesus, what kind of question is that?"

"Sorry. Had to ask." Park took another drink. "Did you drive up here?"

"Greyhound."

He nodded. "Okay. It's pretty late. I'm going to head home. I have another place downtown. You can stay here tonight." He took his phone out. "I'll give you my number. Just in case."

He even made sure I had enough money to get home in the morning. So much for The Friend being "kind of a douchebag." Another lie, I guess. When Park looked at me, there was something sad in his eyes. I refused to see it as pity.

Then I was alone in this apartment where I had fallen in love with a man who didn't exist.

At first I curled up in bed, but I felt like I was going to vomit. So I dragged a blanket to the couch, but we'd had sex there, too. And in the bathroom, and the kitchen, and pretty much everywhere in this fucking place.

I started to cry, standing in the middle of the loft, surrounded by memories.

No. Fuck that.

I booted the PC in the small office area. Guest log-in. Browser window. Google search: *eric wilke westchester illinois.*

His face.

A hundred different photos of him, thirty-something, twenty-something, teen-something. Him in high school: debate team, drama club (not lying about being a nerd). College at NU (also not a lie). Then back to high school, to teach. Awards. Honors. Regional competitions. And for what? What class did he teach?

Acting.

There was no brother. Not even an identical twin. This wasn't the fucking Syfy channel. He had been Eric. Now he was Evan.

Why? And why did he lie about it? What else had he lied about?

Where does he go on his days off and why does he sit in his car for hours, talking to himself?

Jesus, was this going to be some *Silence of the Lambs* shit? Did I really want to know what was eating Eric/Evan Wilke?

Yes. Of course I did.

———

I want to talk, I texted him Monday. *Can I come over?*

Yes. Should I pick you up?

I'll walk.

I took my time. If following Hiyam felt like walking to my execution, this was like walking to my own funeral. When I stepped up to the coffin and peered inside, I was pretty sure I'd see the big bloody red thing currently throbbing in my chest.

There was snow on my shoes when I stood at his door, trickling into the carpet, staining it like ink. I thought of Ilsa's letter and the ink running in the rain.

The man who opened the door had a scruffy beard, dark circles like camera lenses around his eyes, and the thousand-yard stare of a frightened little boy.

Turn around, I thought. Run. This is going to hurt. There's no point.

I stepped inside.

Signs of depression: dishes piled in a Jenga tower in the sink; dirty glasses on the coffee table next to the empty Old Forester; the fact that he was in pajamas at two p.m. and had some kind of echidna growing on his face.

"You're living like a slob, Eric," I said.

He didn't flinch. His brow furrowed, his eyes tightening into that beautiful squint. I turned away.

"I talked to Park," I said.

"I know."

"So let's hear it," I said, walking around, poking at things, tickling the garland on the Christmas tree and making it shiver with a furry sound. "Let's hear your sob story. Should I make popcorn?"

"I want you to know something first," he said. "I never—"

"Stop." I spun around, staring at him with my jaw set. "Don't soften me up. Just tell me."

He walked toward me, palms up, pleading, so ridiculous and disheveled and heartbreaking in the cold afternoon light.

"It's not that simple, Maise. There's so much—"

"Let's make it simple," I said, crossing my arms. "Tell me why you lied about your name."

He opened his mouth, shook his head. Swallowed. Started to speak again and stopped. God, how do you ever plan to teach a speech class? I thought.

"I didn't lie," he said at last. "I had it changed legally."

"Is that why you were in court that day?"

"Yes."

"Why did you change it?"

He swallowed again. "There's a situation I needed to separate myself from."

"Jesus. Stop talking in circles and just tell me—"

"I had a relationship with a student."

My arms unfolded of their own will. The ruby in my chest finally split. I stood there full of released light and blood and a hundred crimson shards.

"It was two years ago," he said. "It was completely over when I met you. But it ended badly, and the student had some—issues with me."

The student. The student.

"A high school girl," I said.

"Yes."

"How old?"

He sighed, long and deep. His shoulders had a concave, defensive arc. "Seventeen when it started. Eighteen when it ended."

I didn't really care about her age. I was trying to work up to the "issues."

"What happened?"

He spoke to the floor. "She was infatuated with me. And I made a huge mistake in returning it. I kept telling myself it was just a crush, an emotional affair, that it would never go farther than that. But I was lying to myself. I let it get to the point where we could act on it, and we did. One time."

"And someone found out?" I said, amazed by my detachment.

"No."

"So why—" My mouth fell open. It hit me as he said it.

"She got pregnant."

"Oh my fucking god," I said, my voice suddenly way too loud, way too big for this sad little scene. "Do you have a kid?"

"No," he said. "No, Maise." He only managed to look at me in slivers of glances, like knife slashes.

"What happened to it?"

"She miscarried."

I was going to throw up. "Jesus fuck, Evan. Eric. Whoever you fucking are."

"I didn't abandon her," he said quickly. "She was eighteen when it happened and we talked it over and I told her I'd do whatever she wanted. I was ready to accept all consequences. Her parents, the school, the police, whatever. But she cut me off, and I thought that was it. I resigned. I moved away. And then she came after me. Her friends knew about it, and they tried to make my life hell. Like it wasn't already."

I laughed, dry and hoarse and cruel. "So you changed your name and started over here, so you could do it all over again."

"No," he said earnestly. "Don't you understand? That's why I was so careful with you. Why I kept asking your age."

"You didn't care about my age," I said, spitting the words. "You just cared about not coming inside me."

He lowered his face, his eyes closing as if he was in pain.

"God," I said. For an insane moment I wanted to tear

down the Christmas tree, rip it to shreds. Destroy something beautiful, the way a child would. "I'm so fucking stupid. I thought we had an actual connection. I thought you saw me for who I really am. I'm so fucking gullible I actually convinced myself I was special."

"You are special," he said softly.

"No. I'm just young." I put my hand on an ornament, metallic red, fragile and cool as ice, and squeezed and squeezed until it popped and the shards stabbed into my skin. "You know what? You *are* an amazing actor. I never once doubted you were this character you're playing."

"I know this is a lot for you to process," he said.

I laughed again. "It really is. Did you go see her? Is that why you were in Chicago?"

"No."

"Why were you in Chicago? Where have you been going when you're not with me?"

His brow creased.

"Wesley saw you," I said. "In your car. Talking to yourself."

"He was *watching* me?"

"God, please. You don't get to be offended right now."

"I was rehearsing," he said, not looking at my face. "For talking to my mother. Because you made me realize I didn't want to carry this darkness around the rest of my life." He shook his head, still not facing me. "And Wesley was watching, and reporting to you. That's great. That's really normal and healthy, Maise."

I ground the shards into my palm. "I didn't fucking know. And you should talk about normal and healthy, *Eric*."

"I think we should take some time apart. To process all of this."

"You think *I* should take some time, while you sit here feeling sorry for yourself for seducing another student."

"I didn't know you were in school."

I walked toward him, flinging blood-edged shards onto the carpet. "Isn't that the first fucking thing you should've asked? 'Hi, I'm a teacher and I knocked up a student. Are you in high school?'"

He looked at me now, but his face was all self-pity. "You didn't seem that young. When I talked to you, it was like talking to someone I'd known my whole life."

"Oh my god. Is that the same line you used on her?"

"I didn't use any fucking line on her," he snapped. Good, I thought. Get mad. Show me you have actual emotions beyond regret that you got caught. "She came on to me, Maise. I'm not saying it wasn't my fault, but it wasn't equal. Not like us. She wanted someone to adore, and I let my ego get out of control. It was a mistake. You were never a mistake."

I didn't want to hear any more of this. I wanted to go home.

I started for the door and he didn't lift a finger to stop me. Didn't even speak. I stopped with my hand on the cold knob, breathing crazily hard.

"There's something I want you to know," I said without turning around. "This is the biggest thing that's ever happened to me. You, and all of this. You changed my life. Who I am. How I think and feel and see the world." I breathed out through my teeth. "But to you I'm just another student you fucked. The one you didn't knock up. I guess that's why this was never going to work. We're *not* equal."

I slammed his door behind me the way I'd wanted to in class. Somehow I made it to the bottom of the stairs without falling or throwing myself down them, through the door without punching the glass out, to my room and my bed without harming myself or others, and then I felt something stinging my hand and looked down at the mess of red glitter and bloody splinters in my palm, and I finally started crying.

———

Black days. Days when I stayed up until four, five in the morning, slept till afternoon, got up only to exhaust myself enough to sleep again, dozing in and out until dawn. I did not want to be awake. Awake meant crying like a baby, a pathetic quivering puddle of saltwater and skin. Wesleypedia once told me that the heart and brain are 73 percent water. Even our bones are full of it. It made sense, then, why I couldn't stop fucking crying. My body was made from this stuff. Hydrogen, the same thing stars burned to shine, smashing atoms together until they fused in a brilliant burst of light, the same thing it felt like my heart was doing to the water inside me.

———

On New Year's Eve, Hiyam sent her driver to pick me up. In her bedroom, surrounded by peach satin and white wicker and the virginal flora of girl perfume, I sold her an eight ball for two Cs. She said I was robbing her until I watched her do a line off a hand mirror, her eyes switching on like lightbulbs, bright and empty. Hollow glass.

"Fuck me. Oh, fuck me." She sat back, laughing. "God, O'Malley. Get me more."

I went home and slept through the turning of the year.

On the first day of second semester, I stood outside Room 209 with Hiyam and a few other kids while the third-period bell rang. The class was dark, the door locked. A note taped to it read:

Film Studies has been discontinued. Please see your guidance counselor for course reassignment.

Hiyam raised an eyebrow at me, smirking. In an alternate universe, I pushed her off the roof.

After school, I went to his apartment. His car wasn't in the lot. His name had been scraped off the mailbox. No Christmas lights on his balcony.

He was gone.

I walked home in a daze, so out of it I didn't even notice what was sitting on the doormat until I accidentally kicked it.

Louis, the sad little pony, looking at me dolefully with his too-human eyes.

I picked him up and sank to my knees, hugging him to my chest.

JANUARY.
   Dull. Gray. Dead.
   I spent lunches in the library writing college application essays. Sometimes Britt would join me. Sometimes she would ask, timorously, about Mr. Wilke. She'd heard he'd gone to another school. She'd always thought he was so nice. I stared at her as if she was talking about a stranger.

   She was.

   Hiyam and I ended up in Art Appreciation together. When she asked if I wanted to hang out after school, I laughed in her face, loud and cold, and for a moment she actually looked hurt. Then she smiled and said, "You bitch," in a way that was both scoffing and admiring.

   Every now and then I'd pass Wesley in the halls. He kept his head down, but he was too tall to hide. I looked at him and felt nothing. No hate, no regret. Just dull gray deadness.

Hiyam kept pushing me for larger amounts of coke. I told her no. Gary had prepped me for this: if I ever got caught, I wanted to be charged with possession, not intent to deliver. Both were felonies, but possession for a first-time offender would likely result in probation. Anything more than an eight ball would look like intent to deliver. Plus he didn't trust me with that much powdered cash.

"You're a smart girl, sweetheart," he said when I met him in a restaurant, "and that's why I don't trust you. You'd rip me off and disappear, and you're clever enough to get away with it."

He asked what I thought of his product, and I told him I had no idea. I didn't use. This made his eyebrows go up.

"*Very* smart girl," he said.

Now that my two-faced teacher was gone, I could've stopped dealing. Hiyam was no threat. But part of me thought: Fuck it. I'd never gotten a call back from all those job apps. Wesley, whose family had money, who had the luxury of stalking me with his expensive camera, was the one who got a job. I got fuck-all and a mom who stole my college fund. The universe seemed intent on presenting me with narrow, unsavory options. Maybe it was time I accepted it.

For a horrifying moment, I could understand how my mother made certain choices. Sometimes life just shoveled endless shit in your face until you threw down your spade and said, *Fuck it, I'll find another way.*

I sat in my classes, staring at the bleak brown landscape pulverized by snow, decaying from the inside. With Him, winter had been glitter and auroras and feathery snowflakes falling out of the sky. Now it was smashed up and filthy, banal. Rust and rot and endless gray.

Things I didn't expect to do my senior year:

Become a drug dealer.

Become my mother.

Find and lose the love of my life.

———

One Saturday I went downstairs and Wesley was sitting in my living room.

"The fuck is this?" I said.

"Babe," Mom said, "he says he wants to apologize."

"Maise," Wesley called.

I was halfway back up to my room. "What," I said. Not a question. The banister creaked under my hand.

"You have every right to hate me. What I did was wrong, okay? Really, really wrong. I'm sorry. Can I talk to you, please?"

Mom stood watching us both with interest.

"This isn't a soap opera," I snapped at her. "Go amuse yourself elsewhere."

Her eyes narrowed dangerously, but Wesley's pleading look assuaged her. She wandered into the kitchen.

"So talk," I said.

"Here?"

"Do you want to come up to my room? Do you want to pet my hair and put your arm around me and tell me it's all right? Just say whatever the fuck you have to say."

Wesley grimaced, shrugging uncomfortably in his duffel coat. "Look, I know there's no excuse, okay? But I want you to know I'm sorry, and I feel like shit." He lowered his voice. "I thought he was using you. Hurting you. I guess I wanted to see it that way, and I tried to make you see that, too. It was wrong and I'm sorry, Maise."

I stared at the wallpaper running along the stairwell. In normal families, there'd be pictures here. Mom and Dad.

Nan and Pop. Beloved daughter. Our wallpaper just had a yellowish film of cigarette smoke.

"Why were you at the carnival that night?"

"Summer job. I ran the darts booth."

I laughed. I'd probably looked right at him and not given him a second thought.

"Why didn't you tell me?" I said, glancing at him. "You always knew it was Evan."

I still thought of him as Evan. It was his middle name, according to Google.

"I don't know." Wesley sighed, cheeks puffing out, hair flopping over his eyes. "Because it was your secret. I wanted you to tell me yourself. I wanted you to trust me with it."

"You didn't deserve my trust," I said.

He looked at the stairs.

"This is all moot anyway. I've got to study."

Wesley wiped a hand across his cheeks.

Oh my god. Was he actually *crying*?

"You were right," he said, still facing the stairs, his voice deep and shaky. "You were right when you said you're my only friend. You're the only person I care about who's not family. I don't expect you to ever trust me again, but I'm sorry. I miss you. Mom misses you. She was so pissed—don't worry, I didn't mention Mr. Wilke, but she's told me how stupid I am a million times." He sniffed. "I wish I could undo it. I put your private life on display for everyone. I thought I was saving you but I was just being a fucking creep. It's messed up. I know that. I'm sorry."

He finally raised his head but managed to face only the banister, not me. His eyes were glassy, a sheen of wetness on his cheeks.

"It's not an excuse, but you're right. I'm younger than

you, Maise. Way younger. You're years and years ahead. And
I didn't mean to hurt you or screw things up with him. I'm
just a fucking idiot kid."

He swallowed, his Adam's apple bobbing.

I swallowed, too. My throat and the back of my eyes felt
tight, pinched. "Siobhan didn't call you stupid. I know her.
She probably called your actions stupid."

"Isn't that what I said, Captain Obvious?" he muttered
miserably.

I stared at him. "No," I said, and started to laugh. "You
didn't, you sorry asshole." My laughter died as quickly as it
had come. "You didn't screw it up with me and Evan. You
were right about him."

Wesley finally looked at me.

"He isn't who I thought he was. And I guess I'm not who I
thought I was, either." I shook my head. "You know who I am?"

"Who?"

"Same as you. A fucking idiot kid."

———

Slowly, over weeks, Wesley and I started talking again. Eating lunch together, sometimes walking for miles when the
roads were plowed, the fields flat and quilted with snow, our
breath trailing mist as we talked about postgraduation plans.
Siobhan invited me over for Valentine's Day dinner and I
melted into her arms, struggling not to cry. She didn't say
a word about Evan but I knew she understood everything,
and just seeing her, this amazing person I looked up to who'd
survived her own affair with a teacher, was enough.

"To the only love that lasts," she said when we raised our
champagne glasses. "The love of family and friends."

I clinked my glass with theirs, but it rang hollowly.

Hiyam's audacity knew no limits.

"I've got big plans for spring break, O'Malley," she said as we sat in the back of Art Appreciation, waiting for the bell. "I need you to come through for me."

She hooked her elbows over the back of my chair, leaning close to my ear.

"Get me a key."

I burst out laughing. "You're hilarious."

"I'm totally fucking serious," she hissed, scraping a fingernail against my jaw. "You know what kind of cut you'll get? You and your creepy boyfriend could move to Hollywood."

She had taken to calling Wesley my creepy boyfriend.

I turned around. "There is no reality, parallel or otherwise, in which I would do this. You're delusional."

"I'm disappointed, O'Malley. I thought the chance to blow this shithole would appeal to you."

"It does. But I don't believe even you have that kind of money."

Her face turned sly and vulpine. "That's where you're wrong."

"Right. Your dad'll just let you take twenty grand out of your trust fund."

"I've been withdrawing small amounts for years. I've got thirty K he doesn't even know about."

I rolled my eyes. "Whatever. I'm not risking my life for your *Scarface* fantasies."

"You should reconsider," she said, leaning forward, "or I'll have to reconsider whether this arrangement is working out."

I stared her dead in the eyes. "He's gone. I haven't seen him in months. That threat means nothing to me."

"I didn't mean him going to jail," Hiyam said, smiling. "I meant you."

"Hiyam's blackmailing me again," I said to Wesley as we sat on milk crates up in the water tower. "She's threatening to narc."

I'd told him everything that had happened with Evan, including the blackmail and dealing. He listened without judgment. He said it would make an incredible movie. I couldn't disagree. We spent hours thinking up titles. *Snow Globe City. The Lights Every Night. Unteachable.* In a way, this was his penance for stalking me: acknowledging the secret I'd bottled inside for so long. Listening to me crying, laughing, raging, sighing over it. I could finally talk openly with someone who knew me, who knew how much of my life it had consumed. Now that I hadn't seen Evan in months and had started to forget the feel of his body, the chemical trance it had put me in, the thing I missed most was simply hanging out with him. Watching movies together. Walking through St. Louis, pretending to be characters from films. Staying up all night talking in bed. The way we'd be sitting silently in the car or a theater and see something ridiculous and look over at each other, smiling. The way we'd look at each other in class, through the absurdity of the lives we had to live, and sigh, knowing we'd be in each other's arms that night.

I missed the mundane things most. The precious minutiae I'd taken for granted.

Wesley had asked why I still wore the Claddagh ring if it was over, and I stared at it, not even realizing. I'd taken it off but kept it in my pocket, touching it sometimes, like a talisman.

"How can she narc on you when she's the buyer?" he said now, shooting a stream of clove smoke at my face.

I chipped at the ice on the driftwood with my shoe. It was so cold my eyelashes felt like a brittle fringe of frost that could crumble away in the wind. "I don't know, but I need to get out of this. It's like I'm in the middle of *Goodfellas*. This is way too serious to be my life, Wesley."

From up here the world was white on white: white ground, white sky, the clouds shining mutedly and rippling with silver like mother-of-pearl. There was a crystalline tension in the ground waiting to be shattered, all the buried living things raring to burst free and breathe again. That same feeling was in me. I was tired of this chrysalis of ice and frozen tears. I wanted out. I wanted to feel the sun again.

Wesley had taken Computer Animation as his art elective. He didn't have a camera glued to his eye anymore—now he was always lugging his laptop around, doing kinetic typography: text unfolding and cascading and flipping, word into word, a visual poem. I was pretty sure he'd shifted focus because of me and the stalking. I knew he missed looking at the world through a lens.

"Hey," I said. "I just got an idea."

"You have that crazy Irish glint in your eyes."

I leaned toward him, doing my best Gary Rivero. "I've got a job for you, sweetheart."

"Maise, I'm your friend, but I am not getting involved in the trafficking of controlled substances."

"No," I said. "I need your particular skill set. And more importantly, your willingness to be a creep."

He shrugged self-consciously. "What did you have in mind?"

————

March. Acceptance letters. A small pile of cash growing in my private bank account. A dream of freedom and Southern California sun.

And always, in my pocket, in my skin, in the back of my mind, the hollowness where he used to be. The empty circle where my finger used to fit into the ring. The crimson flakes and ruby dust strewn across the ledges of my ribs.

There were words for this feeling, but none of them conveyed the bone-deep ache of it, the grinding of cell against cell. It pulled my body into itself, a black hole consuming me from the inside, turning my bones supermassive, as heavy as I was on the Gravitron that night. When I thought I would finally collapse into myself I realized it was him, pulling at me. My skin stretched tight. My heart pressed right up against the bars of my ribs. I lay in the snow and watched the stars and even the Earth wasn't strong enough to hold me down. A greater gravity pulled at me. And pulled. And pulled.

————

It was a strange-looking building, more like an aerospace firm than a high school, steel struts curving gently against the sky with a sense of unfolding wings. The campus was huge, and I spent nearly an hour walking around before I found the car I wanted. I was cold in my wool leggings and skirt and light coat. I caught my reflection in a car window: the bones of my face too prominent, too chiseled, the hollows faintly violet. Not eating well. Not sleeping enough. The cold got in because there wasn't enough stuff between my bones and skin, just nerves hanging like spiderwebs, silvery and thin, undisturbed.

I sat on the hood of the car like I had a lifetime ago.

Kids milled around the lot, yelling and laughing. Two cheerleaders walked past, one brown-skinned and one tan, ultrawhite fluoride smiles. Go Terriers, I thought.

He wasn't paying attention and didn't notice me until he was a dozen feet away.

He stopped, the tension in him slowly unraveling until he stood there, slack and shocked. Jeans, dress shirt, blazer. Smooth-shaven, his hair shorter than it used to be. That face I had been seeing in my dreams.

I swallowed as he walked toward me. His eyes never left mine. The closer he got the more bewildered he looked, and I thought, ridiculously, He doesn't recognize me, but he dropped his messenger bag on the ground and raised his arms and I slid off the hood and hugged him, viciously. We stood like that for a long time. My eyes were closed. I breathed too deeply, drinking in the familiar smell of him, insanely thinking I could hold it in me, preserve it. The chest rising and falling against mine felt like warm summer earth, radiating stored sunlight into my bones. I never wanted to move again.

After a minute or forever or two he leaned back and looked at me, still wearing that bewildered expression.

"Hi," he said in a soft voice, half breath.

The last three months of my life rose into the air and dissolved like mist.

"Hi," I said.

He touched my hair gingerly, let his hand drop. Pulled me close again, then leaned away and touched my face. He couldn't seem to figure out where the proper boundary was.

Answer: there wasn't one.

He unlocked the passenger door and looked at me and I got in. I closed my eyes again as he picked up his bag and came around. The car smelled so much like him, like warm suede and candle smoke. Like home.

I had promised myself not to cry until I'd said something appropriately dramatic, but I was about to break that promise.

Evan got in, still amazed/bewildered/stunned, and saw my face. He reached for me.

Then I was incoherent for the next ten minutes, sobbing my stupid heart out, clinging to his jacket, saying, "I'm sorry, I'm ruining your jacket," and when he laughed that beautiful kind laugh and said, "Ruin it, it's yours," I cried even harder, accepting his invitation.

It's somehow a lot easier to be courageous when you're a weeping mess. When the waterworks stopped I slid away, burying my face in a tissue, everything a million percent more awkward. I had utterly forgotten why I was here. I had just wanted—needed—to see him, to touch a little, verify his existence. Well, mission fucking accomplished. Now what?

Evan seemed to sense this and started the engine.

He drove aimlessly for a while, glancing at me with giddy confusion.

"Do you want to get some coffee?" he said.

Slow head shake. Meaningful eye contact.

His gaze lingered on me. Then it shifted back to the windshield and stayed there.

He pulled up to an apartment complex. I followed him upstairs. We didn't speak. Dingy white walls, boxes on the floor. An unlived-in feeling. He walked straight to the fridge and took out two bottles of Blue Moon and leaned there while I leaned on the counter across from him. We each took exactly one sip before we put them down and met in the middle of the kitchen. He clasped my face in his hands, his thumbs hard against my cheekbones, holding me still as he kissed me so, so lightly, as if pressing his lips to a dandelion whose seeds he might accidentally scatter.

Then he stopped, looking at me.

For three months I had forgotten what the sweet hot rush of blood in my veins felt like. How alive my body was, not only in the obvious places but in my thriving red marrow, the chill prickling my scalp, the curl of my toes. I'd become as numb as if I was the one snorting all that coke. When Evan touched me I became aware of kitten-soft wool rubbing against my shins, the fine hair on my forearms standing on end, his hands unbuttoning my coat as gently and intently as if removing a bandage.

"Wait," I said. "No."

His hands dropped.

God, what was I doing? What was this? I took a step back, walked out of the kitchen and through the apartment. It looked like an art gallery without art. Geometrical patterns of light and shadow slapped across white paint and hardwood. I went through every room, seeking signs of life. Mattress on the bedroom carpet. Beer bottles lined up on windowsills. Shampoo, toothbrush, razor. My reflection in the bathroom mirror, mouth swollen and claret red, eyelashes lacquered with tears, more alive than anything else here.

"Is this what you wanted to see?" Evan said behind me. "My shell of a life?"

I turned around and walked past him. My footsteps echoed violently in the empty rooms. If I spoke too loudly, glass might shatter.

"I didn't come here to gloat," I said.

"Then why did you come?"

"I don't know." I turned again, hands raised. "To see how you're doing. If you like your new job."

"If I'm over you."

Yes. "No."

He stepped closer. His face was blank, his words a soft growl. "I'm not over you. I dream about you every night. I watch that fucking video over and over just to hear your voice. Does that make you happy? Is that proof I cared?"

This was the first time he'd ever seemed truly angry at me. I made my backbone iron, refusing to flinch. "No, I'm not happy. I'm fucking miserable. My life is a huge joke."

He walked off, paced a bit, came back.

"Don't do this," he said. "Don't come here to fuck with my head and play games. You don't test someone's love by leaving them." He rocked on his toes, his fingers clenching and unclenching. "It was so easy for you to end it. So god-damn easy. If I didn't know better, I'd think you used me. You had your fun playing at being an adult and then it got difficult and scary and you bailed."

My fist was in my coat pocket, trembling. "I didn't bail. I didn't go anywhere. You're the one who left." I started to laugh, humorlessly. "And it was difficult and scary from the fucking beginning, Evan. Wesley was right. He saw how messed up it was."

Evan laughed back, and his was cold. "You said you didn't know how to have a grown-up relationship. Well, here's your first lesson, Maise. When it gets hard, you don't run away."

"Save the lesson for your students. You're not my fucking teacher anymore."

We faced each other, blazing and feverish, a blade of hot

kitchen light slanting between us. Dusk bruised the apartment with deepening shadow. If I'd had a car, I would have stormed out. Calling a cab was a lot less dramatic.

"What are we doing?" he said suddenly, in a harsh whisper.

"Being stupid," I said.

"Yes."

I opened my fist in my pocket, letting the ring tumble out. I rubbed the smooth groove in my palm where it had marked me.

"I'm fucking starving," Evan said. "You want some dinner?"

"Yes."

We ate Chinese food on a blanket on the living room floor, using cardboard boxes as tables. He had to unpack a lamp. We split a carton of beef chow mein and finished our beers, then opened more, sitting across from each other and not touching except for when he handed me a bottle, and my arm tingled as if I'd hit my funny bone. Safe subjects: his new class (interesting, mostly about managing stage fright), my new class (boring, mostly about managing boredom). I told him how ridiculous it was being "friends" with Hiyam and he told me about his new students, one of whom was a dead ringer for Wesley ("Maybe he's outside right now, filming an exposé on us," I said, and we peered through the blinds, laughing, his hand brushing my leg). We laughed easily, effortlessly. It was all too absurd. There was really no choice. We carried the leftovers to the kitchen and I stood at the sink, rinsing my hands, and Evan came up behind me and breathed against my hair. I didn't move. Cold water on my skin, his heat on my neck. A live wire ran up my spine straight to my brain stem. I turned and he lifted my face and kissed me, and I let him, my wet hands falling to my sides. My chest felt tight and heavy. He let go and I dried my hands and kissed him again, harder. Beer and almond cookies. Buzzing fluorescent light, linoleum smacking beneath our shoes. My shoulder blades knocking against the fridge. The kiss grew intense and we stopped simultaneously, pulling away.

"What are we doing?" I said.

"Being stupid."

He didn't sound sincere. I swallowed.

"I should get home," I said, thinking, Ask me to stay.

He didn't say anything.

In the cab I clutched the ring so hard it felt like it was carving through my bones. I was almost home when my phone vibrated.

Come over this weekend, he texted.

Immediately, I replied, *Yes.*

When I got there Saturday afternoon, Evan and Park were carrying a couch up the front walk.

I ran to hold the door for them. Evan merely said hello, but Park grinned and winked at me. I navigated them up the stairs. Park brought up the bottom and pretended to doze off, bored, then snapped awake and did lift reps with his end of the couch, and I laughed.

"Show-off," Evan said, out of breath.

The apartment almost looked like an actual apartment now: tables, chairs, framed posters. Evan said he'd had his furniture in storage because he wasn't sure how long he'd be here. Our eyes caught and held for a moment, then I went to the kitchen to grab beers. The two of them stood there in a shaft of dust-spangled sun, sweaty T-shirts plastered to their torsos, tipping their throats back to guzzle longnecks, and I sat on a box with an appraising look. Park laughed and did a few bodybuilder poses, veins bulging, then went to shower.

"So you're staying here," I said to Evan.

"Not sure yet. But I think I'll live here a while, instead of merely surviving."

I looked away, sipping from my bottle. My other hand was buried in my pocket, clutching the ring.

Park showered like a marine. He was out in three minutes, immaculate and combat-ready. "Borrowed a shirt, E," he said. "I look better in it anyway."

Evan and I glanced at each other, smiling. "E" seemed to fit him. Both old and new.

Park took off for St. Louis, and I spent most of the day helping Evan get settled. The whole time I thought, Tell him. Tell him not to get comfortable. Tell him you're going. But I couldn't. He was starting to seem like his old self, relaxed, that flashbulb smile catching me unpredictably, always making something in me go still, dazzled. The light waned and we didn't touch the lamps. We sat on the couch in the last dregs of dusk, searing blood-red rays slowly cooling into cobalt. I lay against Evan's chest, my head moving slightly with his breath, as if drifting on gentle waves.

"I can't tell if this is a beginning or ending," he said.

"What does it feel like?"

"Both."

We ordered a margherita pizza and drank chianti and sat on the floor, watching indie films on his laptop until we became more interested in making out than watching. It was relaxed, too, not meant to lead to anything, slow and light and sweet, our mouths brushing and parting as if we kissed accidentally while trying to whisper to each other.

"Why did you leave me?" he said as I knelt over him, my knees astride his waist. The only light was the bluish glow from his laptop, painting us on one side. My hair coiled in dark tendrils around his neck.

"Because I saw us the way everyone else did. I thought I was just a type to you. Student. Young girl."

"Teacher," he said of himself. "Older man."

I shook my head, my hair rippling. "Why did you let me go?"

"I didn't want to." His voice was very soft, a contoured breath. "But every reason I had for holding on was selfish. And every time I felt weak, I watched Wesley's film, and saw what I'd done to you."

"You didn't do that. The situation did that. To both of us." I swallowed thickly. "It was more good than bad, Evan. Far more good."

He stroked the side of my face, the shadow of his arm moving over us. "Why did you come back?"

Because I love you, I thought. But I'm going to leave again in a few months. For good this time.

I was going to tell him. I really was. But he pulled me to him and kissed me, and the lightness of it became him lightly lifting my shirt and me shrugging it off as if it was smoke drifting away, then rolling down my leggings, unbuttoning his shirt, opening his fly. His dick was hard and hot in my hand and all the old feelings came flooding back, his solidity setting off a tripwire in me, a sudden intense vibration. He let me touch, his eyes closed, a faint groan coming out of him like he'd relinquished his hold on something delicate. I was in a trance. I wanted him but I was also outside myself, watching this happen to us. It was all me. My body atop his, my legs spreading, my fingers digging into his shoulders as I took him inside of me. The sound I made was full of pain and a sort of intolerable relief because I had missed this so much. It was less like fucking than nursing an ache, cradling him in that bruised, tender place inside me. I moved over him slowly, my bare knees burning on the cold wood floor. He still had his jeans on and they rubbed the insides of my thighs raw. The laptop cast our shadows on the wall and I turned my head, watching the slim, sinuous lines of my body joining to his, the rolling curve of my spine, my hair slithering and lashing like some strange spidery creature. He felt so thick inside me, so excessive. Pushing me to the limits of my skin. To the edge where my body met the world, where reality blurred with internal fiction, and I wasn't sure who I was anymore aside from hollowness and fullness, ache and relief, repeating over and over. It had been so long that I couldn't control myself, I started to come and gaped at him with a ridiculous look of surprise. His expression was serene, dreamy, the only change being his hands tightening on my hips when he came.

We stared at each other, motionless. Something flashed between us and broke open on his naked chest, leaving a glittering scar. A tiny diamond. Then another. Then another.

"Maise," he said, touching my wet face.

I couldn't stop. I pushed myself off him and folded my legs beneath me, his come running warmly between my thighs. I covered my face with my hands. He sat up and pulled me close, holding me. After a while I felt a hot point on the crown of my head, trickling down through my hair, and realized he was crying, too.

It was different afterward. I said good night without kissing him and tried to sleep on the couch, watching shadows tilt slowly across the room as the Earth turned beneath the stars, but when I was still awake at two in the morning I crept into his bedroom. He was awake, too, sitting up in the dark. Faint light drifted through the blinds like luminous breath, a sigh of night air. I climbed onto the mattress and sat beside him without touching. Our feet rested side by side.

"Can't sleep," I said.

"Me either. I kept thinking about you out there, wishing you were in here."

Tiny firefly wings flitted in my chest. I imagined my heart pulsing, a miniature red glow.

"Wish granted," I said. I kicked his foot, gently. "Remember the stepping stones in St. Louis?"

"We pretended to be pioneers on the Oregon Trail."

"You lost all your bullets and food. You had to eat the oxen."

"Yeah, but you died of dysentery."

I laughed. "Live hard, die young, leave a disgusting corpse."

He kicked my foot back. "Heard from any colleges yet?"

Deep breath. I faced him.

"I got into USC."

Evan sat bolt upright. He turned to me, laughing in disbelief, his hand finding mine and squeezing so hard it hurt.

"I got accepted to a bunch, actually," I said. "So did Wesley. We decided on USC." Another breath. "I'm going to LA, Evan."

"I am so proud of you." His voice was a loud whisper. He was smiling.

"Did you hear what I said?"

"Yeah, I did."

"Then why are you happy? I'm leaving."

"I know."

I wrenched my hand away. "So you're fine with it? You don't care if I go?"

He touched my bare leg. He was shirtless, his body like carved marble in the eerie, milky light. "I care if you go," he said. "More than you know. But I'm happy for you. This is your dream, Maise."

It was. But I had another one, and it was about being loved, completely, for who I am. Body and mind. Flaws and strengths. Fears and dreams.

"You could at least pretend to be morally conflicted," I said.

He laughed. "I would never ask you to forfeit your future. And you would never do it anyway."

"No, but sometimes being asked feels nice. It feels like being needed."

His fingertips moved over my thigh, making my nerves shimmer with warmth. Then he took my hand again, softer now. "I'm not pulling the age card, I swear. But there's something I believe. You should love something while you have it, love it fully and without reservation, even if you know you'll lose it someday. We lose everything. If you're trying to avoid loss, there's no point in taking another breath, or letting your heart beat one more time. It all ends." His fingers curled around mine. "That's all life is. Breathing in, breathing out. The space between two breaths."

Wesleypedia told me once that you take about seven hundred million breaths during your lifetime. Not until this moment had that number meant anything to me. Now I was counting every single one.

"Come with me to LA," I said.

Evan smiled, lowering his eyes.

"I'm serious," I said.

"I know."

I reversed his hold on my hand and clutched his fingers in mine. "This is real. We're still in love, and I miss you so much, Evan. I miss seeing the world with you. I miss your body, I miss your voice and your laugh and your smile and the way you make me feel like a child, in the best way. Afraid and full of wonder and totally alive. This is me telling you, without reservation, that I love you. Come with me to LA. Let's find happiness."

Even as I said the words, I knew they weren't quite right. We didn't need to go anywhere to find happiness. It was here, now, and if it ended in June when I got on a plane, the only choice was whether to be happy or miserable in this moment.

"Let's take it slow," he said. "We've only just found each other again."

I winced, turning away, and he touched my face and turned it back.

"You're right, though. I am still in love with you."

No kiss. No bombastic love ballad swelling from hidden speakers. Just a simple declaration in a dark room that was beginning to lighten.

I leaned against the wall and talked to him all night. I didn't want dawn to ever come.

———

"Where were you this weekend?" Wesley said.

I popped the last of my grilled cheese into my mouth and gave him a long look. The cafeteria was loud, kids nervy and restive, dying to go wild during spring break next week.

"In Carbondale," I said. "With Evan."

"Did you sleep with him?"

"Yes."

Wesley didn't blink. "Are we still going to LA?"

"Yes," I said, and took a sip of 7 Up. "I'm not giving up my future for a man."

"Even a man you're in love with?"

"Even a man I'm in love with."

He shrugged. "Guess I'm more romantic than you, then. I'd give up my future for true love."

"That's not romantic, that's stupid. You sound like one of those girls whose only career aspiration is housewife."

"I like to subvert gender roles," Wesley said, and I laughed.

In the lab later, I pulled him aside to a quiet corner. "How are we on footage?"

"Pretty good. Still waiting on your pièce de résistance."

"Friday," I said. "Do or die."

"Do, and hopefully not die."

"Here's the deal," I told Gary, sitting with him at the back of a restaurant. "If my friend comes through, then Yvette is even with you, and I'm out."

Gary's eyes narrowed shrewdly as he smiled. "Everyone says that, sweetheart. 'I'm only in until I get X amount. As soon as I hit X, I'm out.'" He took a hit of scotch. "It gets its claws in you, one way or another. You get addicted to the merchandise or you get addicted to the money."

"Well, I'm different. I don't want either."

"You've made a pretty little sum so far, haven't you?"

"Yes, but I'm not keeping it."

He stared at me over the rim of his glass as he drank. I could tell he was curious about me. Someone my age who was so sure, so practical.

"Your choice," he said. "But if you worked for me over the

summer, you could go to Hollywood with a nice nest egg."

I knew I could. The temptation was real, and torturous. Every night I weighed it in my mind. Siphon what I could from Hiyam and Gary and their ilk, and go to California with full pockets, without the pressure of fighting other starry-eyed fledglings tooth-and-nail for shitty jobs and shittier apartments? How could Evan say no if I told him he had a year to find a job, a year while we lived freely in the sun? But I couldn't. It was a trap, not a shortcut. The more money you made, the deeper in you got with these scumbags. They'd collect dirt on you. Then it became an endless game of bluffing, everyone constantly poised to destroy each other *Game of Thrones*–style, and your only choice was to keep working your way up, waiting to be dethroned. That's what Mom never understood. It was a zero-sum game. Your gain came at the expense of someone else, and eventually someone else would gain at your expense. The best you could hope for was to live and keep playing a little longer.

Or you could walk away before they had you that deep.

"I know what I'm doing," I said.

Gary gave me that sharky smile. "You know, sweetheart, sometimes I think you do."

———

Hiyam wore a dress conservative by her standards, a heart-shaped neck framing a pillow of satiny bronze cleavage, her hoop earrings flashing. On the cab ride to the restaurant I thought about hooking her up with Park and began to laugh. Totally his type: the uberhot alpha girl with a planet-sized ego to match. He'd be trying to ditch her within two minutes flat.

"What's so funny, O'Malley?"

"Nothing."

"Then maybe you should shut the fuck up, or I'll start having second thoughts."

I wiped the smile off my face. "Hiyam."

"What?"

I looked her straight in the eye. "I'm going to see Evan tomorrow. And I'm going to fuck the shit out of him, just like I did last weekend." I raised my eyebrows innocently. "Do you want me to say hi?"

She frowned. This must be confusing for her, the slave showing backbone, willingly divulging information. She didn't understand I had nothing to fear from her anymore.

"You still see him?"

"Yes."

"So you really do have a thing. It wasn't just, 'Fuck me, Mr. Wilke?'"

"Oh," I said lazily, "I still say that."

And I burst out laughing at the look on her face.

"You crazy bitch," Hiyam said, part misgiving, part awe.

In the restaurant Quinn gave us both pat-downs before we sat, which Hiyam seemed to find equally offensive and erotic. I traded glances with the tall, dark-haired boy in a borrowed waiter's uniform. Hiyam, being Hiyam, never noticed him. He was just the help.

"Mr. Rivero," I said, "I'd like you to meet my friend, Hiyam Farhoudi."

II

S T. Louis was still sleepy with winter, the grass like frosted
straw, the sky an anemic blue and the Mississippi muddy
green, sluggish but unstoppable. Skyscrapers glinted harshly,
mirroring the cold white sun.

Park took us to a club that let under-twenty-ones in and
his bartender friend looked the other way when I drank from
Evan's glass. We watched Park flirt with a gorgeous mixed-
race girl, cinnamon skin and laughing eyes, but he left her
with a frown and came back to us, saying she wanted Evan's
number. I nearly choked. When I kissed Evan I tasted the
whiskey and cola we were sharing. He took me out on the
floor and Park joined us. They both danced with me, Evan's
eyes hypnotic and his smile slow and our bodies edging
closer and closer until Park wrapped a ridiculously muscular
arm around my waist and picked me up, spinning me away.
Evan laughed and let me go, and I danced with strangers for
a while until he slipped behind me, his mouth at my ear, his

erection pressed against my ass, saying, "Everyone's in love with you." A couple guys were staring at me, and so was a cute pixie-haired girl, and I smiled. Cones of hot colored light flashed in my face, scarlet, violet, indigo. I was drunk as much on whiskey as on the liquor of sweat and cologne. We caught our own cab to the loft. Evan pressed me into the soft leather seat and put his hand between my legs until I gasped and the cabbie threatened to kick us out. I tipped him double and we rushed upstairs. The elevator made me shriek with surprise, forgetting the haunting, and Evan laughed and kissed me and once we got inside he picked me up, turning with me in his arms. "What are you doing?" I said, and he said, "Being in love," and I started kissing him again and he let me down to focus on the kiss. We broke apart and moved around the loft aimlessly, picking things up, flipping switches with a restless, agitated happiness. It's all still here, I thought. All the things we touched and all the things we felt. It was too intense, being near each other, and we orbited from across the room, keeping large objects between us.

"What if this is it?" he said in front of the windows. Beyond him the night sky was an oil painting of deep, swirling blues, starless, the bright streets sketching a map of light across the city.

I sat on the arm of the sofa, ankles crossed.

"What if this is all we have?" he said, coming closer. "What if you go to California, and I never see you again?"

"Then I'll make movies about it for the rest of my life. About a girl who falls in love with her teacher and loses him tragically and never loves again."

He looked at my hand on the couch: the Claddagh ring on my finger, its heart turned toward me.

"Why won't you come to LA?" I said in a hushed voice.

He took a deep breath. He kept looking at the ring. "Your life is just beginning, Maise. You have so much ahead of you, so many new things. And you're already way too damn cynical. Don't argue, it's true."

I closed my mouth and narrowed my eyes.

He smiled. "I don't want to take that from you. The thrill of discovering things for yourself. Of feeling like the world is new and made just for you."

"That's the exact opposite of how it is." I was shivering suddenly, shaking. I felt an understanding building in me after a long, arduous unveiling. Revelation. "You're right, I *was* cynical. I thought I knew everything, I thought the world was vulgar and crude, all cheap thrills. You couldn't make me any more jaded than I was when we met." I let my arms fall, let my spine hold me, a slender fin of bone. How had it borne the weight of so much cynicism all these years? "You changed that. You're the one who made it new for me. If I hadn't met you, I would've gone off to college thinking everything was the same. I would've become hardened and walled up and—" Just like my mother. "Empty. A perfect shell, protecting nothing."

"Maise," Evan said.

"Don't you see how different I am now? Didn't you see it in my film, and every day we spent together, and apart? The world *is* new when I'm with you." I took his hands in mine. "And I've seen how you light up when you're with me. It's the same for you. We're both kids with each other, and this world is made just for us. So that can't be your reason for saying no."

"Am I saying no?"

"You're not saying yes." I pulled him toward me. "Do you really want to teach high school in Southern fucking Illinois the rest of your life?"

He gave me that patented furrowed brow.

"And," I said, pulling him closer, my voice lowering, "do you really not want to fuck me, every day, in our house full of sunlight and Santa Ana winds, in Southern fucking California?"

His hands moved to my waist, sliding beneath my shirt. "I want to fuck you right now."

Do it, I told him with my eyes. *Please, please do it.*

We undressed each other, cool air and warm hands gliding over skin. He laid me on the bed on the icy silk sheets, and the gravity that had threatened to throw us into collision finally did. I held him close as he moved inside me, hard and deep and with an urgency that felt somehow final, and we gave ourselves to it, fully, without reservation. No future and no past, only an endless now. Afterward, as we lay with our limbs tangled and stared at the pipes on the ceiling, his words ran through me. What if this is all we have? This closeness, this space between breaths, holding each other like air in our lungs, the oxygen metabolizing into our blood in a thrilling, ephemeral rush?

How could it ever, ever be enough?

"How was your spring break?" Hiyam said, dropping her Cheshire grin on me.

"Best I've ever had," I said, smiling back. "You?"

She rolled her eyes, tossed her hair, bared her smooth coppery neck to me. She laughed at the ceiling. Kids sitting nearby stared.

"In-fucking-describable," she said.

Translation: coked out of her mind.

I kept smiling, but she didn't see the way it deepened in my eyes, the dark flash.

"Hey," I said. "What do you have next period?"

"American History."

"Ditch and meet me in 209."

She lowered her face, curious. "Why?"

"I've got something for you," I said, and patted my pocket.

Hiyam laughed her rich, sultry laugh. "You freak."

Green light, I texted Wesley after class.

Hiyam caught up with me on the stairs to the second floor, where I'd unknowingly made my way to the class that would change my life. Part of me still expected to open his door and catch him glancing up from his desk, smiling. I'd kissed him in here like I meant to devour him, let him push me against the whiteboard and fuck me. God, I thought. Was that really my life? It seemed like a dream now. A movie.

There was no Evan inside the dark class. There was, however, a Wesley, sitting with his laptop on the dais at the back. The projector was on, its lamp burning hot as a quasar.

Hiyam's eyes drifted from him to me. Intrigue, suspicion, but no fear.

Not yet.

"I didn't know you nerds were into this," she said.

"Into what?" I said, waiting for her to walk in so I could stealthily lock the door.

"Getting high."

"We're not," Wesley said, moving the mouse cursor over a video.

"We're into revenge," I said. "Have a seat."

Hiyam was so fucking confident, so used to getting away with everything, that she laughed and sat at her old desk, crossing her legs as if we were back in Film Studies, vying for Mr. Wilke's attention. Now they both knew it had always been mine. I took the teacher's chair, propping my feet on the desk.

"And now for our final victim," I said, echoing Evan, "Hiyam Farhoudi."

Wesley clicked play.

I'd seen this a dozen times, so I mostly watched Hiyam's face. She shook her head knowingly, a smirk curling in the corners of her mouth, when the first frame came up:

Farhoudi residence. New Year's Eve. Hiyam snorts coke off a mirror in her princess bedroom.

"You little shit," she said without taking her eyes from the screen.

The scene cuts to black, and the title comes up in caps, just like Wesley's first film. This one, though, is called *Addiction*.

Hiyam's burgeoning smirk faded.

There is no soundtrack, only live audio. Hiyam's laughter. The click of a credit card against glass. Her hard snort and the delicate sniffs that follow. She smiles at the camera, high as fuck, not realizing why we're recording her. I get her to show me the thirty grand in her secret account. The pills and weed she has stashed all over her room. She loves the attention. She admits to Wesley that she's blackmailing me. I watch her lick her finger and stick it in her nostril to get all the white. She looks at the camera and says dully, "Ever sucked coke off a guy's dick? It's called a blowjob." She bursts out laughing.

Then, finally, my pièce de résistance.

Hiyam smiles at Gary Rivero in the restaurant, oblivious to Wesley and his hidden camera, and the mic in my sleeve captures the deal for a half kilo of cocaine.

The film ends. There are no credits.

"So," I said, rocking my feet side to side, "class? Thoughts?"

Hiyam scooted her chair back with a metallic screech.

"Sit down," Wesley said. "We're not done yet."

"Shut the fuck up," she said.

I spun my chair to face her. "I'd like to hear what the star thinks about her film debut."

"You dumb cunt," she said, moving toward me. "You can't do shit. My father will destroy you."

I stood, waiting calmly for her to reach me. I felt so much like the teacher, all the knowledge and power in my hands.

"I doubt it," I said, my voice light. "Because we sent him the same video an hour ago. You gave me the idea yourself, with your semester project. Your dad seemed to really care about you. He wouldn't want you throwing your life away on drugs. You should be getting a call from him very soon."

"You," she said. Just that: pronoun, no epithet.

"Let me guess. 'You won't get away with this. You'll regret this.'"

She leaned closer. Her breath smelled like wintergreen. "You will regret it. I'll make sure of that."

I leaned close, too. "You know, I feel sorry for you, Hiyam. You have everything, all this money and opportunity, and you're miserable. You want to live without feeling anything. Why even bother if you're just going to numb yourself? I've had it way worse than you ever will, and I wouldn't trade it for the world."

She had the dignity to keep her mouth shut. She stared at me with dark, murderous eyes, then whirled and stalked to the door. It took her a moment to realize it was locked. Wesley muffled a snort.

Hiyam shot a glance back at me and said, "Did you even fuck him in here that day?"

I smiled at her pityingly.

She slammed the door.

"God," Wesley said, heaving a huge sigh. "Did it work?"

I was shaking. I wasn't sure when that had started.

"Don't know," I said. "I guess we'll find out."

All I really wanted was for her to leave me and Evan the fuck alone. She could buy her coke direct from Gary and scrub her brain blank with it for all I cared. I'd told her dad I just wanted this to be over—I wanted to move on, go to college, not live with this sword hanging over my head.

I prayed he'd understand.

"At least the hard part's over," Wesley said.

But this wasn't the hard part. Confronting this junkie was easy. There was one more I had to face, and she wouldn't surrender before drawing blood.

I sat in the kitchen waiting like I had so many nights when I was little, hungry, bored, alone in the house. When I thought of my so-called childhood, that's what I pictured above all: a sylvan girl with bramble hair and spooky green eyes, kicking her bare, dirty feet on a kitchen chair, waiting. Waiting. Waiting. That girl should have been running in the woods with a boy, scratching secrets into the walls of an old wolf den, howling, chasing him, wild and free. Not sitting in a room that smelled of marijuana and drain cleaner, her belly growling. On good nights Mom came home with food, a bag glistening and transparent with french fry grease, smelling like heaven, and I'd go to bed with salty-sweet lips and sleep like the dead. On bad nights she came home stoned or with a man or not at all. Those nights I didn't sleep much. I listened for her key in the lock, or grunting and the bed knocking against the wall downstairs. Once a pair of heavy footsteps came to my door. I lay in bed, terrified, paralyzed. I thought they'd finally gone when the door creaked open, and I screamed, and Mom came running, still drunk, hitting the guy in the back until he left.

I always locked my room after that.

You, I thought, timing it with the ticking clock. You. You. You.

She walked in at midnight. My ass was numb, and my heart, too. I looked at her woodenly. You have my face, I thought. What have you done to it? It's so old and sad.

"What's going on, babe?" she said, pulling a tallboy from the fridge.

"Sit down, Mom. Please."

Hiss, crack, fizz. I could hear her swallowing, working that dry, burned throat. She sat across from me.

"Gary says you took care of things," she said.

I nodded.

"How the hell'd you manage that?"

"Don't worry about it. It's my business."

"Your business is my business, babe."

"No." I leaned forward, looking her in the eyes. "It's mine."

For a minute I thought she'd pick a fight, but I guess clearing her debt temporarily cowed her. She picked at the tab on her can instead.

"Mom." I waited till she met my gaze. "I got into college in Los Angeles. I'm leaving the second week of June."

She said nothing. Her eyes were flat, unblinking. She took a swig.

For the first time I realized my mother might be jealous of me. Of my unspoiled life, all the possibilities I still had to make something of myself.

Deep breath.

"I saved some money. Enough to replace what Nan gave me." I opened the folded paper on the table and slid it over to her. Until a second ago it had been mere junk.

Mom's eyes bounced off the paper to my face. "What is this?"

"Read it."

She mouthed the words. She stopped at *Rehabilitation Center*.

"It cost every penny I had, but I got you in for sixty days. It's a good clinic, Mom. They're willing to take you June first."

She looked at me like I was a potted plant that had just started talking. "What the hell is this?"

"I'm trying to help you," I said, my voice straining.

She pushed the paper at me, pushed her chair back. "This's some intervention shit."

"It's voluntary."

"You ain't making me do nothing, little girl. I call the shots. I'm your mother."

My palm hit the table, the ring making a sharp clack. "You lost the right to call yourself that years ago. This is not a negotiation. This is your last chance to fix your fucking life before you're too old and brain-damaged to remember it was ever different." I stood, glaring down at her. Somehow this woman always brought my accent out, and I let it take the reins of my voice. "This is my offer, Mom. Take it or leave it. You complete the program, you stay clean, and I'll come see you for Christmas. If you don't, I'm out of your life forever." I hit the table again, softer. "Do you understand me? You will never see me again."

She was breathing shallowly, fast. She stared at some central point on my face, not quite my eyes. "This how I raised you? To make fuckin' threats about disowning me?"

"No," I said quietly. "This is how *I* raised me."

Green slowly crept back into the world, reawakening it as my own body reawakened. I spent spring weekends in St. Louis with Evan, walking along the cobblestoned wharf, listening to the world thaw. If this was all we had, then I would love it unreservedly. When we stopped to watch the boats I leaned back against his body, my neck arching over his shoulder, my face to the sun. I could feel it kindling in my bones. A cold breeze whipped off the water, smelling of mud and fish, and gulls shrieked and their cries echoed eerily under the stone arches of the Eads Bridge. We walked through sun and shadow and sun again. Our own shadows were long and thin, stretching far down the wharf.

I didn't bring up LA again. My cards were on the table. His move.

The sky was a crisp azure on graduation day. They held the ceremony on the football field, the grass lush and emitting a rainy perfume, our royal blue gowns gleaming in the sun.

Hiyam wasn't there. She'd been pulled from school, finishing her year with a private tutor. Mom wasn't there either, as expected. But the Browns were, all of them—Siobhan, Natalie, and Jack the professor, a man in his sixties, still handsome in a Clint Eastwood way, straight brow and deepset eyes beneath a wing of silver hair. He sat next to Siobhan, and they chuckled together over private jokes. Once I saw

Jack touching the small of her back, looking at her with an old, smoldering fondness.

"Dad's current girlfriend is twenty-two," Wesley whispered to me as we sat through Britt's valediction. "Please tell me you'll never date a dinosaur like him."

I flicked his ear, hard.

Evan was there, at the back of the crowd. When they called us to the stage for our diplomas I screamed my head off for Wesley, and on my turn the Browns cheered wildly, but the only person I saw was Evan, standing at the back, the sun slanting in his hair and outlining him in gold, clapping so hard he drowned out everyone else.

Afterward we ran the usual gauntlet of family hugs. When we slipped away and reached Evan, he was surrounded by half our old Film Studies class, eagerly telling him their plans. Rebecca was going to art school in Georgia. A few kids were heading to NYC for theater. Everyone was impressed when we said we were going to LA, and Wesley basked in the attention while I met Evan's gaze, something twisting in my chest, a strangling vine. The boys shook his hand and the girls hugged him, and when it was my turn I breathed in his ear, "You changed my life, Mr. Wilke."

His arms tightened around me, and he whispered back, "You changed mine."

Wesley looked at the two of us, then away.

The crazy thing was that after all of this, no one knew. No one gave me a second glance or raised an eyebrow. They talked excitedly about Hollywood and New York. They asked Evan about his college days. The rumors had died down without Hiyam fueling them. Now he was just a teacher, and I was just another student, not connected to him in any special way. I drifted across the grass, leaving him there in the sun and the warmth of their attention, closing my eyes and letting the light soak through, blinding me with my own neon-red blood.

Wesley left with Natalie the day after graduation, heading to California. I had plans to take a plane the next week. Carbondale graduated later than us.

I stayed with Siobhan after her kids left. We made Manhattans with maraschino cherries and sat on the back deck, talking long after sunset. She planned to travel now that Wesley had left home. She wanted to see Europe, write a novel, date a young Italian ("At least three times younger than me," she said, "to get even with Jack"), live for a while in a villa by the sea. She knew I was waiting for an answer from Evan.

"I am not the wise woman you think," she said, tilting her glass. Starlight skimmed off the rim and shot into her eyes, sparkling. "But I will tell you this: don't put your life on hold for someone, or you'll wake up at forty-two with an empty house and a terrifying sense of freedom and no energy or innocence left to enjoy it."

I wanted to hug her so much. "If Wesley doesn't call you every week, I'll beat the shit out of him."

"Perhaps you should do that anyway, as a preventive measure."

I laughed, she cackled, and we got drunk under the leaves and stars.

When I got home, I discovered two shocking things.

One: Mom was gone.

She'd scrawled a note on the back of an envelope and left

it on the kitchen table. Her childish, blocky handwriting: *Checking in to clinic. Sorry I'm a shit mom & no good with words. This letter came for you.*

I blinked the sudden tears out of my eyes—I was drunk, that was the only explanation—and turned the envelope over. My name in florid, scrolling letters. Return address: Javad Farhoudi.

Shocking thing number two: a letter from Hiyam's dad.

I opened it, my heart going at light speed. A smaller slip of paper fluttered out. I focused on the larger one.

My deepest gratitude for your discretion and concern regarding my daughter. You have given both of us a second chance. I hope this small gift helps you transition to an exciting new period in your life.

The smaller slip of paper was a check.

For ten thousand dollars.

I started laughing, breathless, crazy laughter, and then I jumped up and did a sort of whirling dervish dance around the kitchen, saying, "Thank you, sweet Jesus, I fucking love you," and could not stop laughing with hysterical joy and relief.

And then the only thing left was him.

We spent that last week in St. Louis. Summer was in full bloom now, the city wild and drenched with color, the sidewalks breathing warmly beneath my sandals. I tried my best to live in the moment. To not think about the fact that there were only five more days before we might part for the last time. Then four. Then three. But the tension was always there, a wire tightening in me, pulling my limbs and neck taut like a puppet, and when I looked up at the Arch

I thought, That's how I feel. A terrifying upward pull, away from terra firma.

One night in the loft, Evan was pouring a drink in the kitchen when he suddenly put the bottle down and walked over to me, sinking to his knees. He clutched my legs, his face pressing to my shins, stubble grinding against smoothness. I was bewildered, and when he said, "God, what am I doing?" my confusion became fear. I stroked his hair tentatively, asked what was wrong. He looked up, his face full of panic, and said, "I can't do this to you. You don't know what you're doing, Maise. You have a life to live, not a broken man to fix." I stared at him, horrified, starting to cry as I realized what he was saying, and that quickly he flipped a switch and became the one comforting me, apologizing, soothing me with promises that he was just tired, stressed, not thinking clearly. But that night we both lay awake, staring at the ceiling, silent. I thought, Who fixes broken people? Is it only other broken people, ones who've already been ruined? And do we need to be fixed? It was the messiness and hurt in our pasts that drove us, and that same hurt connected us at a subdermal level, the kind of scars written so deeply in your cells that you can't even see them anymore, only recognize them in someone else.

Two days.

The wires finally snapped at lunch.

I sat on a patio in front of a plate of something I couldn't even process as food. The sunlight ricocheting off the concrete was blinding. Silverware flashed, all sharp edges. Everything was bright and incomprehensible.

My fork clattered to the plate, catching Evan's attention. His skin had tanned slightly, and in the sun his eyes were so vividly blue it didn't seem the right word anymore—they were *azul*, the color of the Mexican Pacific, so pure it almost hurt to look at. He put his fork down. He looked so beautiful sitting there, a fine scatter of sand on his cheeks, the sun drizzling his hair with light, gold on gold.

"Stop acting," I said quietly. "Stop pretending you're not scared."

"I'm scared," he said, his voice also soft.

"We made it through the worst, Evan. School's over. This should be the easy part." The summer sun was in my blood, shining through my skin. "Why can't you let yourself do what makes you happy?"

"It's not that simple."

"It really is. You drop the bullshit and tell me yes or no."

His gaze broke away from me, his eyes tightening. "Just because it's complicated doesn't mean it's bullshit."

"That's exactly what it means."

"You know," he said, focusing on me again, "you talk like you're so jaded and wise, but sometimes you're pretty naive."

My mouth dropped. I felt like he'd punched me. I swallowed, and said, "I'm eighteen fucking years old. Excuse me for being naive."

Evan leaned across the table, lowering his voice. "That's right. You're eighteen. I'm thirty-three. I'm a grown man, Maise. Fifteen years older than you, fifteen years' worth of problems and bitterness and second-guessing myself. You don't need that. Not when you can have a clean slate in California."

Adrenaline pumped through me, turning me cold, my hands and feet tingling. Finally. This was finally all coming into the open.

"Like I don't have my own problems?" I shot back. "How about my junkie mother and deadbeat dad? And the guys I was with before you, who I just wanted to be nice to me?"

My voice cracked; I swallowed again. "And Wesley stalking me, and Hiyam blackmailing me, and every crazy thing that's happened this year?"

"What happened with Hiyam?" he said, frowning.

God, stupid slip-up. I hadn't told him about the black-mail, knowing he'd use it as another example of how he was ruining my life. It was a story for another time.

"The point is, I don't have a clean slate. All that shit comes with me. It's part of who I am. Your problems have always been part of you, and I accepted them. That doesn't change now."

"You're young, Maise," he said gently, giving me that mournful look that took me apart inside. "You don't know any better."

I could not believe this. I could not believe, after everything, he was playing the fucking age card. Reducing me to a number.

"Fuck you," I said.

I stood up. The lion in me wanted to flip the table over, listen to the glass and china shattering, see the shocked faces, but it would only prove his point about my age. I turned around and walked out. I had no idea where I was going, no idea where or who I was, just a meaningless blur of blood cells floating over white-hot concrete. I knew what he was doing. Trying to piss me off, make me leave him. You fucking coward, I thought. If you think you're so wrong for me, own it, and let me decide. Don't try to do what's best for me. Don't try to teach me.

I ended up in one of those urban parks that were every-where downtown, this one all swaths of green velvet grass and trees centering on a plaza with a huge pool. In the center, a bronze Olympian runner stood frozen midstride, plumes of white water pulsing to either side of him. Behind the statue you could see the Old Courthouse and the Arch, a visual timeline of history. I sat on the coping, dipping a hand into the cool water and pressing it to my neck. Breathe, I told myself. I smelled wet metal. I watched the sun chip shards of light into the pool's surface.

Evan eventually found me. He stopped a few feet away, his hands hanging loosely, his pale short-sleeved Oxford glowing with sunlight. He stood there while I stared into the pool.

"You look so beautiful," he said. "So beautiful and far away."

Do something, I thought. Jump in the water, propose to me, tell me you're moving to South Africa. Don't just let me go.

But he only stood there, breaking my heart.

I got up. Headed toward his car, across a street bordering the park, my sundress snapping at my legs as I walked fast. Evan caught me before I crossed and touched my shoulder and I stopped right in the middle of the street.

"Don't leave like this," he said.

The muscles of my throat were tight as a noose. "This is it, Evan. This is how it's going to end. Not on some romantic runway at midnight. It's going to end in broad daylight, on a crowded street, with people—shut up!" I snapped when a car honked behind me. "With people hurrying us so they can go pick up their laundry. Is this how you imagined it? Is this really how you want it to end?"

He looked at me miserably, his voice thick. "I don't want it to end."

"That's not good enough," I said. The car veered around us and zoomed away. Everything had a hot, harsh shimmer. Or maybe the shimmer was in my eyes. "If you're not on that plane with me, it's over. And I'm not holding my breath a minute longer to find out. Are you coming with me or not?"

This is what he said:

Nothing.

Not a word to stop me, to explain himself, no matter how futile it would be.

He just gave me that aching, tender look that ripped me to shreds.

"Give me your keys," I said. "Give me your *fucking* keys."

He did.

Autopilot engaged. I opened the trunk, pulled my bags out. Some of my clothes were still in the loft, trivial things, toothbrush, lotion. Nothing I cared about. Not that I cared about anything anymore.

"Maise," Evan said, "please."

I dropped my bags into the street. Cars were honking again, edging around us. I ignored them. I knelt to unzip one of the bags and yanked out that fucking stuffed pony I'd won almost a year ago and hurled it at him. Good-bye, Louis. Then I bounced to my feet, flagging down a taxi.

"Maise," Evan said again.

I didn't look at him. The cab coasted over, popped the trunk, and I shoved my bags in. Threw myself into the backseat and slammed the door. I couldn't feel anything. My brain registered the hot sun-baked leather, but my body was numb.

"Where you headed?" the cabbie said.

"Just drive," I said. "Drive around for a while, please."

He pulled away, and I lasted all of eight seconds before I started crying, openly, horribly, lowering my head and shrouding myself in the dark curtain of my hair. The hem of my dress turned transparent with tears.

Mr. Driver didn't say a word.

The brain is an incredible multitasker. At the same time that it's piercing itself with superheated needles of anguish, it's ruthlessly making plans, weighing contingencies, plotting out a future, giving zero fucks whether it'll ever see it. On the day I die, it'll be calculating what to have for dinner as it bombards itself with pain signals from my amputated legs or my clocked-out heart. And so, when I stopped crying, I wiped the snot off my upper lip and took out my phone.

In sixty seconds, I had an address for the driver.

Park was waiting in the cool green shade of an elm outside his building. He took my bags as I paid the fare.

"You'll be all right," the driver said.

I laughed, sniffling. "Thanks. I will."

Park led me upstairs without a word. He had a condo a few floors up, pristine cherry hardwood and sleek modern furniture, tracklights, art on raw canvases, everything in shades of gray and touches of chrome. A view of the Arch through enormous windows.

"This way," he said, still carrying my bags.

He showed me to a bathroom. It was so white I squinted, hard lights hitting the mirrors. It looked like a place where androids slept. I scrubbed my face, brushed my hair, tried to tease out some vestige of my humanity instead of looking like a decomposing waif.

When I came out, Park was at the granite kitchen counter, sipping a beer. "Drink?"

"Water, please. I'm really sorry to show up like this."

He made a quick, dismissive gesture, handed me a glass, and looked at me with muted curiosity. Men, I thought. They'll never ask, even if they're dying to know.

Fifteen years. Was that really what it came down to? I'd

been with Evan for the better part of the past year, so why was age a problem now? Because he'd be committing himself to something, I guess. Uprooting his life, leaving his friends, the easy jobs and low cost of living, all for a city full of broken dreams and a screwed-up eighteen-year-old who'd already left him twice.

I took a deep breath and drank. When I thought of it like that, I couldn't blame him.

"The first time I met you," I said, "you thought it was happening again, didn't you? The same as the other girl."

Park's eyes narrowed. He took a moment to answer, sipping his beer first. "She came to me, crying and begging. I thought she needed help. It was all an act. Eric—" He caught himself. "E felt so guilty, he refused to see it. Look, what he did was wrong. No question. He knew, and tried to make it right. But she didn't want that. She wanted to hurt him, and that's wrong, too."

I shifted uneasily.

"Anyway, I was moving to St. Louis for a job and offered him a chance to start over."

"How long have you known him?"

"Since college. We were roommates."

"Why was that girl trying to hurt him?"

Park spun his bottle on the counter. "She felt powerless. She tried to take some of the power back, but everyone loses in a situation like that. It just had to end."

Maybe that's what I was doing, too. Maybe I was just a hurt, fucked-up, obsessed little girl, trying to take the power back.

"You know," he said, peering into his beer, "I've known E half my life. He's family. Even my mother loves him, and she is impossible to impress. Like, doesn't carry the gene." Park grinned at me, let it slowly fade. "He has changed so much since he met you. He talks about getting back into acting. Helping you launch a movie career. I haven't heard him talk so much about the future since college. He's finally looking forward, not backward."

I wanted to scream. I wanted to cry. Instead I just stood there with my fists in balls, brimming with unbearable futility. In the movie version of my life, these were the words that Evan would have said. He would've stood beneath a window and shouted them up to me and the whole city would have paused to listen.

But this isn't a fucking movie. It's my life. There's no script. The scenes are choppy and sometimes pointless, the dialogue rarely witty, the subplots meandering off into nowhere. Evan isn't my knight in shining armor with perfect timing and a stainless steel past and I'm not some damsel in distress who needs saving, anyway. We're just two messed-up people who don't get their happy ending. Happy endings are for movies, and fairy tales.

"He can talk about the future all he wants," I said bitterly, "but it's not going to wait for him to start."

Park gave a quick laugh. "You sound like my mother. She would like you, too."

He went to shower, and I stared out the windows at the Arch looping over the shining blue thread of the Mississippi, like a silver shoelace. My anger was brittle and quickly crumbled. I couldn't imagine getting through the next two days. Not in this haunted city, not with the laughing ghost of a girl who thought she was getting away with some grand secret. Funny, how easy happiness had been when it was us against the world. Guess that was the trick after all.

I took out my phone.

When Park came back, I said, "I rescheduled my flight. I'm leaving tonight. Can you drive me?"

"Of course," he said, but apprehension flickered in his eyes.

I checked and rechecked my bags, texted Wesley that I'd be arriving early, watched TV with Park on his absurdly large screen. My new departure time was nine p.m. It was a long drive.

"I guess we should go," I said when the sky began to turn lavender.

Park paused with my bags at the door. "You sure about this? Maybe you should wait, sleep on it."

"I've been waiting for months," I said, but what I thought was, I've been waiting my whole life. I was so sure this was different, the kind of love story they made movies and books about, but in the end it was just a summer to a summer, a dizzying breath of honeysuckle and whiskey and candle smoke, inhaled, held, let go.

Park told me funny bar stories on the way to the airport, trying to take my mind off things, and I laughed but I felt outside myself, an observer. The camera watching the girl. He walked me inside the terminal all the way to the TSA checkpoint, because he said no one should go to an airport alone. That almost made me cry. He said he'd tell Evan I got here safely. I hugged him good-bye, and he winked.

Lambert International was as cold and bright as a hospital, everything sterile white. I was freezing but I walked slowly to my gate, wanting to prolong it all, listening to the voices on the PA talking about gate changes and delays with an intense reverence. Lives changed here, stories beginning and ending. Somewhere lovers met for the first time after talking online, touching each other's faces with amazement. An Afghanistan vet with sand in her boots hugged her husband and kid. And a girl headed west, chasing the setting sun, without the man she loved. It was so surreal. It was going to end in an airport after all, just like Ilsa. I stared at the signs, the names of cities, but I was lost inside myself. Regrets Only Beyond This Point.

I checked in and sat watching the planes glinting in the sunset, sleek painted steel against the fire in the sky. I listened to Sophie Barker's cover of "Leaving on a Jet Plane" until I thought I was as sad as I could get, then switched to "Maps" and found out I could get sadder, and started laughing at myself, ridiculously, and then they called us for boarding.

Okay, I thought, walking down the gangway. This is it.

Good-bye, Rick. Good-bye, Captain Renault.

Good-bye, Eric Evan Wilke.

God, get to your seat without crying, Maise O'Malley.

I was in the first row of coach, window seat. When I buckled my belt I thought suddenly of getting in the front car of Deathsnake and my eyes went blurry. I turned to the window, forcing myself to focus through my reflection. In the deepening twilight, the runway lights looked like the carnival fireflies that night in August, distance making them beautiful. *Wish you were here.* Someone took the seat next to me and I tried to school my face. God, the last thing I needed was people thinking I was crying because I had a bomb strapped to my chest. In a few minutes, I'd be getting the world's best view of the only place I'd ever lived or loved, but I'd be seeing it all by myself.

I could still smell Evan on my clothes, my skin, as if he was right here. I should have fucking changed.

The captain got on the PA, announcing our flight like a movie. Tonight's feature is *The Rest of Your Sorry Life.* I couldn't tear my eyes from the window, wanting to drink in as much of St. Louis as I could, knowing that somewhere out there, one of those infinitesimally small lights was him. I wondered if he'd look up and see the planes crossing the sky like shooting stars, knowing one of those lights was me.

"You're pretty brave," the guy beside me said, "sitting up front by yourself."

The floor fell out of the universe. I was in free fall.

I turned.

All I saw was blurred gold and a small, hopeful smile, and the haze of city lights through the window across the aisle, twinkling. I couldn't speak. I could only contain the heart and lungs that were beating inside me, that filled my whole body until I was nothing but breath and blood.

The camera zooms in on the shine of an eye, the tremulous quiver of a lip. He's smiling but his eyes are wet. She's crying but her heart is infinitely light. Background noise recedes. Music fades in, swelling.

Spontaneously and simultaneously, they reach for each other's hands.

Cue ending credits.

ACKNOWLEDGMENTS

"Writing is easy," said someone far wiser than me. "You just open a vein and bleed."

I wrote *Unteachable* by candlelight, wearing headphones, with a sweating glass of whiskey at my side, on a crappy laptop on a bare mattress in a dingy Chicago apartment last summer. It was basically my last stab at publishing. I'd been rejected for years by traditional publishers, struggled to find an agent, been told over and over that my writing was good but they just couldn't sell my books in the current market, etc. I wrote adult fiction, YA, everything. Always the same nice comments scrawled on rejection slips. I kept waiting for someone to tell me what to write. Tell me what to change. Tell me the secret. Please.

It seems strange now, because to me there's so much light and hope in this book, but *Unteachable* came from a very dark place. I was on the brink of giving up my childhood dream of being published, and only a handful of good friends were there to support me in that darkness. Bethany Frenette,

Ellen Goodlett, and Lindsay Smith: you are precious to me beyond words. Thank you so much for talking me through the endless nights of self-doubt and depression, for giggling at the absurdity of it all, for crying and raging and laughing and sighing with me. I love you girls. You are the best bad influences ever.

And of course, thank you to my partner, Alexander, who kept me sane and loved me even when I was a frothing fountain of self-loathing. You are the sweetest boy on Earth. I'm lucky to have you, buddy. I love you.

When I self-published *Unteachable*, something incredible happened. People actually read it. Lots of people. Way more than I imagined even in my wildest dreams. They talked about it, reviewed it, loved and hated it, recommended it to their friends so they could discuss it together, and suddenly my silly little book blew up like a fantasy come true. I am still humbled and awed by all of you who put so much passion into reading and reacting to my work. Thank you, from the bottom of my heart.

Thank you to the book bloggers who got the word out in the first place: Aestas at *Aestas Book Blog*, Jenny and Gitte at *Totally Booked Blog*, Natasha at *Natasha is a Book Junkie*, and Lisa and Milasy at *The Rock Stars of Romance*. Thank you to those who picked up the torch: Emily May at *The Book Geek*, Wendy Darling at *The Midnight Garden*, Steph Sinclair at *Cuddlebuggery Book Blog*, Dahlia Adler, Sara Betz (my Fairy Bookmother), and so many others. Bloggers like you are the reason writers like me are able to achieve their dreams in this chaotic, ever-shifting publishing landscape. Thank you so much for bringing my book to the people I'm lucky to call my readers.

Thank you also to the fine citizens of Goodreads. Your passion for books and your hilarious, poignant, GIF-tastic reviews are a huge part of modern book discovery, and I'm grateful to be part of this new world with you guys. Shout-outs to Ana Rita (Master Yoda approves), Ash, Baba, Cam (*grazie, tesoro*), Faye, Katrina, Litchick, and only about a bajillion others.

I wish I could list every blogger and reviewer who's covered *Unteachable*, but I think Atria might frown on that. You are all in my heart.

Thank you to the amazing authors I've met during this journey. Mia Asher, Syreeta Jennings, Mia Sheridan, and all the FB crew: you're my girls. Colleen Hoover and Gail McHugh, you are still the titans I look up to with awe. M. "Bunny" Pierce, you are a wonderful human being and I ♥ you oh so much. Mad love to my Twitter crew who makes me laugh and/or keeps me sane by humoring my insanity—I wish the best for all of you on your own writing journeys.

Thank you to my badass agent, Jane Dystel, for hooking me up with the awesomest editor a writer could ever ask for, Sarah Cantin at Atria. I feel like I'm in the best possible hands with you guys, and I'm so happy to be part of the Atria family. Let's make beautiful books together.

My gratitude could go on forever. Whoever you are—you, reading these poorly written acknowledgments—thank you, too. Thanks for picking up my book, for giving me a chance. Whether you know it or not, you're part of making my dream come true. I am honored and so goo-ily, gushingly grateful that I get to write words for you. How awesome is that? Blows my mind.

Thank you for reading.

All my love,
Leah Raeder
May 2014